Flipping Heck!

S.D.Hayes

First Edition: August 2013.

ISBN: 1491222727

The acknowledgements bit…

To Rachel and my long-suffering family, who have put up with constant ramblings about penguins for over a decade, I hope your patience is finally rewarded.

To my friends, who didn't take fifteen paces back and mutter "You must be weird" when I told them what the story was about, thanks for the encouragement.

To Carrie Hynds for being a superb editor, who again didn't think I was weird (I hope!), thanks for helping me improve the story.

Graham Williams, who took a very short brief and created cover art and illustrations that far exceeded my expectations, is simply amazing! Find his details at the end of the book.

Finally, my thanks go to the characters for mostly doing what I asked of them without too much complaining. Those who didn't complain will find parts in the sequel.

10 things to know if you read this book

1) Penguins do not like icing sugar.

2) Penguins do not fly.

3) It is impossible to fit nine penguins into a Mini, so stop trying.

4) When awoken by a penguin cooing to an alarm clock, the correct action is to go back to sleep.

5) Penguins do not respect fish with half-finished make-up, they eat them!

6) All the places mentioned in this book are fictional, except London, Siberia, Antarctica, the Arctic and practically everywhere else.

7) There has never been any event in the Penguin Games recorded on camera.

8) To the best of human knowledge, no camel has ever swum the Atlantic.

9) The Crown Jewels were never swapped with a bucket of fish.

10) The Mona Lisa, World Cup, and any other item mentioned herein were never stolen, or accidentally borrowed, *as described,* and should they ever be so, the author denies all responsibility. Whatever the characters get up to in their own time is their business.

11) Gorillas do not have personal manicurists.

12) The author cannot count.

Chapter One:
The Nightmare Begins

Would you faint if you came downstairs one morning and found penguins in your lounge?

No?

Really?

Penguins – you know, the short, dual-flipper, black white and yellow creatures?

Are you really sure?

Not even ones that are a genetically abnormal five-foot tall?

Hmmm, perhaps this is the wrong book for you. Put this one down gently and look for the shelf marked 'Unusual Hobbies and Interests'.

Right. Apologies for that slight delay to the opening of the chapter. If you are brave enough to still be reading, let's get started, shall we?

Good. Onwards.

Any normal person would faint, and Don, the person in whose lounge we begin our story, was no exception. A perfectly normal reaction, to a perfectly abnormal event. So, having opened his lounge door and seeing the handful of non-human creatures therein, Don fainted.

"I told you," said a voice above him, as Don's brain allowed him to slowly become conscious once more.

"It's no good; we'll have to wake him."

Please don't, murmured Don's brain to itself, *I'm nice and comfortable.*

"Mr Castor... Mr Castor... Wake up."

Don's brain registered a soft tapping on his cheek, an instant before his nose registered an extremely powerful fishy smell, which made him sit up.

"Eugh... What? Hey?"

Not bad for Don's brain. Not bad at all, especially given the shock he had received. Three words, all on the right topic. He cautiously peeked out of the corner of one eye.

Cue fainting episode number two.

A minute later, Don kept his eyes closed as he came around. He counted to ten and then, telling himself that everything would be back to normal and penguin-free, he opened them.

Penguins, in his lounge, including one whose flipper was hovering just above his face, clearly ready to tap him again. Four penguins, to be precise, occupying the neutrally beige ten-by-twelve-foot space that Don called his lounge and office. The worn sofa had two of the black and white creatures resting back on it, whilst standing next to the old seventies cabinet that held Don's chunky black television another, fatter penguin stood. Between his flippers rested the TV remote.

This time Don's brain knew it was pointless to faint once more, so it kept him awake, although it did allow him to look and feel extremely shocked. It also allowed him to notice the fluff on the cream carpet and remind him that he needed to hoover.

"Sorry to surprise you like this, Mr Castor," came a soft east-coast American voice from the other side of the room.

On autopilot, Don turned to find the owner of the voice. *Now I really must be dreaming*, he told himself, as he caught sight of a woman standing next to his armchair. The fact she was standing next to the armchair, rather than sitting in it, wasn't what surprised him. It was the fact that there was a woman in his house. With the exception of a recent visit from a TV licence inspector, he hadn't had another soul in his house for months. Clients included.

'Castor Investigations' was the proud title on the small name plate affixed to the wall next to his front door. 'Don Castor, slightly balding, late thirties, mediocre P.I., only one accidental client in past three months' would have been a more accurate sign, but also more expensive and probably not the best advertisement for his services.

"Sorry, I don't understand. What's going on?" Don

asked, his eyes fixed on the statuesque and smartly dressed brunette so that his brain wouldn't have to deal with the penguins for a second or two. He could vaguely see one out the corner of his eye, so squinted slightly and tilted his head to block it out.

"As I say, I'm sorry to surprise you like this, Mr Castor. Allow me to introduce myself," said the woman, coming forward and holding out a shapely hand. "I'm Carlota, Carlota Pey. I represent the group."

As she said this, Carlota gestured around the room with the sweep of a hand. She was clearly indicating that 'the group' were the very creatures that Don was trying to tell himself didn't exist. Now he was really worried. He had tried to rationalise the situation by telling his brain that the penguins were all in his head and that Carlota was the only other person in the room. Quite why Carlota was there didn't matter, if it got rid of the penguins.

"We're sorry for the interruption."

Hearing Carlota using the word 'we' meant that either there was someone invisible in the room, or the penguins were real. His brain thought for a moment, never a totally good idea, but came to the eventual conclusion that an invisible house guest might not be any better than a penguin. At least he couldn't sit on a penguin, after all!

Think Don, think. What's going on? he demanded of himself, dredging through his brain for a clue. He had been in bed, dreaming about cake, when his alarm clock had woken him up at 6 am, as it normally did. Why 6 am? I have no idea, I'm merely the author. Quite why it went off at this time, Don had never actually thought about either.

His normal morning routine was to groan, roll over, yawn, groan some more, scratch himself in one or more places, and then suddenly fling out a hand to slam down the button on the alarm to silence it. After that, he would go back to sleep for an hour.

Most mornings, Don's attack on the clock went astray, resulting in him slamming his hand down hard on the oak of his bedside table. He had attempted to solve this in typical Don fashion by getting a bigger clock, a smaller table, and now only missed one day out of every two. He considered that progress.

The alarm woke me as normal, Don recalled, and so he knew his day had started as it usually did. He remembered, because today had been a 'miss' day and his hand still hurt. He had started to go back to sleep, but then something had changed. He heard his television playing the theme tune to some breakfast show or other. Don never watched breakfast television, mostly because he was always asleep when it was on. Clearly today was different.

He *had* thought, as he dragged himself out of bed, that he could go downstairs, turn it off, crawl back up the stairs to bed and get back to sleep. That was, until the penguins completely derailed the plan!

Still, Don rationalised, using logic we will simply come to know as 'Don-land', if the TV had woken him then he must be dreaming, as it never woke him up. See? Makes perfect sense.

"Mr Castor? Don? May I call you Don?" Carlota's smooth voice interrupted his daydream.

"You can call me anything you want," Don replied cheerfully, now that he had decided this was simply a dream that he could go along with.

"Okay, well, Don, as I said this must be a great shock for you. Let's go into the kitchen and get you a drink. You look like you need it."

"Yes, let's!" nodded Don. "Lots of ginger beer!" Quite why he was moving towards *Famous Five* territory, not even the author is sure. You did read the disclaimer re: the characters' actions, didn't you?

Carlota gestured towards the kitchen door, and Don turned to start to move towards it. From behind him then came another voice.

"Norgid, check Elyd is okay, will you?"

The voice appeared to come from the penguin standing next to the TV, a large flipper still resting on the remote

10

control.

"Will do," was the reply, as a penguin started to waddle towards the door.

Don looked at the first penguin.
Then he looked at Carlota.
Then at the second penguin, now waddling out of the lounge door.
Finally, Don turned back to Carlota again.
He couldn't bring himself to ask her whether she had heard the penguin. After all, if this was a dream, then of course she would have heard it. Thinking that the argument was too confusing, Don simply gave up. He rose and headed towards the kitchen. Maybe if he saw what the penguin was up to, it would help.

"I think I should explain what's going on for you, Don," said Carlota, as she followed Don into the kitchen. She quickly examined his kitchen drawers, and found a couple of paracetamol.

"You look like you need these," she smiled, handing him the tablets. Don took them mutely, looking around the kitchen as he did so. He registered Carlota's smile, the whiteness of her teeth, and remembered he should have phoned his dentist. Then he realised she had continued talking.

"...need you to do a job for me, well... us. You could say I represent their interests," she said, gesturing towards the lounge. "I thought you may be able to help me, or rather, us."

"You represent the penguins?" Don asked. He wasn't really interested in the answer, but thought he would go along with the dream to see what happened. His only disappointment was that Carlota would also disappear when the dream was over.

"Yes. They saved my life," Carlota replied.

"Saved your life? How?"

"It's a long story – which I'm sure I'll tell you later, when there is a gap in the plot that needs filling. Anyway, as they had helped me, I wanted to return the favour, and when they told me what was happening, I decided to help. You see Don, what they need is…"

Carlota didn't get any further as Don's brain decided to overload. The combination of listening to Carlota's words, and watching a penguin talk to his chest freezer caused Don to convulsively burst out laughing, though whether through happiness or hysteria, he couldn't tell. He laughed, or rather he made his normal horse-sounding whinnying noise. He laughed so hard that one of his window frames rattled.

Part of his brain registered that he needed a new window frame, whilst the other part allowed himself to feel glad. He had definitely proven once and for all this was a dream.

After all, no penguin would talk to a freezer!

"Don? What's the matter?" asked Carlota, her voice full of concern.

"Nothing. I just know I'm dreaming now. After all, why would a penguin talk to a... wait a minute..." Don blinked hurriedly, "one... two ...?"

Finally, Don realised why he had spent a couple of minutes watching a penguin talking to his freezer.

"Hello Mr Castor, I'm Elyd. Pleased to meet you."

For a long moment, Don just stood there, trying to tell himself that there was not a penguin sitting up in his chest freezer. He blinked a few more times, but the penguin remained.

"If you don't mind, it's getting a bit warm,' said the recumbent creature, lying back down. Carlota walked over to close the lid, whispering "It reminds him of home".

So desperate was Don to prove that he was dreaming that he rushed over to the freezer, pushed past Carlota and flung the lid back open again, longing for the penguin to have disappeared. Alas, the penguin simply stared back up at him and then held out a flipper.

"Hi."

"Let's get you sat down and then I can explain things properly," said Carlota, as Don backed away, defeated.

He allowed her to guide him slowly back into the lounge.

He was no longer sure that he was dreaming. A thin bead of sweat started to form on his forehead, and with more than just a tad of fear, he sat down.

"There's no easy way to say this, Don," Carlota started. "I'm hoping you will be able to open some doors for us."

"Doors? Where are you going?"

"No, not in that way. Call it more of a shopping trip. You can get anything if you can get to the right people in London. I know who we need to get to, but don't know enough people here to move things along. That's where you come in."

"How?"

"Well, I'm guessing, being an investigator, you get to know lots of good and not-so-good people."

Don just nodded. Carlota had, in one line, summed up pretty much everyone in his favourite and decidedly dodgy pub.

"Well, we need to buy something, something... difficult to get hold of, and dangerous."

Now Don felt cold. In part, he knew that this was because he had forgotten to put the central heating back on after he had finally been able to pay his gas bill. However, his central heating wasn't the main reason for his lack of internal warmth. Even he knew that the word 'dangerous' was not a good word. His knuckles were white against the armrests of his chair, fingers gripping as if they held a winning lottery ticket, as he whispered 'The Question'.

"What do you want?"

From across the room, a voice came from behind the back of Don's swivel chair.

"It's really rather simple, Mr Castor," came a stern voice. The chair slowly swivelled to reveal a clearly no-nonsense penguin. It was built like an ox, or at least as much like an ox as a penguin can be with a beak, no hooves, oh, and flippers … and markedly less hide and muscle, and a different height, and … oh all right then, it was built like a … well, a well-built penguin!

"Plutonium, Mr Castor," stated the penguin, too clearly to be mistaken. "We need you to get us one kilo of plutonium."

As Don fainted once more, his mind registered a voice above him.

"Not again! We're not going to get anywhere at this rate."

Chapter Two:
Further Into The Madness

When our poor detective finally re-awoke, the smell of fish in his nose once more, he sat in shock, the words echoing repeatedly in his head.

Ten kilos of plutonium?

As you will see from the above, paying attention is not one of Don's talents, but imagining things certainly is. Suddenly, he had a vision of the nation sitting down to watch evening TV only to have their favourite programmes interrupted. He could imagine a roughly edited video of a penguin, ammunition belt slung over its shoulder, rifle in flipper, standing next to a nuclear warhead, demanding everyone obey its commands. For a moment, he almost laughed at the thought, until he realised that there really were penguins in his lounge. Who knew how far they would go? Luckily, his fears were soothed.

"Don't be mistaken, Mr Castor. We don't want to take over the world or any nonsense like that. We just need it for our own use, that's all," explained a voice beside him, perfectly reasonably. He turned. A penguin. He turned back and fixed his eyes on an unusually tidy area of carpet as he somehow found his voice again.

"Your 'own use'?"

Now what am I doing? I'm talking to them! He groaned.

"Yes. We will explain that later. Carlota told us that you might know how to get in contact with people who can get it for us."

Just then, a penguin waddled back into the room. Don recognised it as the fat one called Norgid who had been talking to his freezer. He saw that it was clutching something between its flippers and, looking closer, he saw that it was a can of sardines. He watched in fascination as Norgid deftly flicked out a sardine and expertly swallowed it, all in one swift move. Sardine followed sardine and before long, the tin was almost empty. Clearly, here was a penguin who liked his food. At least, Don had assumed it was a male penguin, but as he was not an expert on the subject, he could not tell for sure.

Don's guess at penguin anatomy was right, as he was to learn later. The only thing that puzzled him was that the can of sardines had not been left open anywhere, and he was sure Carlota had not opened it in the short time they had been in the kitchen.

"I used that electric can opener of yours. I couldn't get my flipper under the ring-pull. You were so out of it I never had chance to ask either of you, did I?"
It took Don a moment to realise that although he was looking at Carlota, she was not speaking.

17

"Oh I see... here, hold on a second. Did I say that out loud?" Don asked in puzzlement as he turned back to Norgid.

"Say what?"

Don became aware of Carlota laughing.

"No, you didn't," replied Norgid to his question.

Don waited for an explanation from Norgid, but none was forthcoming. He turned back to Carlota.

"They're telepathic, Don. They can read your thoughts. He must have read your mind."

This was a good explanation, but sadly, Don could have done with hearing it a few seconds earlier, as he had just thought Norgid was a stupid blubber ball.

"Stupid is a bit steep," said the ox-like penguin. "Lazy and a blubber ball, definitely; but not stupid." Don decided not to think anything about the penguins again. So much for his innermost thoughts.

"Yes, they are rather shallow," chimed in another of the group.

"I hope you don't take offence," Don muttered, in the closest he ever came to an outright apology.

"No, we will leave it outside by the front gate as usual," joked the penguin, as it sat reading through the previous weekend's *Daily Eye* supplement. Suddenly it fell silent, as it turned the page and saw an advert for a wildlife magazine. Don had never seen a penguin blush before, but realised he must be seeing it now. The yellow flashes on the side of its head began to get brighter as it stared at the colour penguin in the picture. Finally, the embarrassed penguin hid its head behind the pages.

"Maybe I should introduce you to everyone, Don," said Carlota. "First off, this is Torac," she continued, gesturing to the well-built penguin.

Torac struck Don as a very direct penguin. Possibly it was the ramrod-straight back, flippers held tight to its sides. Or maybe it was the two eyes staring at him over the beak. He hadn't been stared at like that since fifth year Chemistry with Mr Burns.

On impulse, Don offered his hand. Torac walked forward, and extended a flipper to shake it. Don realised the plot was finally leaving reality (just as well really, it gets in the way far too much), but felt like he had broken the ice.

"Norgid you already know," continued Carlota, pointing to Norgid sitting on the end of the sofa, still eating sardines.

Next, she moved on to the penguin with the Sunday supplement, which was sitting in Don's favourite squashy armchair with its flippers up in front of the fire. Actually, penguins have feet, but Don had only just come to accept the penguins. He could not cope with realising they had feet too. Nevertheless, whether it had feet or flippers, the penguin had moved on to browsing through one of Dons' selections of London guide books.

"Have you got any thyme?" asked the penguin before Carlota could introduce him.

"All the time in the world," quipped Don, vaguely pleased that he had managed to make a funny joke for once. Besides which, he thought, it was true. This had to be a dream, so there was all the time in the world.

"Oh, good, Henec will be pleased. Our herbs go off too quickly. I'm Perec by the way."
Don was puzzled by several things that Perec had said, but as he couldn't work out whether to be more puzzled as to why 'theirs' went off too quickly, or why he wanted the thyme, or where this Henec character was, Don simply decided to think nothing. After all, three things at once to think about were too much for Don, even under normal circumstances. He decided to meet the next penguin, leaving Perec to his reading. Problem solved.

As they approached, Don could see that the next penguin was fidgeting around. In fact, now Don thought about it, he realised that the penguin had been fidgeting all the time. Before Carlota could make introductions however, the penguin hopped up and started talking.

"Please Mr Castor, please, I know you think this is a dream, but it really isn't. We are really real, and you aren't dreaming this. We are here, and we really need your help. Really. Please!"

Don could see that the poor penguin was agitated and, for the first time, thinking about what they had said so far, he could see why they would need his help. The thought of them trying to arrange face-to-face, or in their case, face-to-beak conversations was laughable.

"Exactly," said the penguin, clearly reading Don's mind. "The nine of us could never do it, which is why we need the two of you to help us. Carlota has been great, but we are so short of time, so we need you."

"Stop worrying," said Torac to the penguin. He turned to Don. "This is Senik."

Don barely took in the creature's name, as he was thinking about something else entirely. Suddenly, he walked over to the sofa, and looked behind it. No penguins. He checked behind the armchair. No, no penguins there, either. Behind the televsion cabinet? In his desk drawers? The drinks cupboard? Still no additional penguins. Then, to make sure he did not make a mistake, he slowly looked around the room, counting all the penguins in sight. Torac, Perec, Norgid, and now Senik. One, two, three, four.

"At last! This must be a dream," Don said triumphantly. He felt relieved that he had finally broken the spell. Unfortunately, so relieved that he missed the obvious yet again.

"What do you mean, Don?" asked Carlota.

"You said that there were nine of you, but there

are only four of you in here. So this has to be a dream."

For quite a while, there was silence, which Don took to mean he was right. He waited for four penguins, and a human, to disappear back out of his lounge. He found the thought of Carlota's disappearance less than satisfactory.

Unfortunately, as you no doubt know, Don was wrong. The silence was in fact while the penguins mentally discussed which of them it would be who would have to destroy Don's false hope, and also whether he really was smart enough to help them. In the end, it fell to Torac.

"Don. I'm sorry to disappoint you, but there are nine of us and this isn't a dream. Yes, there are four of us in here, but four more who you haven't met yet are elsewhere, and you must remember Elyd in the freezer."

"I've forgotten to let him out!" exclaimed Perec, at the mention of Elyd's name. He quickly hopped up and disappeared towards the kitchen.

Don turned back to Torac.

"Where are the other four?"

"Upstairs."

"Upstairs?"

"Yes. We decided to split up just in case you went crazy when you met us. They'll be down shortly, or we can go up and meet them."

Don was just about to argue when Perec came back in followed by Elyd, who, it appeared, had a slight issue. His

22

beak was completely frozen shut, a problem curiously lacking at the South Pole. Something about it being a different type of ice.

The penguins, Don and Carlota tried everything they could think of to get the beak unstuck again. Even when Torac took the remaining sardines, much to Norgid's disgruntlement, and waved them three inches from Elyd's face, it still did not come unglued.

"Why not stick your beak in the fire until it melts?" suggested Senik, after they had tried all the sensible solutions. Whether he meant the beak or the ice melting is unknown. To Elyd's relief, no-one took the suggestion seriously, mostly because they had no idea how to get penguin beak ash out of the fire.

"I've got some chisels somewhere out in my shed."

"I don't think that's a good idea, Don," answered Carlota, whilst Elyd made several sounds that appeared to be along the lines of 'Don't let him do that!'

Eventually, it was Perec who found the solution. He was casting his eyes around the room when they returned to the Sunday supplement. He reached over, and pulled out the wildlife advertisement that had caused him so much embarrassment earlier, and held it in front of Elyd's eyes. Instantly, Elyd's beak parted like lightning and the amazed penguin began to make a kind of purring noise in his throat. When he realised that he was only looking at a picture, the purring was muted to a low hum, and the glow faded out of his eyes, but at least his beak problem was solved. Don was pleased, although he did notice chunks of ice melting into his carpet.

A short while later, Don found himself with Carlota and Torac in the lounge. From upstairs came the sound of waddling feet as the remaining inquisitive penguins, including four that he had not yet met, took a tour of his three storey townhouse. He caught the occasional sound of drawers opening and closing, and also at one point, the sound of running water. He thought better than to ask why. Wise Don.

"Just out of interest, call it professional curiosity really, what do you want a kilo of plutonium for?" asked Don. It seemed like a fair question.

"It is. To run our colony."

"Run your colony?"

"Well," answered Torac, "it's a long story. You see, it all started about five years ago. We'd lived just like penguins throughout time, up to that point. Then the Baron arrived."

"The Baron?"

"Yes, Baron von Canton Ess. Have you ever heard of him?"

"Baron Ess? The name does ring a bell, I think," Don said as the clock struck the half-hour. "Wasn't he that

24

slightly eccentric scientist or something like that? The one everyone thought was behind stealing the 'List of Ten'? He went missing when they did, and hasn't been seen since?"

"Yes, that's him, although he didn't actually steal them; it was an accident."

"An expensive accident," commented Carlota. "I can't remember the total value of the paintings, statues and other objects that had 'disappeared' along with him. It was a small fortune at least."

"I know, but he hasn't yet found a way to get them all back to their right places, without getting himself traced, which is why he still has them," Torac told them. "He was working on a big experiment which went wrong, and he knew he would be arrested if he was found, so he decided the best thing to do was run. No-one would have believed his explanation, anyway. So he chose to flee."

"But how could he survive?"

"To be fair, he's actually fairly clever at most things. He gets supplies somehow, although he won't tell us exactly what's involved. Anyway, he could survive no problem, so he fled to Antarctica and set up base. Problem for us was that he set it up right in the middle of our ice-ball stadium."

"Your what!?" Don exclaimed, almost choking on his drink as he thought *an ice-ball stadium*?

"I know, we were pretty annoyed as well, it was the Cup Final," Torac added, leaving Don even more puzzled.

By now, however, our poor detective was beginning to realise that 'puzzled' was going to be the natural order of things.

"He was fairly shocked to see us, as you can imagine," Torac continued, "but we soon agreed a deal. We have lived happily with him ever since... well, almost. He's needed help with his experiments and we've kept him company. And, to be fair, he's done things for us too."

"How could he help you?"

"Little things, like heating our social areas. That's why we normally seem to waddle around on the ice, you see. It's not because we like to, or it's natural. It's because our feet are so cold. Waddling keeps them warmer than walking normally would."

"So what's gone wrong that you need the plutonium for? Has the Baron left?"

"Oh no, he hasn't left, at least, not the last we knew. You see, part of the deal with the Baron was that he would give us as little hassle as possible. The small experiments we could deal with. Some of them were really fun, like the iceball that said 'ouch' every time it was kicked, and the jokes we had with the rock-fish. We didn't even mind when we noticed that we had all grown too. What you humans know as Emperor penguins are a good foot shorter than us normally."

"So what's wrong?"

"Well, lately, he's started to dabble in matter

transfer again – at least, that's what he calls it."

"Matter transfer?"

"Yes, it involves taking something and swapping it with something else. That's how he ended up with all those treasures. It wasn't deliberate. It was simply an experiment that went wrong. He thought he had solved the earlier problems and could put everything back in its rightful place. Finally, he planned this really big experiment. Because of the magnetic field it creates, we all had to gather together in what he thought would be a safe area. Listening to him was a big mistake, although possibly better than if we hadn't."

"Why?"

"The experiment failed, very badly. When we realised what had happened, we held a meeting and decided to go it alone. We have everything we need thanks to the Baron, except for the plutonium."

"Go it alone? I can see the headline now," commented Carlota, "'Penguins Set Up Nation State'. Of course, I couldn't sell that to any editor without being considered completely insane."

"Oh, we know how to take care of all that, unlike you lot." Torac replied. "Everything is fully renewable, no waste, no pollution, no harmful effects, but it's too complicated to explain, something the Baron helped design. Once we have all the materials together, it will work."

"One thing I don't understand, though," said Don, feeling that someone had to stand up for humanity, even though he was sitting down.

"What's that?"

"Well, I know you made a deal, and I know he made a mistake, but couldn't you give him a second chance?"

"That's a bit difficult considering the circumstances, Don," Torac answered wearily. He then proceeded to explain with a reason that left Don's humanity stranded, knee-deep in water. In a ditch. Next to the hard shoulder of a minor road, somewhere very deep in the back of beyond. It was too shocking to be explained at this point in the story.

"What? All of you?"

"Yes. So, you see our predicament. That's why we need your help."

"And what do I get out of this deal?"

"That's where I come in," Carlota replied.

For a moment, Don put a very curious translation on the reply, until she continued.

"The penguins will give us the 'List of Ten' and a few other items that the Baron took. We will find some way to get them recovered. I'm sure we will come up with something if we try hard enough. After all, I am a journalist. We can always say that we tracked the Baron to somewhere fictitious and he fled but left the goods."

"That way, we get the fame and the reward, and everyone's happy," Don concluded. To him, it seemed a very good arrangement, especially the fame and reward parts. They were two of his favourite words, alongside food and sleep.

"That's the idea. It's not going to be easy, though. It mainly rests on you to start with. If you can't get hold of the plutonium, then we are back where we started."

"Don't worry about that. I have a few friends who owe me favours from an old job. I should be able to find them and see who they could put me in touch with."

Don didn't stop to realise that this meant he had accepted the case. Carlota and Torac shared a glance.

"Now that you've accepted the case Don, there's one other thing that might be a problem," mentioned Torac.

"What's that?"

"Well, whomever you deal with is bound to want to know whom you represent. They might ask to meet us, and that means being prepared."

"That shouldn't be a problem. As long as they get something for the plutonium, they will do business."

"No, I don't mean that. Look at us. We are penguins. How exactly are we meant to sit across from anyone?"

Don just groaned at the realisation. So did Carlota.

"All I can think of for now is trying to disguise you somehow," Carlota commented after a short silence.

"Disguise us? How?"

Torac had a point. Taking penguins shopping is not the easiest job in the world. Think of shopping for the absolute best fancy dress costume in the world for the most difficult child. Are you thinking of that experience? Good. Double that. Now, times by nine. Exactly. As usual though, Carlota looked on the bright side.

"Well, it could be worse, you could be elephants."

Chapter Three:
Take Me To Your Leader

With the introductions to the initial group completed, and leaving Elyd to melt over the carpet, Torac led Don up two flights of stairs, to meet the remaining members of the group.

"They decided to wait up here to make sure that you didn't have too much of a shock," Torac explained as he hopped onto the top floor landing and waddled towards a door at the far end. "I mean, we knew it would be a shock, but four of us were better than eight!"

Don wasn't totally convinced that finding eight penguins in his lounge would have necessarily been any worse than finding four, but decided not to argue the point. At least the group had tried to minimise the shock of first contact.

Torac reached out a flipper and pushed down the handle on the bedroom door easily, more easily than Don had expected.

"Living with the Baron, we learned a lot of human skills, Don," Torac explained, reminding Don of the penguin's in-built human mind-reading ability as he followed the smaller creature into the room.

Until recently, the room had belonged to a lodger Don had taken in. A weird guy named Todd whose sole contribution to society seemed to have been spiky green hair, a nose ring, and an unshakeable belief that he was going to be the 'next big thing' in the rock world. Despite his musical tastes, Todd had been a neat freak, reflected in the room in which Torac and Don now stood. The bed had been left washed and made. The chair on which he had sat to pen his 'hits' was tucked underneath the small wooden writing desk. Even the wall on which he had stuck posters of his rock gods had been whitewashed to eliminate the chemical stain of the Blu-Tac.

About the only thing that was spoiling the neatness of the room was the fact that four penguins currently occupied the middle of it. They were arranged in a reception line, with the tallest of them standing ever so slightly in front of the others. As Torac approached them, he shared a look with the tall penguin, and then gave a single nod.

"Don, this is Sevac. He's the leader of our group." Introduction complete, Torac stepped to the side and slightly behind the taller Sevac, who extended a flipper. As he did so, he stared up at Don with intense black eyes, his back ramrod straight. Even as Don held out his hand to shake the offered flipper, he had the distinct impression that he was being assessed, and couldn't help wondering what the verdict was.

"I'm sure you will do fine, Don." Sevac's crisp voice matched his demeanour. "Thank you for taking our case. I know it must have been quite a shock, which is why the four of us stayed up here. Well, it was also in case you went crazy. We had to be able to continue the mission."

There was no apology in Sevac's tone as he explained the real reason why they had stayed in two groups, just simple fact stated very directly as the penguin stared at Don with jet black eyes. Don still felt that he was being measured up by those eyes, and found himself unexpectedly promising them that he would get the job done. Sevac must have been able to hear the thought as he gave the poor detective a nod of re-assurance.

"Of course you will," said the penguin as he half-turned and pointed with a flipper to the smaller but wider penguin beside him. "Now, time for you to meet the rest of the group. Let me introduce Henec."

Don moved sideways and extended a hand before he saw that there was no flipper coming out to greet him in return. Instead, he was surprised to see a large book balanced on one of the flippers, the other inserted in it, probably to keep its place.

"Good to meet you Don, sorry my flippers are full. Can I ask? Do you have any fresh herbs?"
Don wasn't sure what puzzled him most about the newly introduced Henec. A penguin, with a book. A penguin with a book that it had at least opened, and judging by the

flipper position, had probably read. A penguin that could read.

Don reached his normal three new items processing limit and paused for a moment, his brain resetting.

"Henec is a chef. He'll probably take over your television while we are here."
Alongside Sevac, Henec nodded in agreement and now Don caught sight of the book's title. It was a recent present from a grateful client, '101 Ways to Cook Without Fish'.

"We need the variety," Henec explained once he saw where Don was looking. "As you can guess, even with assistance we don't get to eat that much that doesn't have some sort of fishy influence. Hopefully I can try a few things while I'm here."

"Sure, help yourself," Don agreed, then realised a split second later that he had just given a penguin free rein of his kitchen. With knives and all sorts of equipment.

"Don't worry, he'll be careful," Sevac placated as he waddled past Henec to the final two penguins who Don saw were glistening. Rivulets of water were sliding off their black pelts onto the cheap carpet, forming an ever-darkening patch on the beige material.

"Finally, we have Dara and Nela."

"Hi Don," chimed two voices in unison as the two wet penguins both raised a flipper, one of which had a towel waving on the end of it. "Don't worry Don," continued one of them. "The carpet will dry out. Next time we won't have to hide in here. We didn't expect you to agree to help us so quickly; otherwise we wouldn't have used your bathroom."

Don looked from one penguin to the other as he tried to find some sort of distinguishing feature. Unlike Torac's bulk, Senik's nervousness or Sevac's height, the final two penguins looked identical. Now, to be fair, I dare say that if you or I looked at two penguins you would be hard pushed to tell them apart, even if they were in your lounge, or spare bedroom in this case. Don had felt reasonably confident that he would remember those he had met, but the final two looked impossible to tell apart.

"That's not really surprising, we are sisters," one of the two explained, reading the mental thought. "Anyway, we are normally together, so just call one of us and we'll both be there. Now, as you've met us, we'll get back to the bathroom if that's okay?"
Don wasn't sure why they wanted to go to the bathroom, and thought it wise not to ask. Instead, he nodded and moved to the side, allowing the two penguins to waddle past him, one of them still carrying the towel. As they walked, they left little claw impressions in the carpeting, along with a steady trail of water drops.

"Sorry about the water, Don. After being on the go for so many days, I thought letting them relax was a good idea," Sevac commented, as Dara and Nela left the room and turned right towards the bathroom. "They'll probably spend most of their time in the bathroom, those two. Just think about using it and they will come out whenever you need."

Don nodded again. "And why exactly…?"

"It'll appear later in the book. Let's just say they are practising and everyone will find out when the author is ready."

With that future minor plot filler established, Don, Sevac, Torac and Henec left the room and took the two flights of stairs back down to the lounge. The remaining penguins were now relaxed on the sofa, crammed together, watching *This Morning*.

"Where's Carlota?" Don asked, looking around and realising that the reporter was now missing.

"She said something about shopping," replied Perec, the television remote sitting underneath his right flipper on the arm of the sofa.

"I think her exact words were, 'he has nothing in his cupboards. I don't know what he eats'."

Don thought it vaguely ironic that it was Norgid who mentioned food. Even though Don had only been upstairs with Torac a few minutes, there was now an empty circular

36

salmon tin sitting on top of the equally empty sardine tin next to the corner of the sofa.

"What? Have you any idea how long we have been travelling? I need my food. And she is right, what do you eat?"

"I get by. I don't eat much."

By now, Don was familiar with the penguins' ability to read minds, so perhaps it was as well that he didn't think that his lack of food was mainly tied to his lack of clients, and thus money. It might have damaged their opinion of him somewhat, which given that he hadn't even considered getting them to sign a contract would not have been a good thing.

"Carlota said to let you know that she would be gone for a while," Elyd piped up, the last of the ice crest fading from the top of his black head as he sat next to a still-fidgeting Senik on the red fabric sofa. "There are a few things she needs to try and arrange about getting us back down to the Antarctic once you get the goods. She said that she would shop on the way back. If she isn't back by six, then consider getting us out of the house."

"Get you out of the house? Why?"

"We all think that we've got here undiscovered, but it doesn't hurt to be sure. If anyone were following Carlota, then she'd not want to lead them back here. After all, it was only because she knew how to check if she was being followed that we met in the first place."

37

Don, with all his seating occupied with black, white and yellow creatures, perched himself on the edge of his newly white-gloss painted windowsill. A comment from a recent private client about how Don must use 'shabby' as part of his professional disguise had finally caused him to examine the décor of his office. With a critical eye, he had taken in the cracked and flaked paintwork of the window and the yellowing old-fashioned wallpaper and realised he needed a decorator. This was why the penguins had found a smart, if possibly too beige, lounge.

"So how did you meet Carlota?"

"Well, it was going to be a long story," replied Sevac.

"Was going to be? What do you mean, was going to be?"

"Apparently we have not got time now. Something about the author wanting to get on to the next bit."

"Well, I guess I'll just have to hear the short version, then."

"We held a Council, agreed what we thought was the best way to proceed – even though the odds were minimal – and then the nine of us were chosen to set out on the quest."

"Oh, kind of like Lord of the Rings!"
Don pointed proudly to the extended DVD box set.

"Yes, just with a lot less wide-angle helicopter shots. We had two missions. The first, to get the colony transferred back somehow. The second, to get plutonium so that we could be self-sufficient."

"Sounds a good plan."

"It is. Anyway, we ended up in Siberia and were working out what our next move should be. We realised that we couldn't help ourselves to what we needed from your nuclear plants. They were too tough to get into. We were in hiding, discussing what to do, when we came across Carlota. She managed to smuggle us out of the continent and into the UK. After that, we arrived here and waited in your shed last night until your neighbours had gone to bed. Then we ... well, Carlota ... picked the lock on your back door."

"Ah, I was wondering how you got in."

"She is very good with whatever she used. Didn't take long at all. After that, it was a case of waiting for you to get up. In the end, we started watching TV to catch up. It's been a few weeks since we last saw a news round-up."

Don was momentarily taken aback, but then remembered just how closely the penguins had integrated with the Baron and human life. Obviously, they had kept up-to-date with the world via satellite television or something similar. From the nods he received in Mexican-wave style from the penguins on the sofa, he knew that he was right.

Just at that moment came the chime as Don's front door bell rang.

Chapter Four:
Flight

The ring of the front door bell caused a penguin pile-up in the centre of the lounge. They all hopped up en-masse and collided with each other as they looked around.

"Wait, wait… it's okay. It's just a potential client," Don called over the sound of rebounding blubber, as he watched Senik dive behind the sofa, literally clearing it and disappearing beak first. Perec was busy squeezing himself behind the TV cabinet, leaving just the black dome of his forehead in view, while Elyd simply muttered 'freezer'.

"No… no need," Don called, then realised that he could just think the words and save the author's stock of quotation marks. He mentally pictured the phone call, a new client who needed his help on a case, arranged long before the penguins had turned up to disturb the sanctity of his lounge/office. "Honestly, it'll just be my client. Why don't you all go into the kitchen and I'll bring her in here. Then you can either stay there, or go upstairs," he continued, as the doorbell rang again.

Sevac nodded and gave a single deep booming note. Instantly the remaining penguins in view froze. Then, without further word, a group of well-organised and disciplined penguins were suddenly waddling, single-file, into the kitchen. From upstairs came a rhythmic thud, thud,

thud as two more penguins came hopping rapidly down the stairs to join their compatriots. Don headed the other way, ambling slowly into the hallway towards the front door. He glanced back to confirm the door from hall to kitchen was closed.

"Sorry to have kept you, welcome to Castor Investigations," he announced before the front door was more than half way open. Standing on the doorstep was a mouse. Not an actual mouse – how would one ring the doorbell, after all? – but a woman who Don simply labelled Mouse before she had even opened her mouth.

If anything, Sevac may have had an inch of height on her, and he certainly had a more penetrating stare than the eyes that looked at him briefly and then quickly looked away. She was encapsulated in a thick red duffel coat, its wooden toggles showing years of wear as they strained to retain the small but wide body underneath. The duffel ended in a thick pair of grey woollen tights, inserted at their feet into a pair of tiny brown crocs, beside which sat a brown carpet bag.

"Mr Castor?" The timid squeak came as no surprise. The question did, however. "Have I got our appointment time wrong? I'm sure we said eleven?"

"Yes yes, of course," Don agreed. "Come on in."

It was only as he turned and stood back to let the Mouse in that he caught sight of himself in the hallway mirror, and understood her hesitation.

"Oh, please excuse the attire. I adopt the Yo-Mak-Oopy school of an ancient detecting art. It helps generate Chi ahead of each new appointment."

"Oh, I didn't realise that," the Mouse replied, pushing past Don into the house and shutting the front door behind her quickly, as if she was afraid that the Chi would escape out of the door and go flowing off down the street. Quickly Don stepped past her to prevent her headlong march towards the kitchen door.

"Unfortunately with all the rain that we've had recently there is a water leak in my main office," Don blatantly lied as they walked the few short steps down the hall.

As the Mouse had not read this book, there was no problem with Don's usual excuse as to why he was showing the client into his living room. He ushered the Mouse into the lounge/office, and to a battered leather chair that had only witnessed a handful of clients in the past year.

"Can I get you anything? Tea, coffee, some water perhaps?" Don asked once his new client was settled into the chair, her legs so short that her feet didn't reach the floor.

"No, I'm fine thank you," came the squeak once more, and so Don walked around to the other side of the desk and into the chair that Carlota had been occupying just a couple of hours before.

"So how can I help you Mrs...?"

"Baker. Ms Caroline Baker."

"Right, well, how can I help you, Ms Baker?" Don asked as he made a show of opening a drawer and pulling out a crisp white legal pad. From directly behind a 'Don Castor Investigations' nameplate on the far edge of the desk he then picked up a silver fountain pen, leaning forward and adopting his 'intent detective' look. Shame he missed the fact that ink had pooled in the lid of the pen and was now running down his hand.

"I was wondering whether this was the right place to come," began the squeaky voice from across the desk. "But then I saw that you have one too, so I know you will understand me."

Don sat and watched as Ms Baker reached down to her side and picked up the handles of the large carpet bag, bringing it up to sit on her knees.

"So how many do you have?" she asked as the slowly unzipped the bag.

"How many what?"

"Cats, of course," Ms Baker said, as from the depths of the carpet bag emerged a bundle of black fur and whiskers. "I knew as soon as I saw the tuna tin on the floor. Rascal always liked a tin of tuna in the morning... didn't you, my precious?" Her face buried into the cat's fur as she ended the sentence and she gave the poor creature a little shake.

It was only then, as Don put together the tuna can and the word 'cat', that he took a good look at the black and white bundle and spotted that something wasn't quite right.

"Yes you are, Rascal. Oh, yes you are. Mommy always gives you your favourites, doesn't she?"

"Erm, Ms Baker..."

"Oh, yes you are."

"Ms Baker... umm... Ms Baker!"

"Sorry. Yes?"

"Ummm... is Rascal alright?"

"Alright?"

"Yes, he seems a bit... stiff."

"Well, of course he's stiff. He's dead."

Don took a mentally calming deep breath as he began to wonder just what type of slightly mad person was sitting opposite him, waving a dead black and white moggy in the air, odd strands of fur dropping off to float down onto the carpet. As they fell, Don tried to think of the quickest way to get the woman back out of the front door. He already had talking penguins to deal with; he really didn't need a dead cat as a client.

"I'll pay you whatever you want. I thought five hundred pounds advance would cover most of your initial expenses?"

Don sat back, thinking just how nice this new client was. For something to do with a dead cat, five hundred pounds seemed a bit excessive a fee. Given the lack of suitable clients, notwithstanding the nine non-humans in the kitchen, Don was not in a position to argue.

"That should be a suitable amount for initial investigations. Obviously, an advance is not returnable, you do realise that?"

"Oh, certainly."

From elsewhere in the depths of the cat-carrying carpet bag came a chequebook and pen, and before Don could say anything, a crisp cheque was lying on his walnut desk, made out to D.C. Investigations for the delightful sum of five hundred pounds. Before it could be withdrawn, he picked it up, turned to the silver filing cabinet kept just behind the desk, and slipped it into the middle of a stack of filing envelopes. The envelopes were for show – the cabinet was always empty – but it made a good impression of being successful.

"So, how may Don Castor Investigations help you, Caroline?"

***

"She wanted what?!" asked Carlota several hours later. She was laid out on the sofa, Don in his swivel chair as they watched *Coronation Street*. "Since when was she the owner of The Rovers?"

"A couple of months ago," Don explained as he glanced at the screen. "Tony had a fling with that girl in the paper-shop, so she kicked him out and sold the house. Bought the pub with the profits."

"I thought you didn't watch it?"

"It's been a slow few months, so I have caught the odd episode. Anyway, yes, she wants me to prove this is her cat. She thinks her next door neighbour has done a swap. Apparently Rascal here and his brother were split, one in each house. My job," Don continued, as he held the stuffed cat aloft, "is to try and determine which of the two this is."

"But she was calling it Rascal and all that a page ago."

"I know, but it seems that she has decided that until I find out one way or another, she will just treat it as hers. Her words were that she just wants closure."

Carlota laughed as she stretched out on the sofa.

"Well, rather you than me for that one. Any idea how you'll go about it?"

46

"Not a clue. I might just knock on the neighbour's door and ask. Apparently she hasn't done that – something about them not getting on."

Carlota finished her stretch and sat up, drawing her legs under her on the sofa as he continued. "Anyway, I'll sort that. I wanted to ask you this morning; how did you get involved with the penguins? I don't imagine they waddled down the street and bumped into you."

"Not quite. Do you have any more of this wine?" she asked as she held out her glass. "I'll trade you a refill for how I met them."

A minute later, two full glasses of wine, Don and Carlota occupied the sofa as she began to explain how it was that she came to meet the group.

"How it was that I came to meet the group was by accident; a fortunate accident for me."

With the use of a gentle flashback, we will join Carlota not long after she realised she was in trouble.

"Come on, faster," Carlota breathed to herself and her car as she hurtled down the narrow road, trying to avoid the precarious drop to her right. But for the moonlight shining down, as moonlight tends to do, she knew she would have been over the edge already, or caught, which would end the same way. Even so, behind her the headlights were growing steadily brighter and larger as her pursuers gained ground.

"Just a little faster," she whispered, almost pleading with the car, although given the fact that the engine was whining even louder than a four-year-old in a sweet shop, she knew it was only a matter of time.

Finally, rounding another tight curve, the road left the cliff-side and started inland. Carlota pushed her foot to the floor in an effort to get the last drops of speed out of the hire car. If only she had gone for the upgraded model! All the while behind her, the pursuit closed in.

BANG!

A sharp pop, a lurch, and suddenly the hire car veered to one side.

"Were they shooting at you?" asked Don.

"No. Typical car found the only pothole on the entire road and shredded a tyre."

"So what happened?"

"I'm sure the author is about to explain."

Back in the dark Siberian wilderness, Carlota fought desperately with the wheel to keep the car on the road. The lurch, along with the thud-thud-thud of the deflated tyre, told her all she needed to know. She looked up hurriedly to see if there was any form of shelter or a way to hide before she was caught. Ahead, she could see the beginnings of the Arhbhoor forest. It was dense (not its fault – it's a forest, so it can't go to school) and very dark.

If I can make it into there, maybe I can lose them, she thought to herself.

Another glance in the rear-view mirror. No doubt about it now, she was being caught up more steadily, and as her car finally drove into the outskirts of the forest, the enemy were only a few car-lengths behind.

Then came a horrendous grinding noise, as the steel rim of the wheel punctured the rubber and made contact with the road. The car started to slow.

Now or never, girl, Carlota told herself. She hastily stuffed the memory card from her camera inside her bra, and opened the driver's door.

Carlota leaned back on Don's sofa and closed her eyes, picturing the scene as she continued narrating.

"As I rounded a bend, I dived out and ran for cover. The car continued onto the other side of the road and into trees, so I thought they would follow it and I could run. Seems though that they had caught a glimpse of me just before I got under the cover of the trees. As soon as they pointed the car in my direction, I turned and ran for it."

This time, the moonlight worked against her, although it obviously cannot be blamed for simply doing its job. It's not as if it can see nearly 400,000 miles to go 'Oh, look, there's someone in some trees who is in danger because I'm reflecting sunlight. Maybe I should change orbit.' That's unrealistic.

"There was so much light coming through the trees that they could see where I was going, and they came after me. I've never been so scared. Then, amazingly, I ran into Torac, literally. Simply bumped into him as I was looking ahead at my eye level, not theirs!"

Once more into the flashback, dear readers.

"Help me," Carlota whispered, not quite comprehending that she was asking for help from a penguin. A group of penguins in fact, judging by the number that suddenly appeared. Without a sound, they formed a wall of black in front of her, hiding her completely from view.

"Hold on, you're penguins? How can penguins be here?"

"We'll tell you later. Now quiet, they are almost here."

The crunching of snapped twigs confirmed this as a couple of pairs of heavy boots thudded towards them. She was slightly pleased to note that they sounded out of breath. *Those keep-fit DVDs really were worth the money,* she thought, allowing herself a light moment in amongst the danger.

"Reportiski runnei heerati?" came the panting, gruff voice of one of her pursuers.

"She went that way," came the reply of one of the penguin group in front of her. In unison, she saw nine flippers extend and point further down into a long dark trail.

"But no-one would fall for that, surely?" asked Don in amazement.

"Well, wouldn't you, if you came across nine talking penguins in the middle of a forest at night?"

"Why only at night?"

"Well, any time then."

"I suppose you are right," Don agreed, after thinking about what he would do in the same situation. "So what happened? Did they come back?"

"I don't know if they did or not. As soon as they had thundered off down the path and were out of sight, the penguins shepherded me off. They actually took me further into the forest in a different direction, just in case whoever was chasing me turned back and headed for the road."

"Okay, I understand now how they saved you but still, how did you end up in the UK? It's hardly a stone's throw from there to the middle of London."

"Well, I could tell you through some dialogue, but I think the author wants to do a flashback."

"Again?"

"I guess he'll do it a few times. Might as well go along for the ride."

"Saves us talking it through using an extremely unlikely amount of highly descriptive dialogue and detail."

"Fancy a cup of tea while he does it?"

"Why not? We can keep an eye on the next chapter in case we are needed for anything."

Chapter Five:

A Ship, A Ship, A Smile For A Ship

Cue flashback...

It had taken a couple of minutes for Carlota's adrenaline levels to return to normal after her rescue by the group of penguins. She was still in a state of shock when what was clearly the group's leader turned to her.

"You can rest now. They can't search this whole forest for you, and they won't have expected you to have come this way."

If the moonlight through the trees hadn't been illuminating the opening and closing beak of a penguin, she would have had difficulty believing that one was talking to her. As it was, she believed it with tremendous difficulty, mostly because they had just saved her life. The feeling of the damp, leaf-strewn earth underneath her hand confirmed that she was sitting on the floor of the forest, not having some weird daydream. Even so, a talking penguin that seemed to understand how humans acted was something she was struggling to get to grips with.

"You aren't in fancy dress, are you?" was the first question that came into her head.

Now, now. Be generous, she was still in a slight state of shock, and normally she wouldn't have asked this question.

"A fancy dress? We don't wear human clothes," the penguin had replied.

"No, I mean you aren't pretending to be penguins?"

"Why would we pretend to be penguins? We are penguins. There's no need to pretend."

"But ..." Carlota started, but then realised there were too many questions she would want to ask first.

"I think the question you are after is; why are we here and why do we talk?"

"Well, that was two of them, yes. I mean, you are real, aren't you?"

"I think you know the answer to that one. You heard those people talking to us. If we weren't real, they wouldn't have done that and I guess they would have caught you."

"I know, but you're..."

"Penguins, yes. I'm Sevac, and I lead our group. And you are?" enquired the penguin as it held out a flipper.

"Carlota, Carlota Pey."

"And you're thinking that you still can't believe you are having a conversation with a penguin. Now you're thinking, how does he know that? What? How is he knowing what I'm... Wait a min. Will you stop it while I think... Ohhh."

And indeed that had been exactly what Carlota had been thinking. The 'ohhh' had been her realisation that Sevac could not only read her mind, but could also read it in real time.

"We all can, Carlota. Penguins talk mostly through the mind. It makes it easier for us to communicate when we have to stand around in snow-storms for you to film us. As we know of your language, I can understand what you are thinking. I can appreciate that this must be odd for you. You aren't the first human I've talked to."

"I'm not?"

"No. In fact, it's lucky you aren't, in a way. If it wasn't for the other one I talked to, we wouldn't have been in this forest tonight."

Carlota said a mental prayer of thanks to whoever the other penguin conversationalist was.

"His name's Baron von Canton Ess. You may have heard of him?"

"As you can imagine," said the modern day Carlota, a steaming mug of tea clutched between her hands, "I recognised the name. I had pretty much the same discussion with the group that you did the first morning you met us. Sevac introduced me to everyone, and explained why there were there."

"They trusted you just like that?"

"Yes. I did wonder about that, but Sevac says it's

56

their seventh sense that enables them to know who is ultimately kind or unkind."

"You mean sixth sense. You said seventh."

"No, no; seventh. Apparently the sixth one is something we haven't discovered yet, but they say that we are close. Anyway, they trusted me, as I'm sure the author is about to confirm."

"We know we can trust you," Sevac had told her, after summarising their predicament. "So do you think you can suggest anything we can do to speed things along?"

"After you have just saved my life? I'll do more than that. I'll help you track it down. There's a detective in London who might be worth going to see." Then, realising that World Cities may not be something in a penguin's normal education, she elaborated about where it was.

"I've seen a few documentaries on London," Henec piped up, adding something about a favourite TV programme containing a highly opinionated British chef. It turned out he wasn't alone as Torac commented about football, Perec about a popular comedy show and Dara and Nela seemed to have a fascination with the Krays!

"London sounds a good place to start," agreed Sevac. "Any ideas how we get there?"

"I think I might," Carlota replied and then outlined her suggestion.

So it was that forty-eight hours later, Carlota and the group of nine penguins stood looking down on a fast-flowing river, twenty miles through the forest.

"This leads all the way down to the Flostagard port," Carlota explained as they all stood on the bank. "If you can swim down to near the port, I'll try and get a lift on a boat and then meet you there. Once there, we can try and find a boat to get across to England."

"Okay. The swim will be easy for us," Sevac had confirmed, "but how will you be able to find us?"

"When I first got into the country I checked out Flostagard as part of the story I was working on. When you arrive, you will find the port is bordered by a long stone harbour wall, extending into Flostagard Sound. Wait for me there and I will find you. After dark, say three days from now. There are enough boats going up and down the river that I should be able to get there by then. I want to stay off the roads for a while, hopefully make the people chasing me think I've got lost in the forest."

"We'll wait there after dark then in three days' time, and then the next two days after that, too. If you don't make it by then, then we'll try and work our own way to England."

"How will you do that?"

"Leave that to us. Three days, then," said Sevac. After a very brief flippered farewell, Carlota watched as one by one the penguins slid down the bank to the river and into the water.

Three days later found Carlota, true to her word, walking out onto the stone wall of the harbour at Flostagard in search of the penguins. Rain was hammering onto the rocks, or more exactly it was actually sort of splashing down, and Carlota briefly worried that she wouldn't be able to discern the black penguins. She didn't want to end up walking into the sea! Fortunately, she didn't have to walk far, as soon a small shape started to waddle towards her.

"You made it okay, then?" Carlota asked as she did a quick count of the penguins in the moonlight.

"I thought the author said it was raining?" Don objected.

"He did, but there was a very convenient gap in the clouds. Anyway, we are interrupting his flashback."

"Yes, we made it without any trouble," Sevac informed Carlota as they stood in the darkness. "The only real challenge has been keeping out of sight during daylight, so we've kept swimming up the coast. There's a small island up there we've been hiding on."

"Without food, though," said a voice mournfully. Carlota guessed this had to be Norgid.

"So? I like my food," the penguin persisted.

"Do we need to get you something to eat then before the voyage? I can't exactly feed you on-board."

"You mean you've found us a ship?" asked Perec.

"I think so. I've got to go and meet the Captain again in an hour to make sure. From what he said, the voyage will be in ten days. Something about wanting to make sure the engine is okay and won't break down on the way."

"Ten days?" moaned Norgid. "Ten whole days?" Clearly the prospect of engine failure wasn't an issue.

"We will need food," Sevac apologised. "We can go without food for quite a while normally, but this trip has already used a lot of our reserves. Sorry."

So it was that Carlota found herself at a hypermarket thirty minutes later, standing and looking as innocent as she could as an improbably large volume of fresh fish, shrimp, prawns and other assorted dead sea-life was passing through the checkout.

"Many fish," the bored check-out clerk commented, clearly content to have someone to talk to this late at night, and clearly confused as to why someone would be making such a late night purchase.

"It's for a friend. She gets some weird cravings," Carlota tried, cringing that this was the best line that the author could give her at this precise moment. She made a mental note to contact her agent. The author meanwhile was still chuckling to himself at the line, but then reading about the agent, decided to give Carlota a better line.

"I work for a caterer's. There's a big wedding tomorrow and our stock has failed to arrive."

"Ah," said the clerk in a knowing tone, clearly someone who was used to wedding day fish supply issues. That seemed to be the end of the clerk's interest in proceedings, mainly because the author wanted to move the story onwards.

With the bags of seafood tucked in the boot of Carlota's new hire car, she made her way to a waterfront bar to meet the Captain who she hoped would provide passage for her and nine stowaways. Well, the Captain would not be informed of the stowaways of course, as technically they would not then be stowaways and this would not work the same way.

Finding the correct vessel had taken most of the morning, and many bank notes. It had to be one that suited her needs, something big enough for her to be able to hide the penguins on board, but not so big that it would need a super-efficient crew, who might notice a passenger being where they shouldn't be, or might check any extra cargo.

"But how were you planning to get the penguins on board?" Don asked as they carried more drinks back from his kitchen. "I mean, surely they would be seen unless you... oh, blast!"

A dark stain started to appear on Don's outfit where he had just spilled his tea, or more exactly where the author had tipped it in response to yet another un-scripted interruption to the flashback.

"No, I had a plan for that," Carlota explained, getting the flashback back on track, and earning a positive character trait bonus into the bargain.

She knew from her first meeting with the Captain of the vessel that tonight was a double celebration for the crew, hosted at a local bar. Firstly it was the twenty-first birthday of the ship's galley-boy, and secondly the crew were celebrating a whole year of trouble-free operations, something that the Captain had intimated was not always the case.

Pulling up in front of the bar, Carlota was pleased to see that it was packed. The inebriated state of the crew was a factor Carlota was banking on, provided she could complete negotiations for her own passage.

"You found us okay, then?" Marcus asked her as she sat down in a free chair. Marcus, as I'm sure you have understood, is the Captain. It seems less formal to use his name, especially as he has been given one.

"Yes, no problem," Carlota replied, deliberately resting her hand next to his on the table. "Now, can I get you a drink?"

"Are you trying to bribe me for free passage?"

"No bribes, I assure you," Carlota assured him.
Marcus laughed, his piercing blue eyes twinkling as they
held Carlota's gaze. Her heartbeat quickened as she
surveyed his handsome, yet rugged, face, and then
glanced down to his firm, muscular torso. She saw his
biceps straining the sleeves of his shirt and wondered
what those powerful arms would feel like as they held her
close to him, as those powerful lips of his reached across
and ...

Hmmm. Apologies, dear reader. Wrong genre. Not really
sure how that last paragraph appeared. An inquiry has
begun, but in the meantime please ignore it. The author
will also ignore Carlota's disappointed sigh, and Don's
vague stirrings of jealousy.

Several drinks later, and after Carlota, who was still sober,
had impressed on Marcus, who was quite drunk, that she
really did see why it was so vital to call a boat a boat, and
a ship a ship, a deal was done and a fee agreed for her
passage. Now, she had only one thing left to sort out. She
got Marcus on his own by generously offering to drive him
back to the port. It was a short trip, so she knew she had
to act fast.

"I have three crates of valuable sculptures. They

are quite big. I need to bring them with me as I'm couriering them for a client."

"That's fine. Like I said earlier, when we sail we are only taking a half load, so your crates can go in the second hold."

"Thanks. I'll need access to them to check the contents are safe against the elements."

"Again, that's no problem. You can have exclusive access to that hold. It's probably for the best, knowing my crew," Marcus admitted as they arrived at the dock.
As I said, it was a short trip.

"After that, there's not really much to tell," Carlota concluded as she ended the flashback. "A friend from the art world owed me a favour so I got him to reserve me some sculptures from an art storage place, got them crated up and delivered to the port. That got the paperwork sorted. Then, it was simply a case of putting the sculptures into one crate with the help of a local dock worker, and once he'd disappeared I put the penguins and food into the other two crates."

"But how could they breathe?"

"I nearly forgot about that, then knocked some holes in them and told Marcus it was to prevent mould build-up on the sculptures."

"Nicely done. And so you got loaded aboard?"

"Yes, and then the night before we docked in the

UK I used the cover of a storm to get the penguins up on deck. As we sailed into port, they slipped over the side and swam to where we had agreed. I picked them up in a hired minibus that night. Then we drove to yours and gave you that little surprise. I hope you don't mind." She grinned.

Chapter Six:
Slip Ups

Several thousand miles away from the nice warm house containing one bemused detective, a reporter, nine penguins, and an abused alarm clock, there was a little question of heat on someone's agenda. Or rather, the severe absence of it. And to be fair, there wasn't really an agenda. Agendas are not really suitable when you are lugging a very heavy camera through snow, and you happen to be quite cold.

To say that Martin was quite cold isn't really doing him justice. Quite cold implies that he was not totally freezing, teeth starting to chatter. Of course, if he was totally freezing, then he would be a solid block of ice, without teeth chattering away. Hence quite cold. Simple logic.

So, having firmly established his less-than-heated status, we need to ask ourselves why Martin is lugging a heavy camera through snow in the first place. I'm fairly sure that you would not do such a thing, as is probably the case with every reader (except that weird one from the start of Chapter One). You would be quite sensible. So why is Martin different? Does he have some form of cold weather or camera fetish? Has he been stranded after an argument and is having to make his way back to a town somewhere?

Is he simply an idiot?

No, No and Maybe, but that's not really relevant to the story.

Martin is a relatively sane person and the only reason he was trudging through the snow at all was that it was his job. The camera probably gives it away, but for the record, Martin is a cameraman for a television company.

"Not a sign, not one," Martin heard Harry, the sound engineer, mutter for the tenth time that day as they made their way disconsolately back to their camp.
Martin and Harry were not alone. Up ahead were Willy, their technician-cum-dogsbody, and Charles Hattenburg. If you aren't into your natural history TV, then you may not recognise the name, and perhaps you can be forgiven for not knowing that Hattenburg is the premier wildlife journalist in Europe.

Consider yourself suitably forgiven.

The group were *meant* to be filming polar bears. This was the third year that they had been in the Arctic, following a particular set of bears. The mission planning had started two months earlier when the bear's tracking collars had shown them moving back towards their end-of-winter grounds, exactly as they had done for the previous two years. Then, four weeks ago, only a handful of days before

Hattenburg's crew were due to fly up to their initial camp, the signal bank tracking the bears had gone blank. It had been assumed that the bank had simply broken down due to the cold. Until, that is, Hattenburg had opened the cabinet for it at the camp and found it working away quite happily, though clearly bored with nothing to do.

And that's how things had remained since. Each day for the first two weeks, the crew had gone out to all the regular spots and dens to await the arrival of the first bears. It was only after those two weeks that they had all come to the same conclusion: the bears weren't late, they were missing.

"It's almost like the place has been stripped bear," Harry had joked at the time. After working together for so long, the others had gotten used to the lack of talent in Harry's jokes, but he still received the usual looks of despair and, in Hattenburg's case, annoyance.

"This isn't the time for jokes," he had lectured his crew back in camp after one fruitless afternoon. "The bears must have moved off somewhere outside the trackers' range. They can't have crossed the glacier, so they must still be near enough for us to be able to track them down. We know they have to stay fairly close to the trail down to that inlet."

"So what do we do?" asked Martin.

Hattenburg had pulled out a map and the other three

gathered round. It was a very simple-to-understand map, given that it was mostly a white mass. A curve at one end marked the inlet leading back to their supply ship.

"We'll start staking out from the inlet back up to the main glacier," said Hattenburg as he traced a finger over the map, "then we'll move east towards that ridge that we surveyed in year one. They can't have wandered too far. They'll need to be near the inlet for food later in the season. Sooner or later we will come across bears, or their tracks."

Well, I guess it wasn't meant to be sooner, Martin muttered to himself, thinking back on that conversation now four long, boring, weeks ago. A couple of hours earlier Hattenburg had, yet again, reluctantly called an end to the day's tracking and once more the group had headed for camp, weary and despondent.

All this, and boring food, too. I don't know why I put up with this, the poor cameraman thought to himself. *Why the author can't give us decent food I don't know.*

The author is on a budget.

"Right. Let's get the equipment stowed and something to eat sorted," Hattenburg ordered as they arrived back at the small wooden structures that served as the initial base. "I don't think we're going to have any choice," he continued, "we're going to have to go mobile. Martin, double-check that the tents are ready to go once you've sorted the camera. Harry, do the same for the sleds."

"Will do, boss," the two chorused. That left Willy to handle the food. Re-heated beans and rice again. It was all he knew how to cook. As they had all discovered at least ten times since they had been in the Arctic.

It was half-way through packing the camera that Martin first thought that he saw movement out of his peripheral vision. Just a quick blur that distracted him momentarily. Long enough for him to notice it, but too quick to see what it was. Incidentally, it was also just long enough to drop the camera pack onto his foot in surprise. Insert several un-repeatable words here. Feel free to pick your own.

Once Martin had recovered from the sharp pain, he took a good look around, but saw nothing unusual. *Must be imagining things.*

A minute later he wasn't so sure, as yet again he saw movement. This time, he glimpsed slightly more. A shape, white with a hint of black, was all he could make out the corner of his eye. He knew he needed to get a better look, but was unsure how to do so, waiting for the author to make up the next bit. Suddenly, he knew what to do. Making sure that there was nothing he could hurt himself with, or on, he whirled around quickly to stare at the shape. Or at least, staring at the shape was his intention.

It was as he started to spin past a hundred and eighty degrees that he realised he may have put too much impetus into the move. As he passed three hundred and sixty, he wondered when he would stop.

He did stop, but that was probably due to falling over and burying his face in the quite cold snow. Still, at least he had learnt how to pirouette!

By the time he pulled his head out of the snow and stared at the spot once more, there was again nothing to see. Until, that is, a pair of snow boots planted themselves down in front of him. Well, the boots didn't exactly do that, their owner did. The owner was Hattenburg.

"You okay, Martin?"

"Yeah, sure. Slipped."

"Well, get inside. Just checked the weather radar and there's a snow storm coming."

***

We are now going to take a small diversion on our way back from the Arctic to the London home of a bemused detective. Our destination, northern Russia; where Karl Stealosky is considering a banana.

Have *you* ever sat and considered the humble banana? No? Don't worry, you're in the majority. The author is going to take a liberty, however, and ask you to consider a banana for just a few short moments.

The banana. Its purpose seems quite clear; it's one of your 'five a day'. However, that's not all. Bananas are extremely useful objects for at least *two* reasons. One, they are a smooth-skinned, normally yellow, curved, edible fruit. And two? They also come in extremely useful if you want to slip into a nuclear reactor plant unnoticed.

For Karl Stealosky, crouched in the darkness outside the Nernyer nuclear reactor plant, it clearly wasn't food that was on the menu. Karl's bananas weren't for eating.

He carried six bananas. Three for entering the plant, hopefully undetected, and three for leaving. He had performed this routine twice before and everything had worked like clockwork both times. Karl was sure that this time wouldn't be any different, mostly because he had managed to read an early draft of this chapter whilst it was still in development.

A quick cut of a fence and his specialist group were in, the four of them having chosen a black spot in the plant's security arrangements. They headed towards the canister area, and sat to await the first guard.

The first guard came around the corner of the administration building right on schedule, fifteen minutes late. On such a cold night, it was normal for the guards to spend as long as they could checking, very vigorously, the insides of the nice warm offices of the admin block.

The guard clearly wasn't concentrating very well, probably looking forward to the warmth of the power monitor station that was a mile away. One minute, he was walking briskly ahead, the next his feet hurtled forward whilst the rest of his body stayed where it was. He landed flat on his back, and just for good measure, and according to plan, the concrete gave his head a little tap and knocked him out.

Karl watched the performance and then dashed across to the fallen guard. He picked up the banana skin (no sense leaving evidence lying around is there?) and checked the area. Then he signalled to the rest of his group, who quickly and silently dashed across to join him. So far, so good.

The second guard fell for it much the same as the first, and the group neared their destination. Unfortunately, the third guard on duty was even later than normal, and the group found themselves waiting in the cold for many minutes until he appeared. If only Karl hadn't skim-read this chapter; they could have brought a thermos!

Finally, the group were relieved to see the guard approaching, but then watched aghast. You see, in a late change to the chapter, and unluckily for Karl and his team, the guard was actually doing his job. He saw the banana skin, picked it up, and threw it towards the bin, then whirled around when he heard a shout.

"Petri, tell the Stores manager I need to see him. His phone's not working again."

"Of course," Petri replied, waving as the man disappeared back into his warm office. He went three steps further and then crashed to the floor. It was a pity that he hadn't checked to see that the banana skin had made it into the bin!

Finally, Karl's group reached the storage container compound. With a precision that showed a very well-rehearsed plan, the men started to re-mark a number of the steel containers in the stores. They were half way through, when they realised that they had spent their time re-marking the wrong ones. Karl clearly had skipped over this part of the story, too. Quickly they rectified their mistake and, with their work done, they left the stores as quietly as they entered.

Getting out of the compound took practically no time at all, and this stage went without a hitch, each time, an unfortunate guard falling foul of Karl's bananas. Under the circumstances, it is hardly surprising that none of the guards spoke about their slip-up. After all, would you feel comfortable telling your friends that you were knocked out by a banana? It's one thing to be knocked out by a heavyweight boxer, but by a banana?

Precisely.

With the job done successfully, Karl's group left the area and headed home. The next morning, when the regular trucks turned up for the container empties, they would in fact be loaded with full ones instead ... full of plutonium.

Chapter Seven:
Shopping Lists

Now, you may not be surprised to learn that Don isn't really into the latest fashions. He still wears the faded overcoat that he purchased nearly ten years ago. His jeans are only stylish by accident, and if you asked him who Versace was, he'd probably think it was the owner of a nearby pizzeria.

Given that he struggles to clothe himself, it should therefore come as little surprise that Don didn't have a clue where to look for clothes for penguins. After discussing the task with Carlota the next morning, he decided to get started on tracking down their little requirement.

"There was an old job I did a while back. I might be able to get hold of someone who seemed to have a contact or two. Let me see if I can track him down."

"Okay, well while you do that I might as well make a start on getting clothes for our lot. I've got their measurements, so will see what I can come up with," she grimaced, clearly not looking forward to the task.

"Okay, see you. Call me later," said Don hurriedly as he headed out the front door before Carlota could suggest they swap tasks.

That was why, a few hours later, Don found himself in the

small, dark, and faintly smelly back room of a small bar in a very dodgy part of London. Then he switched on the light. Now he was in a small, smelly, bright room instead, which was a little bit of an improvement. On a chair that looked like it was on its last legs, he sat and waited. Waiting for Eddie 'Sticky Fingers' Collins.

He was waiting for Eddie thanks to what should have been an open and shut case seven or eight years before, which turned out a bit odd. Off we go into flashback land ...

The boss of a local plumbers' merchants had called him in one day because he had a suspicion that some stock was going missing. Being of an age where computers were more alien than programming a DVD recorder, he kept all his records on paper and paper was easy to destroy. He couldn't prove exactly that anything was, in fact, missing.

"With times as they are, I can't afford to lose anything, so although it's not much gear I need to know what's going on. All I want to know is who's knocking off my piping? You find that out for me, there's a bonus in it for you."

Now given that Don had his usual amount of open cases (zero), from his usual monthly average of clients (one), the idea of a bonus as well as his normal fee was more than tempting. It wasn't as if he had much to occupy his time.

Five nights after taking the case, Don had found himself

wondering whether there was anything to find. For the previous four nights all he had captured was a cold, resulting from the fact that he was in a cold car and kept forgetting his thermos. Then, in the early hours of the fifth morning, something finally happened. There came the unmistakable flickering of a torch where a torch should not have been, unless a torch had learnt how to levitate.

"Finally," he whispered, knowing that where there was a torch, there was a burglar, or an employee doing something outside their job description. Clever detective work, that.

Within a few minutes a car pulled up outside the gates to the merchants' yard. Don quickly got a couple of snaps of the car, and then shots of someone coming out of the yard, arms loaded with copper pipe.

"Showtime."

So excited was Don about a) anything happening at all, b) the fact he was going to get paid and c) the fact he was going to get a bonus, that he decided to do a thorough job and follow the car. After all, he had been awake most of the night; he might as well stay awake a bit longer. So he followed at what he thought was a discrete distance.

Perhaps a discrete distance should have been a bit further away, thought Don later when, turning into a narrow, unlit entrance, he was suddenly blinded by headlights. A further pair came on behind, and our trusty detective realised he was trapped. Oh dear.

Now, don't be too worried, dear reader, as you will have read Chapter One already...

You haven't? Stop cheating and start from the beginning, none of this flicking through nonsense. What's that, you're still in the shop and wondering about buying it? Buy it, now!

Right, where were we? That's right...

Don't be too worried, dear reader, as you will have read Chapter One already, so you know that Don turns out perfectly alive and healthy, but Don was not to know this at the time, so sat in his car, waiting. He was hardly in a position to dictate what should happen, after all.

"If you would be so kind, Mr Castor. Turn off the engine and step out of your car. Please," came an amplified voice.

They knew his name??

"Now, please."

It took less than a second for Don to weigh up his options and decide he didn't have any, so he did as he was told and got out of the car. The car lights went out, but then a torch came on, shining into Don's eyes and once again reducing what he could see.

"Welcome, Mr Castor."

"Thank you. Where exactly am I?"

"You don't need to know that, do you? See?"

"Not really, just curious."

"Tyson's Plumbers' Merchants."

"Oh. Right. Thanks."

"Anyway, you've been watching the yard for five nights now, haven't you?"

"Yes, how did you know?"

"That." The torch had flicked to Don's car.

"Oh, of course."

A few weeks earlier, in an effort to boost advertising, Don had ordered advertising film for the side of his car, on the basis that having no clients wasn't really the sign of a remarkably successful business. He had forgotten that the film had been attached two days before he was offered this latest job. It perhaps wasn't the best idea to do surveillance in a marked car!

Don continued to be blinded by the torchlight. He raised a hand to shield his eyes, but could work out nothing more than the fact that the torch wielder was about six foot tall, and rather wide.

"What happens now?" asked Don nervously.

"You hand us your film, get in your car and tell your *client* that you haven't found anything, see?" came the stranger's low, rumbling voice.

"That's it?"

"Would you prefer a different solution?"

"No, no. That solution's good for me. Just, this is the first case I've had in a while," he told them honestly. "I was hoping to have something to show for it."

He heard a short, hushed conversation, catching only the word 'poor'.

"First case in how long?"

"About three months. That's why I took it. That, and the bonus."

"He was offering you a bonus? Let me guess, he gave you some garbage about stuff going missing?"

"Well, yes, I mean you were carrying..."

"He didn't tell you that he stole the stuff in the first place?"

"No."

"No surprise there. Well, see, he did. He nicked a load of stuff from a job we were doing."

"A job? What sort of burglars are you?"

"Burglars? We ain't no burglars. We're plumbers, see. I told you already. Tyson's."

The torch was moved from shining on Don's face to illuminating the yard of what Don now saw was quite clearly another plumbing merchants.

"We're simply retrieving our property, see? Only we were trying to get it back without attention, see?"

"I guess," Don had agreed, not seeing at all. Five nights' stake-out for nothing, and no bonus. *Feuding plumbers. What next?*

"Tell you what we'll do, see. You tell him you haven't found anything and give us your film; we'll give you the bonus you were going to get. How's that? And as an extra, if you ever need anything difficult to get hold of, you give me a call, see?"

Apart from not 'seeing' why the author insisted on using the word 'see' so much in this scene, Don had realised that the suggested solution involved a fee and a bonus, and knowing that he wasn't helping someone keep stolen goods had felt like a good outcome.

"It's a deal."

"Knew you'd see. See?"

Now, when Don had mentioned to Carlota that he had a contact, he hadn't exactly, specifically, explained that the contact concerned was a plumber's merchant. Mind you, she hadn't exactly asked. Still, the guy had said 'anything difficult to get'. What was more difficult than plutonium?

"You want what?"

"A kilo of plutonium."

"You're joking."

"I'm not."

"You must be."

"I'm not."

"You have to be."

"I'm not."

"Really?"

"Really."

"Oh, alright then, let me make a call."

"Really?"

"Really. I just wanted to be sure this wasn't a wind-up."

"You can get it just like that?"

"Well, no. It's not like I've got it on the shelves – think of the storage! – but I can get you hooked up with someone who can make a few calls. You've met him before, actually."

"When?"

"That night you followed him here. You might say I hired a… night-time property removal specialist to retrieve our stolen stuff, see."

"I do," Don agreed, using the standard universal underworld un-code, the same one that described hit-men as Terra-Firma Personnel Displacement Specialists.

A few minutes later the phone call was complete, following several 'no, really', 'yes, I'm serious', and 'I don't know, probably bonkers' comments. Don was handed the address of a bar, and a name: Eddie Collins.

"Mr Castor, Don, isn't it? I'm Eddie," said a surprisingly well-dressed young man, entering the room and bringing Don and the reader back to the small, smelly but now well-lit back room of the bar very neatly. Eddie's expensive suit and highly polished shoes gave him the look of a young investment banker. Clearly, the night-time property removal business was going through something of a boom.

"Now, let's not waste time," Eddie continued, after shaking Don's hand and sitting opposite him across the table. "I've been told what you are after, but I just want you to confirm it."

"I know it's slightly unusual."
There was a large bout of surprised coughing from the opposite side of the table, and it was some time before Don was able to continue.

"We, I mean, uh... me, I need a kilo of plutonium."

"*I, we*, huh? I guess you are working for clients, then?"

"Yes, but I can't discuss it."

"Oh, that's okay, I know how that game works. You say anything they ice you. Don't worry."

"Why would they ice me? Who says anything about them *liking* the cold? They might like warm places, maybe deserts or something. Maybe they would burn me."

Eddie just looked at him for a moment, obviously thinking that he was one sandwich short of a tea-party, but then gave a shrug which indicated it wasn't any of his business.

"So, a kilo of plutonium. You are sure? There hasn't been some sort of mistake?"

Don could hardly imagine how he could have mistaken plutonium; it hardly sounded like a tin of beans, now, did it? Still, he could understand why Eddie had to check.

"There's no mistake. A kilo, definitely no less. Preferably not much more as the pe... my clients will have made arrangements for transferring a specific amount."

"What do they want it for?"

"That's also confidential. To be honest I'm not totally up with it, but it's a technological thing. Not a weapon, though. They don't intend to take over the country or anything like that."

"So it is a *they*?"

"No names."

"Well, okay, just professional curiosity; I'm sure you know what that's like in your business. Well, this one's going to be a toughie, no mistake about that."

"Can you get it?"

"Possssibly... but..."

"But?"

"Well, the fee for this one's going to be very big."

"You can tell whoever your supplier is, that we should be able to meet any fair offer."

"Okay, your funeral if you can't. And that is real. Give me a couple of days and I'll see what I can do. Now,

85

if you can leave through that rear exit, I have another client waiting."

Don obeyed, leaving by the fire exit. As the door started to close behind him, he heard Eddie greeting his next visitor.

"Ah, Mr Jones. How's the mummy-importing business?"

Don checked his watch. Nearly lunchtime. He headed for the nearest tube station. He had to meet up with Carlota and see how she was getting on.

Chapter Eight:
Actually Shopping

As Don found out when he met up with her at a café for lunch, Carlota had had a morning of mixed fortunes. The basic task sounded simple, after all: buy clothing for nine. Okay, they were not people, but she had a rough idea of what she needed: oversized hoodies for them to hide their heads, large trainers, and a long overcoat to ensure no accidental views of flippered feet. Dara and Nela, the penguin equivalent of sisters, had approved of the ensemble as soon as Carlota had suggested it. Don had left them to it when they started to argue of which of them would be Trinity, and which Neo.

"Sounds like you've got it all sorted, then," Don said encouragingly, privately relieved that he wouldn't have to get involved in the task.

"Well, you say that, but after the morning I've had, I really begin to wonder, Don."

"Why?"

"Well, you see…"

First of all, she had come up against the one large problem in buying goods from a shop: 'helpful' assistants. The term helpful, in case you haven't already guessed, is ever so slightly tongue-in-cheek. If there were any prizes for Non-

Brain of Britain, then almost all of the people she had approached that morning would stand a good chance of being in the top ten. Why couldn't they grasp that all she wanted to do was buy clothes? Surely, that was what they were there for?

When, in vexation, she had said this to one of the imbeciles, he had looked at her in amazement. Clearly, no-one had explained to him that this was the purpose of a shop.

"You want to buy them?"

"Well, of course. Why else would I be here?"

"Well, ummm... Hold on, I'll just need to go and get my manager."

He scurried off, never to reappear, and then up trotted the manager.

"How may I help you, madam?"

At last, someone who is normal, she had thought.

"I want to buy nine of those coats over there."

"Nine, madam. Surely you mean one?"

"Nine."

"But, madam," said the young manager, laying a hand gently on her arm, and lowering his voice as if he was about to impart a great secret, "there is only one of you".

"I know that! I'm buying for nine p... young adults, so I need nine coats."

"Well, madam, I'm afraid we don't normally sell that many items in one go. I'm not sure how we go about it."

"Surely it doesn't matter how many I want to buy. You beep one through the till, then the next, then the next."

"I'm afraid I'll have to call head office to double check. Funny things, these tills, you know. Now, the department I need doesn't open until just after ten, would you like to browse and come to the counter then?"

There were many things that Carlota wanted to do right at that present moment, but waiting around for an hour was certainly not one of them. She gave up and stormed out, restraining herself from the urge to seize the nearest mannequin and place it somewhere the designers had never thought it would fit, when one of the assistants near the door started to approach her to ask if she needed any 'assistance'.

"And if I didn't have to deal with totally brain-dead assistants, I had to run the gauntlet of the NP brigade," she moaned to Don.

"NO brigade?"

"No, the NP brigade."

"That's what I meant, but the author can't type. Who are they?"

"Oh, Don, you should get out more. The NP brigade? The Nosey-Parkers. They're completely vicious.

You'll find them lurking in any High Street. They simply do not ever stop in their search to find out the tiniest detail about a client. The professors of NP, as they call it, can get your address, bank details, favourite way to assassinate a traffic warden, and the last time you cleaned behind the cooker in less than three seconds flat. Five seconds if it has been a bad day."

"Ah, which in the present circumstances isn't the best thing, given the secret we have to keep."

"Well, luckily I'm not a good reporter for nothing," she smiled.

When Carlota had finally found a shop that was actually eager to sell the products it displayed, she was asked why she was buying clothes for nine.

"They are children coming over from Australia, but their luggage was impounded at the airport before they took off; something about too many bright colours not being allowed into the country. I've got to get some temporary replacements until their gear is sent over. They land in a few hours."

Fortunately, the assistant she was dealing with had the intelligence of a snail that could not have even passed the exam for Dunce school. She bought the idea; Carlota bought the clothes.

Carlota had kept coming back to the same problem,

however, and all morning she had been struggling to come up with an answer. Over lunch, she asked Don.

"Jeans; hooded jumpers; size 12s should do for footwear, but how can we cover their faces? I've bought the biggest hoodies I can find, but I still think their beaks will be too long."

Penguins are not very good at disguise unless they want to be disguised as another penguin, purely for the reason that a penguin beak is relatively long, sometimes being a third as long as the body. Concealing such a protrusion is a nightmare, although one that most people do not have to think about first thing in a morning, or second thing either, come to that. Still, this was the challenge that the couple faced as they sat drinking their coffee. Suddenly, the answer came to Don in a flash. The flash, in turn, came off the window of a Circus truck going to set up in Regent's Park.

"We don't have to hide their faces," said Don, in triumph that he had finally solved a problem.

"Why?" asked Carlota, who had caught a glint in Don's eye.

"Easy. We say that they are wearing prosthetic suits, with some techno-babble voice synthesiser that no-one understands, to conceal their identities. That way, they can have their faces exposed, and can speak. We should get away with it, as long as one of them doesn't mess up."

"Perfect! That should work fine. Shame you didn't

think of it earlier, I need not have done the shopping." She was so grateful that Don had supplied the solution that she reached over and gently gave him a peck on the cheek. Don added another memo to his mental notebook, alongside the one which said that he should get new window frames. This one simply said: *Get more things right. Rewards are nice.*

"Of course, they'll have to keep their flippers in their jumpers, so at least the coats and shoes won't go to waste. I don't suppose we can get those contacts of yours to only deal with you?"

"No. That is the one thing I can guarantee: whoever the sellers are, they will eventually want to meet the buyers. It's meant to be standard practice. The buyers have to be there to talk face-to-face."

"Hmm, that prosthetic idea then is really the best option."

"Well, when I next hear from them I can say that they might come in disguise, to protect their identities."

"We'll just have to warn them to be careful when we go for the talks."

"The only problem will probably be Senik. He's more strung up than a violin, and could quite easily blow it all, or rather, *bow* it all." Don laughed at his joke; Carlota just stared at him.

"Hmm," she sighed, shaking her head ruefully. "There's hope for you yet," she concluded.

"So anyway," said Don as he put down his glass of coke on the cheap plastic red check table covering. "How did you get involved in all this? I mean the undercover work and reporting?"

"It was my dad," Carlota said softly, averting her eyes. Her fingers began twirling the stem of her wine glass idly and she paused, then sighed.

"It's always been for my dad, really," she shrugged as she finally looked back at Don. "He was an undercover cop over in the States. Many times as a kid I watched him kiss me and mom goodbye and we wouldn't know when we would see him again."

"Just the two of you?"

"Yes. They had tried for a little brother or sister for me, but it just didn't happen. We were always happy though, just the three of us. Well, and an aunt who used to bake fabulous cakes."

She smiled as a memory came to her.

"This one time, Dad came home from assignment with a huge beard and his hair was black, not brown. I was so scared at this stranger coming into the house. I ran screaming for mom. Took me a few minutes to be sure it was him."

"Must have been tough for you growing up like that."

"He was killed on my fourteenth birthday. Executed just half a mile from our house. An undercover deal that went bad. We didn't find out for nearly a month."

There were no tears in her hazel eyes as Don looked across in shock. No tears, just a sad acceptance of a painful past.

"After that, there was only one job I was ever going to do. I was going to follow him into the police."

"And did you?"

"No. Oh, I wanted to," she gestured with the glass as a police car drove conveniently passed. "That would have been me. Working over in New York. It was all I could think about. But then mom started pleading with me not to. She wanted to protect me, I guess. I couldn't sit still and do nothing though. Ended up going to university to do journalism, and a few years later, that was me doing undercover reporting."

"So you get to work at exposing the truth, and your mom is happy too."

"Something like that. She wants me to settle down, get married, and start producing grand-children. Keeps threatening to fly over to get me fixed up with what she calls *a nice boy*. If she didn't have so many friends back home, she probably would, too." She drained her wine, and glanced at her watch. "Is that seriously the time? Better get moving. Meet you at the Science Museum at four?"

"That should give me enough time," Don grimaced,

thinking of what was to come that afternoon.

Carlota just laughed, sliding her hand across the table onto the top of his, giving it a slow squeeze. Clearly just being friendly, although Don wished it was more.

"Trust me, Don. You can't hide from these things. Now, off you go."

Don's business that afternoon was an appointment with his bank manager. A letter had arrived for him from the bank a few days before and had sat unopened on his desk until the previous day. In an effort to impress Carlota with a show of efficiency, Don had spent the afternoon working through all his old post and papers that had been littering his desk. He found it such tough going that, after watching him struggle for a while, Carlota had offered to help. It was she who had found the letter.

"Don, I think you had better take a look at this," was all she had said after taking a brief glance herself.

"What is it?"

"It's an appointment for you at your bank, tomorrow afternoon."

"I haven't made any appointments."

"No, it looks like they have made it for you. Don, this letter is dated five days ago, surely you looked at it?"

"I've been busy."

"Well, it says here you are due there at 2pm to *discuss your on-going repayment situation.*' "

"Oh."

Arriving at the branch, Don was slightly perturbed to find that his account manager was standing by the entrance door, waiting for him. What was worse, this was not the bumbling Mr Madgewick, his account manager of the past few years, but one Ms Clark, who was holding a clipboard with his photograph on it, as if she was standing guard waiting for him.

It's almost as if she thinks I might try and run away!, Don thought to himself bitterly, surprised at the speed with which Ms Clark had guided him through the bank to a meeting room on the first floor, and into what was clearly the client seat. She disappeared back into the hall, and just before the door closed, Don was sure he heard a whispered voice in the corridor exclaim 'Blimey, he came!'

"Right, Mr Castor. Sorry to have kept you, I just needed to get hold of your files," he heard Ms Clark say as she pushed the door open with her bottom, due to the mass of paperwork in her hands. With a loud thud, she dropped several large folders onto the desk in front of Don. He was concerned to see a sticker on the front of one folder: 'Mr D Castor. Priority.'

"I thought you kept all that stuff on computer these days."

"We do normally, just sometimes we find it useful

to have the evidence in front of us, for circumstances like these."

"Circumstances like these?"

"Yes."

"I don't understand. What circumstances? Where is Mr Madgewick?"

"Unfortunately he went off ill with stress this morning. You do know why he called you in, though?"

"Not really. I haven't asked for any services or anything."

"But you did read the letter you were sent?"

"Ummm... No. Well, I read something about a payment or something, and that you needed to see me. I wondered whether you were going to offer me a new type of account or something."

Ms Clark physically shuddered slightly as Don said this. Clearly, she was either quite cold, or the thought of giving Don yet more money with little chance of it being returned was a horrific thought. Given that Don's usual repayment method was simply to be completely oblivious to the bank seizing half his other accounts to balance his debts, it was probably the latter reason, especially as the bank was always nice and warm.

"Well, Mr Castor."

"Call me Don."

"I'd rather not."

"Oh."

"Anyway, as I was saying. Mr Castor, the reason we demanded to see you is the state of your accounts. Let's start with your business account, shall we?"

"Yes, that's looking good now, isn't it," Don

beamed, thinking of the last cheque he had deposited.

"Not quite. No."

"Ah."

"You do know how overdrawn that account is?"

"Well, I know it was slightly overdrawn."

Ms Clark shuddered again. Her whole body language squealed '*Why me? This guy's an idiot!*' but fortunately she was a professional and so resisted the temptation to scream.

"Right, Mr Castor. Let me summarise things. Your business account is currently seven thousand five hundred pounds overdrawn. Your personal account is fifteen hundred pounds in credit."

"Okay."

"So, you see the problem, don't you?"

"Not really."

"You don't?! Mr Castor, balancing your accounts, you owe the bank six thousand pounds!"

Now Don, whilst not necessarily the smartest cookie in the jar, was also not a fool in the 'owing money to banks' business, in fact he was quite an expert in it. He knew he owed the bank quite a sum, but had hoped a strategy of blissful ignorance would be enough to get him through. It had always worked with Mr Madgewick. He had a sudden inkling that maybe his former account manager's stress might simply be a way of avoiding this very conversation.

He suspected Ms Clark might not fall for the old 'business will pick up' line.

"Well, business has been a bit slow..."

"That is not our concern."

Oh well, it was worth a try, Don thought to himself.

"Well, I do have a high-interest savings account. You could just take the money from that?"

"Mr Castor. Where do you think we have been taking the payments you owed us from? We will be taking the rest of your personal account today to balance against your business account. You will still owe us six thousand pounds!"

"Oh."

"Yes, oh. Now you see the problem?"

"Yes."

Ms Clark's body language changed to *Finally he gets it. He's still an idiot.*

"Do you have any way to repay what you owe, Mr Castor?"

"Well, I do currently have a client."

"A real one?"

"Yes, of course a real one. Why?"

"Well, according to Mr Madgewick, you claimed you had a client this time last year, and it turned out to be a postman who had lost some Valentine's cards."

"The investigative profession covers all aspects," Don said, somewhat defensively, "and anyway, this current client is a lot more important than missing letters."

"So what is it?"

"It's confidential."

"We must have something, Mr Castor. If you can provide a decent reference from your client, then I'll extend your accounts by sixty days. You will have that long to show us that you can get your affairs in order. The reference will need to state how much you are going to be paid, approximately, for your services."

Don had a very satisfying, though brief, mental image of the shock Ms Clark would feel if Don could have told her his fee from the penguins. *'Is a million pounds good enough?'* On reflection, he thought that this might not go down well, given his former lack of million-pound clients, so thought he would get Carlota to draft him something.

"I'll get you the reference over by the end of tomorrow. Just one thing though, I'd like my savings account kept separate from now on."

"I give you my word. In fact, if you wait here, I'll go and get a letter typed up to that effect."

"That's very nice of you."

"It's all part of the service, Mr Castor. We like to look after our clients."

Five minutes later, letter in hand, Don escaped and went in search of a costume for an annual fancy dress party he had wheedled an invitation to a couple of weeks back. The invite was Don plus-one and he was pleased that the plus-one this year would be human. Last year's debacle as 'Alan Titchmarch plus Spade' didn't go down too well. It wasn't his fault that the patio door in question had been there.

He was still unsure as to whether to go ahead with the plan, as it meant leaving the penguins on their own for the night. He felt sure they would find something to do. It was this 'something' that was bothering Don.

"How exactly will nine penguins entertain themselves whilst we are out at a party?" he had asked Carlota earlier that day.

"You're not worried? They are penguins; what could they get up to?"

"I don't know. Maybe you're right. I mean, they needed your help to get here, so what's the worst they could do?"

"They'll be fine. Most of them will probably be watching TV. I'm sure Dara and Nela said something about using your bathroom again."

And they had left it at that. Reassured by Carlota's words, Don went ahead and picked up his costume, before heading to the Science Museum.

Carlota spent her afternoon in much the same fashion as Don, except her struggle with the bank involved her desire to pay some money in. Clearly it had been such a long time since anyone had used the bank for such a purpose that none of the staff seemed quite aware as to what they had to do. All Carlota could think, as she left the bank, giving up in disgust, was that the assistants should have been grateful that their cacti were glued into place, otherwise... Maybe banks and retail stores get their assistants from the same stock?

Deciding that the money she had in her bag was too good to sit in a bank anyway, she opted to spend it instead. She had the same fixation for shopping as Don did for not doing anything at all. Surely Harrods would have some costumes for the fancy dress party, she thought, after accidentally finding herself standing outside the doors, after accidentally catching a bus, two tubes and a taxi across London. She found a perfect costume, then found the less than perfect price tag, but bought it anyway. It cheered her up.

Later that afternoon, the two of them re-met outside the Science Museum and then went inside for a look around so that, for plot reasons, they arrived back at Don's house as night was setting in. They found Henec in the kitchen, up to his flippers in ingredients.

"Ah, I'm glad you are back," the gourmet said to Carlota, as they walked in. "I've got a bit of a problem."

Chapter Nine:
Party Time

"What's wrong?" Don panicked, thinking that Henec was ill, and having visions of having to take him to a vet.

How would I explain that? 'Oh yes, I often have penguins visiting…'

"No, no, it's nothing like that," said Henec as he waved a flipper. "I'm working on this recipe, but it doesn't explain exactly what I need to do. Do I have to put the ingredients in backwards, or on my head?"

"Backwards?" asked Carlota.

"On your head?" echoed Don.

"Yes and yes," Henec replied, pointing to a book lying open on the kitchen worktop. "I'm trying to make this upside-down cake. But I can't find where to turn it upside down. It's really confusing."

Given Don's lack of any positive culinary experience, he was inclined to think Henec had a point.

"Thank you," said the confused penguin, glad he had someone else who agreed with him.

"Oh, Henec," said Carlota, stroking his head softly. Don tried not to be jealous, Henec tried not to show Don he knew what he was thinking.

"It's called an upside-down cake because that's how it comes out."

"Oh. I see. I think I'll stick to meringue for tonight," the penguin decided, muttering something about weird humans.

"Well, don't forget there is a food mixer there if you need it," Don added, helpful as ever, although the penguin's sudden interest in the new gadget made Don wonder whether he should have said it.

"Oh, by the way, the others have just gone for a little swim. Shouldn't be too long. They made sure it was dark before going out. The river's only two roads away."

Don and Carlota took a moment or two to think about this. Somehow, they knew that where the penguins were concerned, a little swim could soon turn into a major calamity, but how much trouble could they get into? After all, it was dark, and they were swimming in a river. They decided that the best thing they could do was to get ready for the party and let the author worry about what the penguins might get up to. It wasn't like there was another option.

"What are you going as?" asked Carlota, as they went to get changed.

"What are *you* going as?" asked Don.

"I asked first."

"It's a surprise. What about you?"

"It's a surprise too. Wait and see," she mimicked. Behind them, the penguin shook his head. Definitely weird!

The penguins' decision to go swimming is worth a mention for a couple of reasons. Firstly, Don and Carlota need time to get changed, so you might as well spend a minute or two waiting for them. Secondly, the following may come in useful if any of you have relatives who are around in a hundred years' time.

Somewhere in a building in North London is a basement. Somewhere in that basement there is a small, pitch black room. Somewhere in that pitch black room there is a particular filing cabinet containing a file marked '*Not to be declassified before 2100*'. It is a very curious file, containing a couple of witness statements, two or three exceptionally grainy photographs, and a summary page bearing the title: *Eyes Only - MOD - Alien Visitations.*

You see, unbeknownst to Don, the area in which he lives is a bit dodgy. What do I mean by 'a bit'? You could go to sleep in your bed and wake up with no roof, windows, walls, or doors. That dodgy. Don, however, lived in blissful ignorance and so had no idea that Detective Inspector Lee Gent and a couple of detectives from the regional crime unit were staked out in a house two roads from his, watching the flat of a suspected drug dealer. He would have been astonished to learn this, in fact. His astonishment, however, would have been nothing compared to that of DI Gent that evening.

Gent had only come out to the house to check up on his surveillance team and see what the latest intelligence was, but ended up covering for one of his team, who had managed to poke himself in the eye with the end of his binoculars. Dusk had been and gone, and now the only light came from a dim orange street lamp, three or four doors up from the flat.

The surveillance team's job was routine: monitor which cars came and went, who entered the flat, what they were carrying. To help keep record, they had a surveillance camera set up. The inconvenient placement of the street lamp didn't help, but there was nothing to be done about that. Moving the lamp nearer to give more light would have been more obvious than a cat sitting in front of a mouse hole with cheese in its paws.

In later years, DI Gent would try very, very hard to re-live the night in question, trying to remember every detail. He was in the process of getting up to get a coffee when he thought he saw movement by the corner of the flat. His left hand was resting on the top of the team's surveillance camera and, on autopilot, his fingers found the right buttons and took a photograph.

"Think we got something here, Dave," he said to his sergeant. Suddenly, he caught more movement and shot three or four more frames. Then he stopped to look at what the camera had captured. He blinked. Looked away. Blinked again. Closed his eyes and rubbed them furiously.

"Something up, boss?"

"Probably just eye strain from the dark," Lee replied.

"Want some coffee?"

"Yeah. No-one's gone into the flat, so let's have a break and then I'll check the camera again."

Sadly for DI Gent, when he checked the camera five minutes later, he found the image hadn't changed. He was expecting to simply see a large dog, or small child on a bike. Instead, what he saw would cause him, in no particular order, to do the following in the next two hours:

1 - Exclaim "What the heck!", followed by more eye rubbing

2 - Find himself drunk, giggling, and whispering into the arm of his sofa *'sssshhhh, it's a secret'*

3 - Book an eye exam

4 - Check the camera for dust or dirt of any kind

5 - Call in his boss, his boss's boss, and a random person everyone would recognise, but no-one would be able to name, and whose purpose is to be completely irrelevant.

As you will have guessed by now, due in no small part to excellent telegraphing by your author, DI Gent was not seeing things, so he could have saved the fee from the eye exam. He did see movement, and it wasn't a dog, child, bicycle, or any combination of the three. When he looked at the initial photograph he had taken, all he saw was a short black shape step out into the dimness. The next shots then caught this shape standing in the middle of the road, gesturing as a group of six or seven other blurred shapes hurried across and over the embankment.

"Do they have kids as lollipop people?" he asked Dave, fairly certain that he wasn't that far behind the times.

"Would make sense – the first one to the road gets the job. Wonder why no-one has ever thought of that yet," Dave mused as he stared into space.

Gent couldn't make sense of the pictures. He knew what he thought he was seeing, but then what he thought he was seeing was impossible, so how could he be seeing it? He knew exactly what to do in these circumstances. He called his superior.

It took his superior an hour to arrive. With a couple of quick glances at the photographs, his superior knew exactly what to do. He called *his* boss. Re-read the previous two sentences twice more. Finally, you have four bosses standing in the room, the author hasn't had to retype it twice, and we reach the problem. They had run out of bosses.

"We need to call in CO88."

"The bingo squad?"

"No, that's CO11, didn't you get the memo? We need 88 – the Department Investigating Mysteries Which Involve Total Secrecy. I don't know about you, but I know that I don't know what's going on."

No-one knew what was going on after hearing that sentence, so they all mutely nodded.

Thirty minutes later, Lee Gent found himself outside the house, in the back of a black van, having a nice chat with someone who had only introduced himself as Phark. Well, 'chat' is perhaps stretching things ever so slightly. A chat would imply an amicable conversation between two willing parties. For Lee, it was a tad more one-sided.

"You don't speak, don't ask questions, just listen. Understand?" demanded Phark.

"Yes. Well, I think so."

"I thought I told you not to speak."

"But you..."

"You're speaking again."

Lee kept his mouth shut.

"Finally. Right, listen very carefully. There is no flat. Do you understand?"

Lee thought about it for a second or two, then nodded, shook his head and shrugged.

"Good. There is no flat."

Nod.

"There never was a flat."

Nod.

"There never will be a flat."

More nods; he was starting to catch on.

"You were never here. There was no surveillance, no camera, no CO88."

Nod, nod, nod, nod.

"Tonight you went shopping for a new hat and then went home and watched a DVD. Last night you did the same thing, and every night before instead of doing surveillance."

Lee never knew he liked hats so much!

"And above all else, there certainly weren't any alien visitors disguised as what looks like penguins in the middle of London tonight. Understood?"

Lee nodded again, and kept nodding as he realised he was a bit behind in answers. The final 'understood' he understood only too well. It was said in the same tone as someone might say '*I wonder what concrete swimming trunks would look like on you*' or '*does my bum look big in this?*'

"Good. Get out of here."

Lee left the van quicker than a heavy metal fan accidentally parachuted into a euro-pop concert, and headed for the nearest pub. He needed a drink.

***

Sorry, folks, Don and Carlota are still not quite ready, but it doesn't really matter as we are leaving London for a short while, hopping back a couple of hours in time, and joining up with Captain Paul Lane, pilot of the transporter Waddling Duck.

Lane had realised that he had a problem. In fact, Lane's problems are quite numerous, but most of the others are personal and it wouldn't be right to reveal them. Besides which, I need him in a couple of chapters' time.

The problem Lane faced on this freezing afternoon was that his aircraft had the hump. Initially, the crew thought it had solved the problem when they had found the camel hiding in between two cargo crates and persuaded it that, whilst yes, it was a good idea to see the world, being parachuted onto ice way below zero was not the way to do it. The camel, too, had got the hump at such information and had charged the cockpit, head down.

Wrong way.

Unfortunately, the chief engineer had dropped the rear

ramp to check a problem with a system on the aircraft. The first that the camel knew of her lack of aircraft interior awareness was when she suddenly realised she was trying to run on thin air. Oops!

There was nothing that she could do except watch the Waddling Duck disappear into the distance as she experienced a short moment of vertically descending motion.

Now now, don't worry. Camels are used to long walks.

Back in the cockpit of the Waddling Duck, Lane and his co-pilot had more on their minds than camels, however. They had their hands full as a few of the cockpit instruments were having a slanging match. Most of the instruments had shut down through sheer boredom, but the two flight compasses were playing their usual game of favourites.

"They use me more than you anyway," claimed the one.

"Well my dear, you weren't the one who got tweaked up yesterday, were you?"

"That's only because you're past it," cried the other one in jealousy. "And anyway, who got sorted out with the size eight screwdriver?"

"That was only because I was having my gauges fiddled with," the other retorted.

All the while that the bickering was carrying on, Lane and his co-pilot, Andy Craft, had to try to guide the aircraft with two compasses, whose sole purpose in life seemed to be to point in totally the wrong direction at all times. Wisely, the manufacturers had foreseen something like this, and so had added a third compass. Unfortunately, this compass was sulking because, in a fit of drunken lunacy, some barmy aircraft designer had stuck it in the lavatory. It just swung its needle to a new heading whenever it felt like it, which was fairly often.

By now, Lane was worried... very worried. Not so much at the fact that he was lost – he was an expert at being lost – but rather, he was worried because he had to make a decision, and that was something he did not do very often. Looking out of the windows did not prove much use. The revolutionary signs pointing to the North Pole were being reconstructed after losing the battle over airspace with a jumbo jet travelling at some 450 mph. No contest. With a misplaced faith in the author, he banked the aircraft to the right slightly, and decided that it would all work out well. Somehow.

Chapter Nine ¼:

This Chapter Does Not Exist

Right, you will be glad to know that our intrepid detective and equally intrepid reporter are finally ready for the fancy dress party mentioned some pages ago. So ready, in fact, that they had already arrived at the fancy dress party whilst we were up in the Arctic.

They are currently standing over by the stereo, next to that pirate with the dodgy eye patch and Cinderella. Don is explaining to Carlota just how he got into his current profession.

"So after I burnt the lab down they decided that I wasn't really suitable for the job."

"That's really harsh."

"That's what I thought at the time," agreed Don. "I mean, I know it cost them three million to rebuild, but even so..."

"So is that when you decided to change career?"

"Well, not quite," said Don as he swiped a sausage roll off a passing food tray. "To be honest, what with the fire, and that earlier issue with the cement lorry, I wasn't getting many interview offers. I was looking through the free ads and saw someone was offering courses on being a P.I. so thought I would give it a go. Own boss, own equipment. Nothing I could damage."

Carlota laid a gentle hand on Don's arm.

"Well, it looks like the right career move, Don. After all, I doubt just anyone could have rescued her Ladyship."

"I like that lizard costume over there," Don pointed. They had moved, as everyone does at some point or other at a house party, into the over-crowded kitchen.

"His tail is too long, though. That's the fourth time I've seen him trip over it."

"No. I think that paperboy is standing on it when no-one is looking."

"Ah. Anyway, why the obvious change of topic? You rescued her, Don. That's why I chose you. You should be proud of that."

Don took a deep breath, and then looked at his toes.

"It was an accident."

"What was?"

"Rescuing her. I've been trying not to think about it around the penguins, but I need to tell someone. It was a complete accident."

"Is this going to be another flashback?"

"I think so. Should give us enough time to grab some of that chilli."

"You'll have to introduce the flashback first."

"Oh, of course. You see, what happened was…"

As with most things that Don did well, it started off purely by accident, when he bumped into a man walking away from a local phone box; Don's favourite phone box, in fact, used whenever he had a disagreement with the phone company about paying bills. The man was in such a hurry that he didn't notice his wallet fall from his pocket. Neither did Don for a few steps, but then looking back he saw the wallet lying on the floor. By now the man was starting to disappear round a corner and so, fortuitously as it turned out, he didn't hear as Don called out to him. Don hurried to pick up the wallet and follow.

For once, Don's instincts actually appeared, and subconsciously he realised that something was a bit odd with the owner of the wallet, although quite what he couldn't tell. Maybe it was the Hawaiian shirt in early spring. Out of curiosity, and the fact he had no work to do as usual, he decided to follow him before handing it back. He considered it good practice; he was bored, and needed the exercise.

Don's instincts were practically standing up, waving a large banner saying 'Something Dodgy' when he ended up at a disused industrial plot and saw the man disappear quickly through a side door into what looked like an abandoned warehouse.

Using guile and stealth, which included knocking over a whole stack of rusting sardine tins, Don managed to find a

117

vantage point where he could look down into the main area of the building. At this point all of his detective skills really came into play, as he realised that the owner of the wallet must be one of the kidnappers of Lady Boi 'With an I', daughter of Britain's wealthiest frozen foods magnate, Lord Thomas Boi. It was one of the few items on the national news that had not escaped his attention.

To be fair, it didn't take that much effort really, as he overheard the words 'ransom', 'Lady Boi' and 'money'. The fact that Lady Boi herself was in full view, strapped to a chair, was too obvious a clue, and Don had initially overlooked that one.

Don took a while to think about what to do. His skill at tracking the man to the site and working out what was going on spurred him on to try even greater things. He decided to raid the building single-handedly. Then he thought some more, and decided to use two hands instead. He opened a nearby door, and sneaked inside.

Creeping through the building, everything went well until Don reached what used to be the reception area of the building and came face to face with a giant of a man. Well, not quite face to face, more like face to upper chest. Just the right height for Don to read the nametag on the stranger's overalls. Charlie.

Don quickly realized he was seconds away from an extreme amount of pain, and decided to seize the initiative. He did the first thing that came into his head. He trod on the giant's foot. Quite brave, for Don, considering fleeing would normally have been his first instinct.

Nothing happened.

For Don, time seemed to stand still as he waited for the inevitable. He couldn't believe that the author had made him tread on the giant's foot! The author simply pointed to the 'suicidal actions' clause in his contract.

Charlie looked at Don.
Don looked scared.
Charlie smiled slowly.
Don looked terrified.
Charlie looked evilly happy.
Don wondered if crying would do any good.

Finally, having had a long journey, the message reached Charlie's brain, from his foot, that someone had done something so utterly suicidal. Then, however, he realised that his foot hurt and, as he hadn't looked at it for a while, he bent down. Don knew he only had one chance and, seizing an extremely conveniently placed desk lighting object, he proceeded to give a whole new play on words to the phrase 'lamp-chop'.

The lamp hit Charlie's head with a loud thump, and Don watched in amazement as his would-be foe slowly toppled over, like some gigantic oak tree, felled in a forest.

Don One, Giants named Charlie Nil.

Emboldened, Don continued to stalk onwards, like some eighteenth century hunter, adding more victims to his chopper and becoming bolder all the while. Finally, he felled the last person standing, which was a bit unfortunate, as Lady Boi had managed to free herself and was on her way to escaping before he hit her!
Nevertheless, when she had awoken from her week-long coma, Lady Boi 'With an I' had been grateful for being rescued, as had her father who had showered Don with his favourite gift; lots of money, and a fair amount of publicity for his business. This brings us very nicely back to the party.

"And that's how it happened. I hope you aren't too disappointed?"

"We all need luck sometimes, Don. Besides, you seem to be doing well so far with this case. Even so, I think we had better keep it to ourselves."

"Agreed. I don't think it would go down well. Especially with Senik."
All the time, whilst Carlota had been listening to Don, she was also watching a penguin wander around the room. *Nice costume,* she thought to herself, but now that she had

seen the real thing, she thought she could see the difference. On a plot-required whim, she grabbed the beak of the costume and pulled. The beak and the headdress came off, its owner somewhat aggrieved. Feeling absurdly pleased, she repeated the movement as another penguin appeared by her side. This time nothing happened, except an annoyed 'ouch'.

"Henec???"

Chapter Ten:
Sending Out An SOS

Don and Carlota stood there in shock for a short moment. Just long enough, in fact, for a normal reader to have had enough time to turn the page.

"What are you doing here?" asked Carlota, once she had got over the shock of trying to pull a live penguin's head off.

"It's the others. There's a problem. They need your help."

Nothing more needed to be said, and the trio headed for the door, then raced down the steps to Don's car. Well, two of them raced, the other kind of hopped, flippers out, trying to avoid tumbling beak first, being not as well blubbered as some of his fellow travellers.

"What sort of problem?" asked Carlota, coiling the tail of her puppy dog costume onto her lap as she tumbled into the car.

"I don't know. Just that they're at the zoo."

Now, as you have discovered, generally it's quite fair to say that Don tends to not be that great at much. However, everyone in life has at least one thing they can do well, be it tying shoelaces, singing opera, or putting nail polish on a fly's feet.

"Don't worry, we'll be there quick as a flash," said Don, saving the author from the beginnings of a bizarre thread.

You see, Don was a very good driver. It was the one thing that he could do, mostly because his short attention span meant he really had to concentrate hard on the road. He had discovered this by accident, or should that be many accidents.

"Don't you know what sort of trouble they are in?" Don asked as he started the engine.

"No, I just got a hit from them."

"A hit?"

"It's a kind of mental text message, except without too much detail. I just knew they were at the zoo."

"Then it's not a text message, if there's no text."

"Well, it sort of is."

"No it isn't, it's a chime."

"Don, I think you're missing the point," Carlota interjected. "How long ago did you get the message, Henec?"

"Must be over half an hour now."

"You use our time?" asked Don, quite surprised.

"Well, no, we use anatiles, but with the Baron around, he taught us how you keep track of time, even if it is weird."

"I see."

Don couldn't think how having sixty seconds in a minute,

sixty minutes in an hour, and twenty four hours in a day was weird. After all, sixty and twenty-four are such common numbers, and so easy to divide and multiply by. He felt that now was not the time to bring this up though; he would most likely lose. Wise Don, once more.

"What on earth were they doing at the zoo, though?" Carlota wondered in puzzlement.

"Probably Dara and Nela felt like a party," Don answered. Henec just nodded.

"It's been tough on them. As the youngest two in the group they are used to being out playing or partying. Our night life is way better than what you folks come up with."

Don couldn't imagine how a penguin could possibly have a night life, but let it go, concentrating on getting to the zoo.

Five minutes later, they arrived.

"They are somewhere over the far side, I can feel them," Henec pointed with a flipper.

"That must be where the enclosure is. Don, drive round and see if you can find us somewhere quiet to park."
A couple of minutes later, one reporter, one detective, one penguin and a host of readers stood by the side of Don's Mini, working at how to get into the closed zoo. Well, you don't need to worry about how to get into the zoo, that's their job.

They were quietly observed, in a sort of uncomprehending

124

way, by none other than DI Gent, who, having had several drinks in a nearby alcohol serving establishment, was now resting in an alleyway.

"I knew I was right," he nodded to himself.

The sight of another small black form (his eyesight was bad after drinking), this time standing with humans, made him certain that some form of alien-human cover-up was definitely happening.

"Right, I think this is how we should do it," said Carlota. "Henec, we'll get you over the fence by that small gate. There's a padlock on it but I can't reach through to it. If you can push that padlock towards us then I should be able to pick it open so we can get in and out without being seen."

So, a minute later, Henec, balanced on Don's shoulders, was about to jump over the railings when Carlota stopped him.

"Hold on, you won't have to."

"Why not?" asked Don, staring into the park, fixed on one spot to try and keep his balance. There was a brief creak and suddenly he found himself looking at Carlota, face to face.

"Someone's cut the lock and then put it back on to look like it's still in place," she said through the fence. "That wouldn't have been one of our lot."

Don considered for a few seconds but then had to agree; after all, where would a penguin hide a pair of bolt cutters? He reached up to help Henec down, but at that point there came a little thud and down landed Henec on the other side of the fence, flippers perfectly perpendicular to his body, like a world-class gymnast on the dismount from parallel bars.

"The Games?" was all Don had to say as he walked through the gate.

"Yes, until I had to retire. Just wanted to see if I could still do it."

"Retire?"

"Too old."

"Quiet," Carlota whispered suddenly, urgently. She pointed through a gap in the bushes ahead. Three men stood beside a maintenance hut, and in the dim orange light of the park's night lights, they could see one of them clearly holding a net, and not the size you would use as a child on the beach. A more penguin-sized net.

"That's the penguin enclosure they are next to, Don," whispered Carlota, her tone worried, as was the rest of her.

"You sure?"

"This visitor map is. That must be why the padlock is cut. If one of ours comes out to see if they can get out, or if we are here, then they will get caught! Those guys must be out to kidnap one of the penguins."

"They've come to steal one for a collector," Henec piped up, in a whisper. A low growl came from the black and white creature as he started waddling forward, but Don stopped him.

"If Carlota's right, then we don't want one to just waddle up to them on a plate, Henec," he cautioned, although where they would have got a plate from I don't know; the gift shop had already closed.

"Those guys must have been waiting for the wardens to finish cleaning and feeding them, that's why they haven't pounced yet."

"We have to stop them," said Henec, in a tone that Don had never heard the normally pleasant penguin use. It made Don shudder, as it was more a 'where shall we leave their bodies?' tone than a 'oh dear, this is a bit of a problem' tone. He felt it prudent to prevent a penguin attack.

"We will stop them; Carlota and I will find a way. You need to hide, though. We can't rescue the others if we are having to stop them from grabbing you."
Grudgingly, Henec saw the logic of Don's argument.

"Okay. I'll hide up there in those bushes. That way I can see what is going on, and still keep an eye on that path back to the gate." Off he waddled.

"Any ideas?" Carlota asked, once the penguin was out of hearing.

"We need to get their attention somehow, make them think people are coming, or the alarm has been raised. Something like that. Don't know how, though."

"That's sort of what I was thinking. I think if we creep round to the other side of the enclosure and make enough noise, they might decide it's too risky and head back to the gate. Whatever we do though, we can't risk them getting into that enclosure. It'd be bad enough if they got any penguin, but it'd be worse if they got one of ours."

"Why don't we head around and see if there's anything we can use?"

As carefully as they could, the duo backtracked slightly and then made their way to the other side of the penguin enclosure, a long oblong-shaped mass of concrete, rocks and pools, with the penguins' sleeping area nearest Don and Carlota's side.

"Can we smuggle the penguins out from this end, do you think? Hide them somehow?"

"Maybe. Damn, the door's locked."

"Can you pick it?"

"I'll give it a try." Carlota reached into an inside pocket of her jacket and pulled out a small leather pouch, which Don saw was filled with thin metal rods and hooks of various sizes and shapes.

"Never leave home without it, fortunately."

"Good idea. I could do with those for when I forget

my house keys." Don had become a regular customer of a local locksmith. In fact, he was overdue for his six-monthly 'keys-left-in-house' session.

"Well, why not get yourself a set?"

"I'd probably forget them," he reluctantly admitted. "Any luck?"

"No. I can't get it. Do you think you could get up on the roof and see if there's a skylight or something?"

"I'll give it a try," Don was surprised to hear himself say.

A fear of heights normally would have asserted itself at this point, and so proposing to somehow get onto a roof was the last words he expected himself to utter.

But then came a slight interruption to their plans.

"What's that sound?"

A rattle. A clunk. A tapping, then splash!

"Food, they're trying to bribe them by using food! Don, quick!"

If you were to ask Don why he did what he did next, I doubt he could really explain it, and nor should he; this is fiction after all, all things are possible. Into the back of his head came a memory, the memory turned into an image, the image turned into a TV programme he used to watch.

The penguin-nappers looked up as a shadow appeared over the pool. An immense figure, backlit by a floodlight behind the enclosure, was towering over them. They all glanced, then looked, then stared, then started to back away, as they heard an unmistakeable cry.

"Let's get the heck out of here!"

Don watched, amazed as the three men turned tail and ran. From his vantage point on the roof he was able to watch them all the way past the bushes hiding what Don guessed was a very angry penguin. He was able to deduce the anger state from the perfectly timed branch that shot out, tripping all the men, who slammed into the concrete. They all hastily got to their feet and sprinted for the exit. A few seconds later, the squeal of tyres told Don that they had driven off. He felt quite pleased that he had done something right once more. Maybe these penguins were a good influence, or maybe it was Carlota.

With the danger finally over, Don made his way down from the roof to find Carlota standing by the side of the enclosure, looking at a group of penguins who were finishing off the fish thrown into the pool. As he walked up to them, he heard Sevac talking to Carlota. As they had suspected, a little idea of partying had started to develop as they had been swimming, and everything had been fine until they found a slight height problem.

"Height?"

"Yes, Don – height."

"I don't understand."

"Well, you see, we slipped in through the gates as a delivery was being made. Don't worry, no-one saw us," Sevac continued in answer to Don's unasked question, "it's just that when Senik went to check, we found the gates locked and then realised we are too small to get over the fence unaided."

"So how did you end up back in the enclosure?"

"Well, we decided we might as well enjoy ourselves, so we came back here and then sent a message to Henec."

"And I found your diary so I knew where to come to find you," finished Henec.

"In the meantime there was nothing we could do, so we thought we might as well make the most of things," Sevac continued, and pointed to the small matter of a penguin party that had clearly just re-started. "The next thing we knew was you guys arriving and those men being out there. You saved us, Don."

"We'd better get out of here," said Carlota, standing guard by the door of the enclosure, which was a hive of noise. It had been nearly ten minutes since the rescue but unfortunately for nervous humans, and penguins, separating a partying penguin from his or her entertainment is like trying to unstick your fingers after sticking them together with the Hold-it-Tight 2107th version of superglue.

Yet, whilst most of the others cavorted around, Don saw Torac and Norgid were having a quiet talk in one corner.

"You're sure about this?" asked Torac.

"I think it's for the best, you know how useless I am at all this."

"Umm... as Romic would say, if you've got cold flippers..."

"Exactly, I'm useless to you."

"Wasn't your choice, unlike us. You're probably right."

All the time whilst they had been talking Don had been growing more agitated. For once he and Senik were doing the same thing; worrying. They mirrored each other as they paced across the floor, with either arms or flippers behind their back.

Eventually, after checking his watch for the tenth time in the past minute, Don decided enough was enough.

"Come on, we've got to go."

Reluctantly and only after several more minutes of penguine chatter they agreed.

What's that? Penguine isn't a real word?

Of course it is. Just ask Torac and he'll tell you.

Anyway, back to the story and finally, after a further delay involving a somewhat ceremonial farewell (during which time Don wore out the soles of his shoes pacing around) the nine penguins, six males and three females were ready...

Three females?

Don checked again. Sure enough, there was one of the zoo group in the entourage.

"Where did she come from?" Don asked, turning to Carlota, pointing out the new recruit.

"From her mother, where else?" joked Dara. "Really Don, I'd have thought you'd know the facts of life by now."

"Actually," took up Sevac, "This is Javanishka. There's been a swap. She's taken Norgid's place."

"Pleased to meet you, Mr. Castor. I hope you don't mind. I know this must be a bit of a surprise."

The last female Don had heard that from, he was beginning to be seriously attracted to. The consequences in this case did not bear thinking about!! The penguins just laughed at his thought and Javanishka did a Perec, blushing deep yellow.

"What's so funny?" queried Carlota, not sharing the penguins' mental skills.

"Don heard that 'I hope you don't mind' statement from you before and now fancies you. Now he's heard it from Javanishka, he's worried!"

If looks could kill, Perec would already have been floating up to that great white ice floe in the sky. After calming slightly, Don realised that he was not the only one who was blushing, once he turned to look at Carlota. The penguins looked from one to the other. They could see what was happening, and were quite amused.

"Oh, come on," said Torac, "Any minute now that funny guy with the wings and bow that you humans seem to believe in will come whizzing in. It's making me sick!"

At the mention of someone coming, Don and Carlota pulled themselves together and they led the new nine out of the enclosure. On the way, the penguins still chattered, much to Don's anxiety.

"What was that you said to Norgid?" asked Javanishka as they reached the fence.

"An old saying in the colony, back home." replied Perec "If you've got cold flippers, go and stand somewhere warmer. He had; he did. Mind you, he's the cousin of one of our leaders. He had no choice."

"Better off where he is," added Torac as he waddled through the gate.

"Well, that's a relief," said Don as they assembled by his car.

"Where next?" asked Dara, still in partying mood.

"Home!" cried Carlota and Don in unison, deciding that enough was enough. It was only then that Don then realised that he needed a bigger car. How could he fit nine penguins and two humans into a Mini? I dare say you would be equally perplexed if you had to decide how to accomplish this feat in the dead of night.

As it turned out, the answer was simple. Elyd, Dara and

Nela went into the boot as the remaining six penguins and two humans squashed into the seats of the Mini.

It was at that point that Alan Dark, a night watchman at the zoo, came around the corner of the reptile compound, just in time to see the last three penguins being loaded into the Mini. For a moment, he was too dumbstruck for this to register, but what he saw next was worse. For as the penguin's assistants finished the loading process and went to get into the car themselves, he caught a perfect view of the driver illuminated by one of the street lamps.

    "Tarzan?!?"

Chapter Eleven:
The Baron's Own Goal

That night, when Don eventually got to bed, he decided to break with his old routine for once. He set his alarm clock for a later time of 9:30, and had the best night's sleep in ages, most of which he spent in dreams that seemed to concern Carlota!

Don's brain dragged him, kicking and screaming, into the light of the new morning, to the accompaniment of an equally screaming alarm clock. Suddenly, the ringing of the clock was muffled, and if Don had not known differently, he could have sworn there was a pigeon in his bedroom.

He remembered that he had penguins in the house and thought anything was possible, so opened his eyes. He was just in time to see Elyd wandering out of the room, clutching the alarm clock to his pelt, cooing to it. Don just lay there open-mouthed, and that was how Carlota found him ten minutes later, still in bed, staring at the door in puzzlement.

"I've just seen Elyd," she said, clearly waiting for Don to explain. Don was hoping she would do the same and said nothing.

"What's he doing with your alarm clock?" she

asked eventually. Don just shrugged, he had no idea.

"I hope he'll take good care of it," said Don, somewhat hypocritically, considering his one-sided boxing match with the poor object every morning. Carlota reassured him on that point.

"Oh, he will. He's become metrosexual, thanks to my Gucci bag!"

"He hasn't?"

"Yes. I wondered at first why he wanted my bag. Then I saw the clock."

From that morning on, everywhere that Elyd went, a little bundle wrapped in two towels and carried carefully in a Gucci bag followed. It was quite a fashion statement, although not perhaps the type you will find on your normal High Street.

Leaving the clock in Elyd's capable flippers, they planned their day. Just to be on the safe side, they told the penguins that they were grounded until further notice. It seemed the safest option, even though they knew no-one had spotted them on their last outing. Well, except for the penguin-nappers, who were hardly going to go to the police. Then, with some trepidation about leaving the penguins in the house alone, Don and Carlota left to secure some important items.

To pass the time, the chastised penguins decided to get to know Javanishka, which they had shortened to Ishy, because it was not such a mouthful and matched her smaller frame. Quite why she was called Javanishka no-one knew, although the author guessed it was probably to make his fingers more tired.

"I've been at the zoo all of my life, as was my mother. There are a couple of newly introduced ones, but almost all of us have been bred there."

"Is it as boring as it looks?" asked Perec.

"Oh, it's not so bad I guess, because we don't know any different. Even so, there's not much to do. Swim, eat, sleep, mate. That's about it."

Privately, more than one of the assembled group thought that a short break to do that would be nice. Perec, in particular, seemed to start blushing at the word 'mate', or maybe it was because the penguin picture from a couple of days previously was still on display. Either way, he went back to hiding his head under a flipper, on the pretext of grabbing a quick nap. He was quite glad when Senik piped up.

"All those people staring in all day," he shuddered. He was one penguin who liked his privacy. The thought of people gawping and pointing at him all day was the stuff of his worst nightmares.

It's a bit like that dream where you are standing in the middle of the High Street, on a busy Saturday afternoon, and you realise you are wearing a shirt and tie. Only a shirt and tie.

Yes, that dream.

Don't worry, I'm sure the other readers won't tell anyone.

"The staring is fine, they aren't really doing us any harm doing that, but the young ones who yell and throw bread are annoying."

"Bread?"

"Yes, apparently we aren't the only ones. They throw bread at everything. Odd creatures."

"That is bizarre. Surely they know we eat fish."

"Well, maybe it's a pastime or something."

"And it's like that every day?"

"Pretty much. That's why I was surprised when Norgid said he would swap, when I asked to come with you. I feel sorry for him."

"Don't," instructed Torac, "he'll love it! Regular food, plenty of sleeping time, and no responsibility. As we said last night, he didn't really have a choice in coming, and he isn't cut out for it."

"But Senik, you said your uncle was also important?" Ishy asked, clearly thinking that he too wasn't really cut out for the task, based on what she had seen.

"Very," agreed Senik, to both the verbal and mental points, "but I wanted to come. I wanted to prove that I could do something worthwhile. It's just that I've been nervous for so long, I forget not to be."

"Awww, that's so cute," Ishy replied and reached out a flipper to softly stroke his head; then, realising the thoughts running through the heads of the five remaining males, she smiled instead.

"I only wish we could have brought you all back here," Sevac apologised.

"It's better this way. Most of the others are terrified at the thought of 'Outside', as we call it. It's just I had heard our feeders talking about a trip they were going on and it sounded exciting, so ever since, I've wanted out. I guess it also means the zoo is less likely to notice anything has happened, except maybe I've put on weight!"

It also saves the author from having to introduce multiple new characters, create their biographies, characteristics and dialogue, not to mention a whole un-required storyline about the press handling the disappearance of multiple penguins from a zoo. Honestly, I'm never appreciated around here.

Oops... back to the story.

"So what exactly happened to make you come here?" Ishy asked. "You said last night that something had gone wrong but I didn't really understand it. Something about a Baron Ess?"

"Well," Sevac replied, "it all started about twelve months ago, during an iceball match..."

Now, if this were a film, there would be one of those *'going back in time, everything going squirrelly, fading, opening on a new scene'*-type effects. And you would find yourself in the Antarctic. Well, not literally of course, as it would be quite cold, but metaphorically. As it is, this is not a film, so simply imagine everything is going as above. Really, it is. And stop.

We are here.

Where's here? Didn't you pay attention to Sevac just now? *"Well,"* Sevac replied, *"it all started about twelve months ago, during an iceball match…"*

…

Seven anatiles down, less than half of one to go, the score standing at 27-25, and Talic Wodan is lining up a penalty, to bring the score to 27-all.

The hush of the crowd is palatable, and the lack of the usual half-deafening racket of cheering and jeering tells its own tale. Never before in the history of Iceball has a final been this close. It's a bit like one of those feel-good movies where, having been behind for the whole match, the weakest member of the underdog team is now showing his true mettle, and is about to score the penalty that will tie the game, and due to the author's very dodgy sports rules, means the underdog team will win.

Talic glances across at the main ice stand, crowded with

penguins, looking, searching for just one face. Finally, he spots her, the girlfriend (or female-penguin-friend to be precise) who, in typical movie fashion is cheering on her hero after eight anatiles earlier saying she was leaving with her parents. Anyway, you get the idea. He, underdog hero about to score (well I'm hardly going to make him miss, am I?), everyone about to go wild with joy. The players from both sides standing all around the penalty area up one end of the pitch, waiting for Talic to take the shot.

He waddles forward slowly and moves the iceball into the correct position, then takes a glance at the penguin he has to beat. Torac 'The Tank'.

"Come on Talic, you can do it," calls the solitary voice of his female-penguin-frie... look, she's his girlfriend, alright, otherwise the author will develop RSI.

"You only need this to win," comes her voice again. No sense in not adding just a bit more pressure onto his shoulders, is there?
"If you score, I'll love you forever."
Talic takes the required fourteen paces backwards to ensure a) he has a good waddle-up and b) he can think about which way to shoot without the Tank being able to read his mind.

143

A deep breath. A pause. Then the penguin controller drops a flipper and Talic starts his waddle-up. Thirteen paces, twelve, eleven, nine, eight, ten (as you know, the author cannot count), seven...

Suddenly, out of nowhere, there comes a loud rumbling noise, and the ground starts to shake.

Maybe I've put on too much weight, Talic thinks to himself.

Six, five, four...

Why's Torac not looking at me? I bet he's trying to put me off.

Three, two...

Why's Torac got his beak open? Distraction tactics, is it? I'll show you!

One.

On instinct, Talic lifts his foot and kicks, watching in slow motion as the iceball flies perfectly towards goal, then soars majestically past a completely stationary and immobile Torac, and finally nestles blissfully and perfectly into the wonderful corner of the goal. The most absolutely perfect shot he has ever played. The shot that now meant his team would win the Final, and incidentally mean his girlfriend would love him faithfully forever (penguins stick by their word).

So why was the stadium so silent?

It had taken Talic a moment to realise this, after having to wade through the superfluous over-use of adjectives in the previous paragraph by the author.

There should be cheering, clapping, at least, he thought, not to mention his team-mates coming up to congratulate him, something to indicate that he hadn't just dreamt up that moment.

"What the heck?" he heard Torac mutter in surprise.

"What? I scored. It was a good shot," Talic replied defensively.

"No. That."

Torac pointed and as Talic turned to look back over his shoulder, and then turned around in shock. Talic finally understood why the stadium was so quiet, as he too stared just like everyone else.

"How did that get there?"

The 'that' in question was something occupying three quarters of the pitch and towering over it. A 'that' made of stone, and wood, and glass just like the places by the ocean that the penguins saw when they went to top up on their fish. Only this 'that' was much bigger, and should have looked infinitely more impressive.

Yet somehow, it didn't. As you know from earlier chapters, this was the Baron's castle, transferred here in panic by the Baron after one experiment too many ending in failure. Not that the penguins knew this – after all, there are no booksellers on the Antarctic – but still, there was something about how the castle looked that told them it was a building that had seen better days. Cracked stonework, missing blocks, the occasional boarded-up window, and a general air of neglect that said the owner clearly didn't pay attention to such things. You could also say that the owner didn't pay attention to where he parked his castle, and you may have a point. At least the author had foreseen something like this and had made sure the landing area was clear of players.

There was a general flow of movement towards the castle as the natural curiosity of the penguins took over, and eventually it was surrounded by a mass of black and white bodies, with most of them gathered at what was unmistakably the front, staring up at the structure in puzzlement. Then, with a very old clichéd creaking noise, the huge wooden doors in the doorway (a good place for them) started to open and a figure began to emerge.

Now, picture if you will, a slightly eccentric scientist. You are at liberty to picture any form of eccentric scientist that you wish, as long as they are male, and vaguely human. This saves the author from having to paint a detailed picture. You know the type of thing… *'out into the blinding sunlight emerged a tall, but frail, figure. His greying hair wildly straggled all over the place, and thin, worn, wire-rimmed glasses perched on his nose, covering piercing brown eyes. A grubby off-white lab coat covered most of his torso, with patched trousers poking out the bottom, ending in worn leather shoes. From a front pocket of the lab coat sprouted a multitude of coloured pens and various scraps of paper.'*

Actually, that's not too bad a description, as descriptions go, so feel free to use that one if you wish, now that it's been typed.

So anyway, out of the door emerged what was clearly an eccentric scientist, blinking into the glaringly white ice-reflected sunlight.

Ah, I guess this isn't New Zealand, said the scientist to himself, slowly adjusting to the glare. Then, he caught sight of the throng of penguins in from of him.

Silence.

The kind of silence you would expect at first-contact between humans and aliens; not that the penguins are aliens, of course. The scientist, who you know, stood staring at the penguins, and the penguins stared right on back at him, neither side totally sure what to do next. It was clear that he didn't pose any great threat; if anything, he looked so lost that they almost felt sorry for him. A very quick mental debate began, had a middle, and then ended as they decided what to do.

A penguin called Romic stepped forward, and held out a flipper.

"Hi, I'm Romic. Welcome to our world."

The Baron promptly fainted.

Chapter Twelve:
Curious Culinary Cuisine

"He fainted? Why do humans always do that when we speak to them? Do they not realise that they didn't invent their language?" Ishy asked in amusement.

It was not the first time that she had seen someone faint. At the zoo, whenever a really obnoxious child would get too close, or be too rude about the penguins, she would swim over and, making sure no-one else could hear, she would say 'hello'. Every single time she had done this, this anatome, (eight times to be exact) the child concerned had fainted into a heap. The zoo blamed the soaring temperatures, the penguins were entertained, and the kids concerned learned a certain measure of respect.

"I don't know, but he went down like a leaf. Kind of graceful. I remember watching it," said Torac, getting us back into the scene. "Romic gave him a couple of taps on the face, and then he sat up."

"What planet is this?" asked the Baron in wonder. After all, it had to be another planet, where the aliens had taken on a form that he wouldn't find too weird, and no doubt using some form of universal translation device.

"No, no, nothing like that," Romic told him. "This is your world. Antarctica, I think you call it."

The penguins could tell what the Baron was thinking, and decided to save time and the author's weary fingers.

"Yes, it's your world. No, you haven't banged your head. We can read your mind. You didn't invent it."

"Oh," was all the Baron could say in reply, his questions answered. "Well, in that case, how do you do? I'm Baron Ludvig von Canton Ess; call me Ludvig."
He extended a hand and shook Romic's flipper. Not to be rude, the gathering of other penguins also extended a flipper and shook an invisible hand, by way of greeting. They could have waved, of course.

"I really hope me appearing like this isn't a problem."

"I think you appearing like this is a shock, but no particular problem. The timing could have been better perhaps, but I guess you didn't know today was the Final."

"The final what?"

"The iceball final."

"Is that a bit like football?"

"What's football?"

"Come in and I'll show you," the Baron offered.

"And that's how it all started," Sevac concluded to Ishy, "by some of us going in and the Baron starting to show us all about his life and the world of humans. From that, we explained how we live and survive, and we agreed that he could stay."

"Sounds like a good arrangement, although what did he get out of it?"

"Company, I think. He had been so engrossed in his experiments that he hadn't had much time for other humans, so I think that when he realised here were creatures he could talk to, who wouldn't interfere with his work, but would share his company, he was happy. We even helped out in the odd experiment."

"He experimented on you? That's outrageous!"

"Not in that way. He often was doing things over long distances, so we helped him by observing things for him, making notes, telling him what worked and didn't – that sort of thing. In return, he heated our caverns, created us a new and better iceball stadium overnight and helped us in other ways."

"You have caverns, like we do at the zoo?"

"Oh yes. It's only the humans who think that we stand around in the cold all the time. We simply draw lots when we know they are coming. Our long-distance races they seem to think are some form of feeding and breeding cycle."

"They really are a gullible species aren't they," Ishy smiled, whilst waving a flipper to the readers. "So overall, he helped you have a better life then?"

"He got me loads of new ingredients to make meals with," agreed Henec.

"And don't forget all those movie channels," Nela

added, before turning to Dara. "I could have been a contender..."

"Sounds like a good deal all round, so what happened?"

As Ishy has not had chance to read this book, a short re-cap from Sevac and Don is now about to occur. Given that you have already witnessed this in an earlier chapter, it hardly seems fair to make you sit through it all again. The following sentence will suffice: Sevac then gave Ishy exactly the same explanation as given to Don regarding their predicament.

"But if he saw what happened, why didn't he get you back?" she asked.

"We don't know," blurted Senik, so tense he could have used some Valium.

"Knowing him, something probably broke," said Nela, to wind up the nervous wreck even further.

"If necessary, we can repeat the experiment when we get back," reassured Sevac. Then he had an incredible sense of deja-vu, as Ishy, in the same puzzled tone Don had used said, "There are only six of you here. Even with Norgid gone, there should be eight in your group."

"Henec and Elyd are in the kitchen," Sevac explained, half expecting Perec to cry "I forgot...!".
Fortunately, it did not happen. Torac and Ishy wandered into the kitchen to look for the other two.

They arrived and immediately thought they were back on the ice of their respective homes. The kitchen was a bombsight, albeit one which was totally white. It was this whiteness that marked Henec out against the work surface like a ... well... like a black and white penguin against a white work surface.

"Oh, hi again," Henec greeted them with a white flipper. "Sorry about the mess," he added, casting a baleful eye around.

"I used his food mixer and forgot the lid. It rather went everywhere."

A great understatement if ever there was one!

"What are you making?" enquired Ishy.

"That," said Henec, pointing to his masterpiece, and masterpiece it was.

On the surface was a palatial cake, appropriately like some sort of ice palace. Ishy was just about to say something when she became aware of a knocking noise and looked round. She watched as Torac waddled the couple of paces required to reach the lid of the freezer.

"Time to let him out," Torac explained to Ishy. "He's been getting a bit homesick."

As Torac opened the lid, up popped a penguin head and the others immediately burst out laughing. A large sliver of freezing ice had started to form on the top of his head forming a crest, making him look like some bizarre form of cockerel. Their laughter was prematurely silenced.

"What the heck has happened in here!" screamed
a voice, the owner of which was Don.

"What's the matter?" said Carlota as she came in

just behind him. Then she shut her eyes, as Don had with the freezing penguin days ago.

Don, admittedly, was no gourmet, but even he kept his kitchen in a better state than this. His conscience was demanding action and he was just about to explode when Carlota turned to him and pointed.

"Ooh... is that for us?" he asked.

Immediately, he locked his conscience in a deep room in his head, and his usual hunger for food took over. His conscience fought back and tried to start a mutiny, but the food department was far larger than any help the conscience could have gotten. Ignoring his conscience's now frantic pleas, Don turned his back on it and calmly accepted Henec's explanation about the lidless mixer, and his assurance that he would clean up the mess.

"I'm starving, when can we eat?" Don asked, eyeing the cake.

"Please," complained Henec, as any chef would at such a *faux pas*, "surely you don't eat the dessert before the main course!"

Don was severely tempted to say yes, but the penguin gave him such a look that he did not dare.

"Ah, you're back," said Sevac as he too waddled into the room. "How did you get on?"

As expected, Senik was hovering at his back like some over-protective mother.

"You can stop worrying, Senik," Don commented,

to ease the poor penguin's nerves. "We've got another meeting lined up, quicker than I thought. Now if you don't mind, I'm hot and would like a bath," and, so saying, he walked out of the kitchen.

Carlota realised immediately that there was something wrong, from the expressions on the faces of the others.

"What's wrong?" she asked.

Upstairs in the bathroom, Don found out. He walked in to find Dara holding his hall clock, and peering into the bath. Naturally, Don looked, too.

"What exactly is Nela doing lying face, well, beak down in my bath?"

"Well...er...practising." Dara replied.

"Practising?"

"Nela holds the Antarctic record for the longest dive in the Penguin Games. I'm timing her."

"How's she doing?" asked Carlota from the doorway. She had come up after having the quick version from Sevac.

"Seven minutes so far," said Dara. "She holds the record for fourteen minutes as it is, so she's doing well. When we go diving to eat, we only go under for three normally, so it takes a bit of a workup."

Then, to wind Don up she repeated the infamous line.

"I hope you don't mind, I know this must be a bit of a surprise."

Don just ignored the jibe, although the penguins did notice a slight reddening of the cheeks of both the humans.

Deciding to retreat downstairs and leave the penguins to it, Don settled for a nice pre-dinner drink, whist listening to Sevac's description of their home life.

"I still can't believe you have a Penguin Games," he finally admitted, pouring himself another chilled glass of wine from the fridge. Every time he thought he had gotten to know the penguins, something new like this always cropped up.

"Oh yes, it is quite a festival," commented Sevac. Henec prevented him from enlightening them any further by shooing them out of the kitchen, flippers flapping.

"I've got a dinner to cook, go on ... out!!"
Quite unused to be harried out of his own kitchen, Don realised that he did not have any choice, as he would not get any cake otherwise. Henec was left to work in peace. Don, after finally managing to evict Nela from his bathroom, took a long soak, whilst Carlota learned more about the Penguin Games.

By six o'clock, everyone was ready to eat. Henec barred all but Ishy from the kitchen, but even from the lounge, they could smell the mouth-watering aroma of the dinner. On one occasion Ishy came in to check with Don.

"Can we have this?" enquired the empress, bearing one of Don's finest bottles of wine (a white; five pounds ninety-nine in price). "For the fish."

"Yes, of course." Then, just to be on the safe side, "You do mean to go with the fish, don't you?" – thinking that he might just check there were no fish floating around in the bath upstairs with a preference for good wine. The penguin just smiled at his thought and question.

"Yes, of course," she said, echoing him, as she returned to the kitchen. Don still went up to the bathroom to check.

The wine was used to form a white wine sauce, to go with the fish, after a salmon soup starter. The meal really was first class, although the penguins' method of disposing of the soup, namely by placing the beak in the bowl and sucking, would have sent any waiter into an apoplectic outrage. Fortunately, Don was not a waiter and instead thought it was a good idea, until he tried it and spilt most of the hot soup into his lap. He went to change his trousers.

For the dessert, which Don had been waiting for, Henec and Ishy came in carrying the cake, and he realised that what looked like one whole cake was, in fact, a small series of interlocked pieces, like a jigsaw. After the polite niceties, which lasted about two seconds, Don took a piece of the cake and eagerly bit into it.

"Eeeuuucchhh! What's this?" Don coughed, taking a large drink of wine to wash out the taste.
Carlota made pretty much the same remark, although the

penguins seemed to find nothing wrong.

"Wits mishlack?" asked Henec with his mouth full. "Sorry, you said you loved them. I must have got the recipe wrong. Tastes pretty good to me though."

"What is it?" Don asked again.

"Fishcake. That was what you said you liked, wasn't it?"

Henec was now really confused. After all, what else would fishcake be, but a cake made of fish? Carlota burst out laughing.

"Oh Henec, I should have explained. Fishcakes are mashed fish and potato rolled in breadcrumbs, and then deep fried."

She looked over at Don, but he was too busy looking at his cake. It was fishcake all right, unfortunately whole and looking back up at him! He drank some more wine.

"Oops!" mumbled the chef.

He quickly removed their cake and went back into the kitchen. He came back with the meringue he had made the previous night. Don cut it nervously, but all was well, no fish.

Soon, there was not a scrap of food left anywhere, and everyone sat back, feeling bloated. It was just as well that they did not go swimming that night. They would probably all have sunk! Instead, everyone relaxed, watching a film. Dara and Nela soon went back upstairs, saying they had seen it before. Don, agape once more, turned to Sevac but realised the answer.

"Don't tell me, the Baron's got satellite."

Sevac nodded and Don left it at that, watching the film and falling asleep half way through. In the bathroom, Nela and Dara practiced.

Chapter ~~Fourteen~~ Thirteen:
Unexpected Discoveries

The next morning, a very bizarre conversation took place at London Zoo. It started when Alan and Charles, known to their friends as the Fishy Brothers, arrived for their thrice-weekly inspection of the penguins.

Day to day feeding was carried out by whichever zoo staff member had arrived latest into work each day. They were given the dubious honour of carrying an extremely large and smelly bucket of fish out to the penguin enclosure twice a day, where a varied group of adults, children, and assorted packed lunches would then watch the penguins eat.

Alan and Charles' role was more healthcare and breeding management, and they were the latest contractors in the zoo. Everything now was private; even the gorillas have their own manicurists nowadays. Alan and Charles had been working in the zoo for the past three years, and had gotten to know their charges very well. They soon noticed anything different.

"Oi, Alan, there's something dodgy going on here." See, told you.

"What's up?"

"We've got an extra."

"An extra? What? Extra penguin, you mean?"

"Yeah."

"Nah, you're still drunk from last night."

"Look yourself, then. Where's he come from?" Charles asked, pointing at Norgid, who was feeling his way into his new and much suited role of total lazybones.

"Blimey. He's a big 'un."

"It's gotta be one of the males has bloated or something. Maybe too much fish."

As you can see, they clearly knew Norgid well!

"Can't be. Look at the markings; he's not one of ours."

"Well, where's he come from is what I want to know. No-one touches our penguins without our say so."

Charles put down his bucket. The brothers had found the easiest way of inspecting the zoo colony was by tempting them out with food. It never failed. Today was no different. The zoo penguins all began to waddle forward, or slipped into the water for a quick swim. Norgid got up and waddled over to the two keepers. He was, as penguins always are, naturally curious, and came to see what they were doing.

"Fifteen, sixteen, seventeen. We're missing one! Where's Flash? Alan, she's gone!"

Charles was naturally upset. He had always liked the penguins and the loss hit him hard. It seemed bizarre that a beautiful, healthy female could have suddenly changed into a lethargic, slow male.

"It looks like it. This doesn't make sense, Charles. We were here Saturday. No-one moves animals over the weekend. Are you sure he's not one of ours?"

"Of course he isn't. Look at the size of him. We'd never let one of ours get that overweight!"

"Hey, who are you calling overweight?" retorted Norgid. Instantly the two keepers looked around, but they could see no-one who could have spoken.

"I'm in here," the voice spoke again. They just stood there in total bafflement. They could hear the voice, indeed, it was rather loud, clearly nearby, but they could see no-one. Then, to their everlasting astonishment, the fat penguin in front of them reached out a flipper, muttering, "Well, if you're going to just stand there, I'll help myself. Overweight indeed. I'm just bulky." He took a fish out of the bucket, whilst they stared. The fish was somewhat aggrieved by this and smacked Norgid's flipper with its tail.

"Just wait will you, I haven't finished my make-up," scolded the fish in annoyance.
It was Norgid's turn to feel surprised. Gently, and very respectfully, the penguin placed the fish back into the bucket and stepped back.

"Sorry," he mumbled.
The brothers had still not quite regained their composure. They had just seen a penguin, which talked, and thought,

and a fish that complained about not being allowed to finish its makeup before being eaten. They did not find the fact that the fish talked at all odd, purely because their brains could not cope with so much going on at once.

"You talk?" asked Alan, clearly not believing what he had just seen.

"Well of course I talk," replied Norgid, eyeing up the bucket again, wondering whether he could grab a fish and swallow it before it had chance to make him feel guilty. Luckily, for the penguins at any rate, the two men started throwing the fish into the small pool, and the penguins quickly dived in to get them. All except Norgid, who stood on the side waiting to talk with the keepers, who had decided that they too had to talk to him.

"Well, this is a right case," said Charles in slight understatement. "What has happened?"

"Simple. We did a swap. Javanishka, that's Flash to you, went with my friends, and I stayed here."

"Your friends?"

"Yes, my friends," said Norgid, feeling that they did not need to know the details.

"Question is, what are we going to do? We should turn you in."

"Oh, come on," said Norgid between mouthfuls, after flicking a fish out of the bucket before it could object. "No-one will believe you. A talking penguin? All I'd have to do is not talk and you'd be made to look like fools.

Besides, if you did anything like that, you'd lose your jobs."

The two quickly realised that this was true. The work at the zoo was hard and the hours were long, but they liked it, and they did not want to lose the contract. Thinking about it, they realised that they did not, in fact, have to do anything at all. It was their job to take care of the penguins in all respects; the benefits of privatisation. All they had to do was modify their record for Flash to show *her* as a *him*, and the problem was solved, although they couldn't help noticing just how many fish he had eaten in a short time.

"I was hungry! Anyway, you are right. You don't really need to do anything, do you? I won't cause any attention."

Charles and Alan put their heads together quickly and, equally as quickly, agreed. They didn't have to do anything.

This was a view that Norgid entirely agreed with. He finished his fish, said goodbye to the brothers, and then went back across to his sleeping quarters. He needed a nap.

***

Someone who wasn't napping at that precise moment was

a certain scientist. No, he most certainly wasn't napping. He was staring out of an upstairs window instead. Now, from a productivity point of view, you might think that staring out of the window is not the best use of time for someone who has relocated a species to the opposite end of the earth (well, two species, if you include the likewise transplanted polar bears). Not too productive at all. And you would be right.

What's that? The author hasn't told you that this is what's happened yet? Really, there were clues. What do I have to do, write it down for you? Actually, that's not a bad idea. Read on.

As the Baron stared across the ice visible from the window, he wasn't running vast and highly complex calculations in his head, nor was he fine tuning a formula to reverse the earlier experiment. He wasn't wistfully wondering what went wrong whilst whistling either, although he may have been wondering at the author's penchants for 'w's.

No, the Baron was having lunch.

Yes, lunch.

Now, now, don't think that! He has earned this lunch. Aside from the fact that characters need to eat too, the Baron had been working very hard. Barely half an hour earlier, and after weeks of revising, testing and planning, he had finally put the finishing touches to a new version of his transferring equipment. A quick bite to eat, and then he would be able to go back down into his basement and carry out one final test. Then, he would be able to bring back the penguins and everything could start to get back to normal.

And I'll be able to go out for a walk, finally, he thought to himself as he stared.

His view currently contained only two polar bears, but he knew there were a lot more out there, all quite hungry, and no doubt not averse to the odd morsel of scientist. Perhaps that was why they all seemed to be staying around about the castle for some reason!

The bears had come as quite a shock to the Baron when he first saw them. Probably this was a side-effect of not knowing just how big a failure his experiment had been.

"It will be best if you all stay in your caverns," he had told the leaders of the penguin colony.

"You are sure we'll be safe there?"

"Totally. Trust me. You would probably be safe as it is, but with the amount of electromagnetic radiation that may come off, your caverns are a nice safe distance away. I'm sure everything will be fine."

And he had been sure, at that point, that all would work.

So trust him the penguins had, otherwise you would not be reading this book. It was because he had told them to get under cover that their absence initially went unnoticed.

"What's wrong with it, Ludvig?" the Baron remembered asking himself as he had climbed the stairs out of his basement-cum-laboratory, on the day of the transfer. You see the Baron, whom hereafter we will call Ludvig (that being his name), was used to the odd failed experiment.

As far as he was aware he had just had another failure in the greatest experiment of his career. Matter teleportation. He could tell that the experiment had failed due to the object he was now carrying under his arm. He reached his long hallway and found an unadorned sideboard. He placed the object on it, before stepping back to admire it.

"Why did it have to be *The Scream*? Any other painting would be fine, but not one that's already been stolen before!"

Quite why failed matter transfer experiments always resulted in expensive items materialising in the Baron's basement, was another mystery he was still to solve. That's what he found fun about being an eccentric scientist, working out what had gone wrong and fixing it. Given that he wasn't the best eccentric scientist in the world, he got the opportunity a lot more than maybe he should have.

Oh well, at least this one didn't cost me a scarf. Food and bed. I'll work it out in the morning, he had told himself as he realised just how long he had been down in the windowless room. So he stayed in, watched a couple of *Friends* re-runs on his satellite TV, ate a late meal and then went to bed, blissfully unaware of the dilemma that he had plunged the penguins into that afternoon.

He was in the same state of blissful ignorance the next morning as he set out from the castle to tell the penguins that they could move around once more. He knew it would take him at least a couple of weeks to recharge the power cells necessary for the transfer, and with the Penguin Games fast approaching, the competitors were practising every hour they could. He took a brisk walk in the very cold air to their caverns, and was slightly surprised to find it eerily quiet when he stepped into the entrance. Given the penguins' natural like for socialising, it seemed strange that there was no sound.

That's strange, given their like of partying I'm surprised there's no sound, Ludvig thought to himself, completely missing the fact that the author had just pointed this out.

"Sorry, I didn't notice."

Well, pay more attention in future. I'm not typing these things for nothing. Now, you should be able to start hearing something.

Ludvig realised that the caverns were not totally silent after all. Every now and then came a sort of soft snuffling, sniffing sound, followed shortly after by a series of clicks.

In all his time and experience on Antarctica, he had never

once heard any penguin make a similar noise, and knew something odd was going on. For a moment he thought it was some form of ritual until, rounding a corner, he came within a few feet of the rear end of a polar bear. He froze and watched as the bear sniffed, then ambled forward a few steps, its claws clicking on the hard ground. That explained the clicking and snuffling noises, although it didn't explain the bear.

"Even I knew that polar bears shouldn't be here."
Who exactly is telling this story?
"Sorry."

Now, geography is not one of Ludvig's strongest suits. After all, he had been trying to send his castle to a private island in the Pacific, not to the southern end of the earth, but even he knew that polar bears are most definitely Arctic, not Antarctic, creatures. With a growing sense of dread, along with an awakening sense of the truth, his mind started to add two plus two and eventually he reached four.

But that's impossible, surely! he thought to himself. There was no way his experiment would be able to do such a thing.

It was at that moment that the bear stopped, and raised its head. Very slowly it sniffed the air, and its head started to turn. As Ludvig saw its right eye make contact with his, he decided that staying in the cavern a moment longer would not be that conducive to a long and healthy life. He legged it, pursued closely by a very puzzled and angry bear, which should have been peacefully asleep, thinking about fish, not stuck in an unfamiliar landscape wondering why it was summer already.

"Impossible. Quite impossible," was all he could say (Ludvig, that is, not the bear) ten minutes later as he sat in safety. He was watching several bears prowling around the outside of the castle within which he was nicely enclosed and protected. The first thing he had done upon reaching the castle was to check his two GPS systems to ensure that he was still in Antarctica. Actually, that's not quite accurate. The very first thing he had done upon reaching the castle, aside from stopping screaming, was to close, chain and bolt the front door, and then ensure there was no other way for any bears to enter the castle. Once *that* was done, he went to check his GPS receivers. These, backed up by the sun appearing at its normal time, and the penguin caverns being in the right place, convinced him that he hadn't accidentally transported himself to the Arctic.

So if the bears are here, then that means… he had said to himself as the realisation of what had happened confirmed itself in his head. Straight away he had headed back to the basement to look over his notes and try to fix the problem.

Now, several weeks later, with his lunch finished, as he looked at the bears, Ludvig knew that he was ready to bring the penguins home.

"Just this final test and everything should be ready to go," he reassured himself. "I must remember the bucket. Let's hope Torac is still with the rest of them up there."

Yes, you read that right, 'must remember the bucket'. This was not for any form of illness or some side effect of the experiment; nor was it because Ludvig wanted to mop the floor. The 'bucket' was also not some form of code for a wonderful Inter-Dimensional Ionising Optical Targeting System. It simply was a humble, if polished, metal bucket and was Ludvig's good luck charm, used in all of his experiments as it was just large enough to have enough mass to transfer, whilst also being very simple to reconstruct. There was the added benefit of it being easily replaceable should anything happen in the 'everything fitting back together perfectly' stage.

"Right. The bucket on the transferring pad, and when I press the button, it will disappear and then reappear on the receiving pad," he said to the empty basement, so that the readers would know what was about to happen.

He pressed the button and, without the loud bang or grey billowing smoke of an illusionist, the bucket vanished from the transferring pad. The non-existent bang noise would barely have had time to finish before the bucket appeared on the receiving pad.

Success.

You may applaud.

Ludvig danced a weird little jig that the author has no idea the origin of.

"Right, Ludvig old bean," he then said, turning to upper class English for one exchange with himself. "Spiffy job, what? Jolly hockey-sticks, we are ready old chum. Five short minutes to power-up the system and then whizzo!"

Fast forward five minutes.

There, that wasn't painful, was it? I bet you didn't even notice. Now, it's five minutes later and Ludvig is ready to return Torac back to the castle. Why Torac? Well, it had to be someone the author had already introduced you to; otherwise you wouldn't know who they were.

Torac had been interested in the Baron's experiments since he had first gotten involved with a joke iceball six months earlier. When Ludvig had then needed a volunteer for the matter transfer trial, Torac had waddled at the chance. He was the only penguin to have *successfully and*

174

intentionally been transferred using the system, and with his DNA still stored in its memory, the Baron planned to home in on Torac and bring him back.

"If I can get him back, I can confirm the location of the others and then transfer them all," he concluded, both to convince himself his plan would work, and update the readers of the logic.

Can you guess what happens next, when Ludvig presses the button and the receiving pad energises?

If you guess it all works fine and Torac appears, go back to page one, you clearly haven't understood how this whole thing works.
If you guess it goes wrong but don't know how, well done, continue reading.
If you guess that onto the receiving pad appears not the bulky black outline (not to mention the rest) of Torac, but instead something quite crown-shaped and jewel-encrusted, then you have clearly read this before, or work for the publisher.

"Hmmm, that's not Torac," confirmed the Baron as he stepped back from his console and stared at what sat on the pad.
To get final confirmation we will just happen to hop many thousands of miles away to the now closed, but still security monitored, throne room in the Tower of London

containing many jewelled objects, two wooden chests, several cameras and a highly-polished bucket.

It is perhaps fortunate that, at the very moment we are in the throne room staring at these items, the security guards are being fortuitously distracted away from their security monitors by an improbably large ship that has sailed up the Thames and got stuck underneath Tower Bridge.

"Thanks for the diversion," the Baron says gratefully to the author as he reluctantly, though hastily, places the Crown Jewels on the transferring pad and starts the process once more.

A blink of an eye later, the bucket is in the Antarctic, the Jewels are back in London, we are leaving this part of the tale behind (before we appear on the security cameras) and the Baron is going back to the drawing board.

Chapter Fourteen:
Who Moved My Ladder?

A few days later, Don was quite excited. The reason for his excitement? A new client. Yes, another one! I know, it is pleasing for him, isn't it? We will share his excitement for just a moment. Feel free to be excited in any way you wish.

Right, moment over, otherwise we'll never get anywhere.

"We'll stay out of the way, don't worry," Sevac had told Don when he announced that the client was coming.

"You're sure the nine of you can stay out of sight, without leaving the house?"
Don was quite clearly thinking of the zoo. Sevac patted him on the arm with a flipper.

"Trust me, you'll never know we are here."

True to Sevac's word, Don couldn't tell that there were nine non-human creatures in his house – well, ten if you include his goldfish – when the client rang the doorbell an hour later. Carlota showed the clearly nervous man into Don's office, which we will all recognise as his lounge.

"Hi, I'm Don Castor. Take a seat," said Don grandly, determined to impress after yet another letter from his bank that morning.

"Thanks, I'm not sure how this all works," said the man as he took a seat next to the TV, settling himself gingerly due to the large cast on his arm.

"Well, you turn it on and there's a remote control to change the channels," said Don, clearly on the wrong track and wondering about the mental state of this new prospective client.

"He means you and him, Don," Carlota whispered as the stranger started to carefully remove his coat.

"Yes, like I was saying, the way this works is that you will provide me an up-front advance, and we have a five minute session detailing what you need me to find out. Then, after I have done some initial investigations, I will give you an initial report. If you wish me to proceed further or obtain proofs, then we agree a fee."

"Will a thousand pounds be enough of an advance? I didn't have time to find out how much it was likely to cost. I noticed your advert said 'reasonable'."

Given that Don usually had to barter for even fifty pounds as an advance, he thought about this for a moment.

"A thousand should just about be sufficient."
A short while later, with a nice cheque sitting in Don's desk drawer and the nervous stranger, Derek, starting to relax, Don decided to see what he had to do.

"So, how can Castor Investigations help you today?"

"Well, it's a bit of a delicate situation. I need you to investigate someone for me, but they mustn't know about it."

"Discretion is part of our business," Don reassured smoothly. "So, who is it we need to investigate?"

"My wife, Mandy."

"Anything in particular we are looking for? What do you think she has done, or is doing?"

"She's trying to kill me."

Don stopped the doodle he had started on his desk pad and decided to pay attention. He was used to the odd case of milkman-itis from worried husbands, although in every case he had ever taken no milkmen were involved (it had always been boiler repairers), but he had never had someone sitting in his lounge fearing death-by-marital-partner.

"You sound sure."

"I am."

"Why?"

"Here."

Derek handed across his phone. Don scrutinised it for a moment. Derek then leant over and turned it on, and opened its photo gallery.

"This is the only physical proof I have."

Don studied the picture, decided he couldn't make head nor tail of it, and passed it to Carlota. He was privately relieved to see she was also puzzled.

"What is it?" Don asked.

"It's the underside of our car," Derek replied, his tone implying that they should know this.

"Oh, is that what it is. I did wonder. And what, you think she has tampered with it in some way?"

"No."

"So why did you lie under your car and take a picture?"

"Because that's when she ran me over in it."

"You actually lay there and took a photo?"

"I had to."

"Why?"

"Because she was still in it and I was worried she might do it again if I got up."

"And why haven't you gone to the police?" Don said this slightly more quietly, as he didn't really want that; it would be bad for business.

"Well, I don't really have any proof. That's what I need from you."

"You have that photo," Don objected.

"All that shows is me underneath the car. It doesn't prove anything."

"He has a point, Don," Carlota agreed.

"And besides, I'm not totally one hundred percent sure, which is why I've come to you."

Don had a minor choking incident involving his cup of tea and a lack of breath at this point.

"You aren't really sure?! She ran you over, not accidentally gave you a paper-cut with an envelope!"

"Well, she *did* say it was an accident."

"She drove the car over you."

"Yes."

"And it was daylight?"

"Yes."

"And you were just standing there?"

"Yes. Well, no."

"No?"

"I was kneeling."

"Kneeling? Why on earth…?"

"I had dropped something under the car and was trying to get it when she started to drive it. I flattened myself to the ground."

Don paused for a moment, sharing a very quick glance with Carlota. Over Derek's shoulder, Don could see the beak of a penguin reflected in the TV screen. Clearly one of the group was displaying its natural curiosity and listening to the trials of human co-habitation from just outside the lounge door.

Derek sniffed.

"Do you want a tissue?" Don asked automatically, reaching for the box that he kept for this very occasion. Not that Don had actually used the box before. His clientele had been somewhat short of crying maidens

181

recently, and anyway Derek was not a maiden!

"No, no I'm fine," Derek replied, waving them away, "I just got a sudden whiff of fish."

A movement in the TV caught Don's eye as he saw the penguin beak withdraw. A few seconds later he heard the soft thump-thump-thump of a penguin hopping up the stairs. Its owner had either taken offence at the fishy reference, or decided Don's chance of retaining the client would be reduced if Derek saw the nature of Don's house-guests.

"It's from next door," Carlota ad-libbed, as the author had failed to get back to the dialogue quickly enough and it seemed wrong to simply freeze for a while.

"Oh, I see. So, do you think you can take my case?"

"Well," Don replied, not quite sure what to think yet, "I'm not quite sure what to think yet. I'd like to know what your wife said. I know you said 'an accident', but what else did she say?"

"She says she didn't see me."

"But she stopped when she did, or didn't hit you?"

"Yes, she says she heard me yell and braked. Then she says she sat there in shock. To be fair, she did then reverse the car off me. She seemed to be upset when she got out of the car and saw me lying on the ground looking at her."

"So it could just all be an accident?" Carlota asked.

"Well, that's what I thought until a couple of days ago."

"And what happened then?"

"I fell off a ladder outside our bedroom window."

"Ah, I was wondering about the cast. I take it you found the rungs had been greased, or something similar?"

"No."

"She moved the ladder to make you fall?"

"No."

"She got someone else to move it?"

"No."

Don decided that this was equivalent to drawing blood from a stone, and thus was much too difficult, so he gave up.

"Okay, I give up."

See?

"If she didn't do any of those, then why do you think it's her fault and that she's trying to kill you?"

"She was in our bedroom."

"I see," said Don in a tone that said he didn't really see at all, and was getting tired.

"Did she open a window and hit the ladder?" asked Carlota, who was equally clueless.

"No, she paraded in from our en-suite wearing the new lingerie she had bought."

Silence. Perhaps too much silence as, at precisely that moment, there came a loud THUD from upstairs, causing

Derek to jump and spill some of his tea.

"It's my cat," said Don automatically, having long

since decided that any unexplained noises would be attributed to a fictitious feline. There came an even louder thud. "He's very fat. Anyway, I don't understand, why did you fall off the ladder?"

"Well, I only had one hand on the ladder at the time; I had my squeegee in the other. I was so surprised when she opened her robe to show me what she was wearing, that I let go and fell off. She never buys new things."

"So she didn't push you, then."

"No, no. She never came near me. I was just very surprised."

"So let me get this right. She may or may not have seen you when she started the car, and didn't go anywhere near you when you fell off the ladder. This makes you think she's trying to kill you."

"Well, I guess when you put it like that, it doesn't sound much."

Don didn't say anything. It was clear what he was thinking as it was all over his face. Given that you cannot see his face however, Carlota will say it for him.

"It is very thin. Are you sure there's nothing else? No other evidence or proof?"

"Well, she has started singing around the house lately. She never used to sing."

Don stood up and decided that this was one client who was a pork chop short of a barbeque but, business being as rapid as a frozen stream, he wasn't about to turn down the income.

"Well," he said firmly, standing and gesturing Derek to the door, "you've given me her details and the advance. I'll do some background checks and we'll meet up in, say, one week?"

"Oh, there was one other thing," Derek suddenly remembered.

"What's that?"

"She got me to sign some papers the other day."

"Papers? What sort of papers?"

"I don't know. Something for the builders, apparently. Normally she does all that, but she asked me to as she was drying her nails. We are having a new conservatory and patio, you see."

"Okay. I'll look into that as well," Don assured him as they reached the front door, "This time next Thursday, then."

"Can we make it Friday instead? We have the foundations for the patio going down Thursday."

"Sure we can."

A quick shake of the hand and Don then closed the door and returned to sanity.

"Why do I always get the nutters?" he asked Carlota.

Chapter Fifteen:
Nine Penguins Went To Market

We could now have a chapter detailing a slightly amusing but highly impractical escapade involving the penguins, a talent show, and some minor publicity. However, to do so would require this being written, and the author would have to be willing to expose the penguins to the possibility of being discovered. This is not a good thing; their mission is meant to be a secret, after all. Instead, we will join Don as he experiences one of the highlights of his year, a trip to the bank when they haven't summoned him.

Despite what you might think, the author is not being sarcastic, as Don also knew as he entered the bank. He tapped an inside pocket to ensure his weapon was secure, and then made his way to the queue for the clerks. He picked up a piece of paper as he waited, and wrote out his requirements.

What's this, you ask? Has Don lost the plot and is now attempting to steal from the bank that already knows him? Given his penchant for not following much, it is possible he's defying the author. Read on.

There was no-one ahead of Don in the queue when he saw Ms Clark behind the safety glass, talking to one of the tellers. She looked up and saw Don. The surprise was evident in her face and Don smiled grimly, his hand tightening in his pocket.

No mercy, Don, he thought to himself as that particular clerk became free.

His pulse raced as he took a slow walk forward, his hand slightly sweaty. Even though he was determined, he still had a brief moment of indecision, just as he reached the counter. Then he thrust the papers at the teller and stared silently at Ms Clark. Then he waited.

Two minutes later, Don walked smartly out of the bank, anxious not to be stopped. The receipt slip for the thousand pounds he had just deposited in his savings account was tucked nicely in his wallet. His secret weapon he tucked in alongside it, the letter from Ms Clark stating that the bank would not touch his savings account to clear his other debts. As he walked down the High Street, Don savoured Ms Clark's look of intense frustration. A good day, and about to get better, for that afternoon, Don, Carlota and the nine penguins were due to have their first face-to-face, well face-to-face and face-to-beak, discussion with their plutonium supplier.

The meeting with Eddie had been the previous evening. Unsurprisingly, this time, it had been a different dingy backstreet bar, another dark then light back room, and another fire exit. The rest of the details, however, had been pretty much the same, except that Eddie's suit was charcoal pinstripe.

"You definitely want plutonium?"

"Yes."

"There's no chance they have made a mistake, your clients, and want something else instead?"

"No. Why? Is there a problem."

Privately, Eddie thought the problem was that the man in front of him didn't see any problem in private clients obtaining and using a kilo of plutonium.

"Your clients aren't Australian by any chance?"

"Australian? No, they've never even been there. That is, I don't think they have. Why?"

"Oh, no reason," Eddie lied.

He didn't want to tell Don that he was taking the precaution of a six month trip 'down under' just in case an unexpected revolution was about to sweep through London.

"So. Are we going to get a deal set up?" Don asked, slightly concerned, because his car was on a meter, the time of which was about to run out.

"Let me make a call," Eddie replied, pulling out a mobile phone and rapidly punching in a sequence of numbers. A very quick, and somewhat one-sided dialogue ensued, featuring lots of 'yes'es, 'no's, and on one occasion, 'kebab'.

"It's on," Eddie told a very relieved Don after putting away the phone. "Tomorrow, 3pm, the old warehouse by the docks. They say look for the one with the table. Apparently it will make sense on the day."

That's how, three hours after his success at the bank, Don found himself in a run-down warehouse, waiting with Carlota and the nine penguins. There had been a hurried and secretive debate that morning between Don, Carlota and Sevac as to whether the whole group was needed. Finally, they decided that safety, and strength, in numbers would be a good idea.

The comment about the table had made sense when the group had finally found the correct abandoned warehouse. They knew it was the right one as a clearly expensive conference table and chairs had been arranged in the centre, along with the obligatory conference flip chart and coloured pens. The group took their seats and they waited patiently. Finally, they heard cars pull up outside.

"Okay everyone, this is it," said Carlota, trying to calm their nerves down, which was not that easy, when her own nerves were jumping about mercilessly. She could not help remembering the last time she had run into, or from, people dealing in plutonium.

"Just remember, don't say anything unless you really have to. Leave it to me." They all nodded vaguely, each knowing that this was a crucial part of the operation. If they messed this up, then it meant starting all over again, trying to find a new supplier. Luckily, their biggest concern seemed to be already taken care of. For some inexplicable reason, Senik, whom they had expected to be shaking like jelly by now, was actually the most relaxed of all of them. The secret lay in the Valium he had taken to steady his nerves, just before setting out.

The door opened, creaking like the bones of an old man, and into the gloom of the warehouse walked the two marketeers, whom the author will introduce to you as Mr Alex Amber and Mr Mike Mauve. Not their real surnames of course, but everyone knows that baddies are usually referred to with colours.

With almost majestic poise, the early thirties, brightly named pair, made their way up to the group, and took their seats at the head of the conference table. They were identical in every respect. The same tanned complexions, the same darting black eyes looking for danger or an opportunity to make money, the same strength of build that warned people not to cross them.

"Good, everyone is here and seated. Let's get on with this," said Mr Amber as he slid into his seat, checking his watch.
Both men were very safety conscious and well acquainted with the maxim of never spending too long in one place, and that is why they came alone. There were others in the

organisation that could take over if the meeting was a trap.

"No introductions," said Mr Mauve. "I'm X"

"And I'm X too," said Mr Amber.

"Where's X three?" asked Perec, trying to change the mood of the meeting.

"Dead. He asked a stupid question," Mr Mauve replied, giving Perec a long, cold stare.

Clearly, he had never heard of under floor heating. Perec looked away hastily and swallowed.

"Right then. What do you want?" Mr Amber asked, getting the meeting back on track.

"One kilo of plutonium, purpose to remain a secret," answered Carlota.

"That's fine with us. How are you going to pay?"

"How much?"

"That depends on how you are going to pay."

Question followed question, answer followed answer, until at last, Carlota realised that she would not get anywhere without giving them a minor snippet of what they had to offer.

"Suppose we were to offer you the only copy of a radical new engine design that would revolutionise world travel. Is that worth enough?"

If this was Carlota's idea of a little snippet of information, it certainly had the desired effect. For a second, Mr Mauve and Mr Amber just sat there trying to grasp what Carlota had just told them, not believing their ears.

"Excuse me?" asked Mr Mauve at last, totally dumbstruck.

"Why?" queried Nela. "The meeting isn't over yet." The man had said he wanted to be excused, and in all the TV films Nela had seen, when someone was excused from a meeting like this, they normally came back with a gun. This just showed the type of films she had watched with the Baron!

"Excuse me?" said Mr Amber to her in puzzlement.

"Not you as well," chimed in Dara, realising her sister's point, and showing her penchant for the same films.

"What the heck is everyone talking about?" suddenly put in Senik.

Under the enormous lack of pressure to cope with, the Valium had temporarily gone to sleep, bored, allowing Senik's usual nervous state to creep back in. Sensing that chaos was about to break out, and that his money depended on the deal, Don, in his usual diplomatic manner, brought things back to order.

"Can we get on with this? I'm starting to get cold."

"Oh, I'm *so* sorry, Mr. Castor," said Mr Amber, his voice dripping with fake sincerity. Then he realised that it was cold and that Don had a point.

"Okay then, we'll sort out things our end and get the shipment. You sort out the plan for that... thing of yours.

We'll contact you for a progress meeting in a few days."

With that, both men got up from the table and walked towards the exit. Just as they reached it, Mr Mauve turned back round.

"Those really are great disguises."

"What disguises?" Senik blurted out, before he could stop himself.

The two marketeers stood there and looked at the highly embarrassed Senik, who was now keeping his head down so they would not see that he was getting steadily more yellow. Then they turned, shrugged and walked out the door.

The group, still seated around the table, listened to the sound of the cars driving off. After the agreed five minutes, they got up and made their way outside to their hired minibus. It seemed much more comfortable than the Mini. Nevertheless, even a minibus was still a hazard, as you are about to find out.

What's that, you are in a hurry? Well, okay then, those of you in a hurry can skip to the start of the next chapter. Really, I don't know why I bother.

Still with us? Right, picture the following:

- It's a gloomy day
- You're late for an appointment you must be at, but will

dislike every minute of. Think parents' day, the dentist's, or being about to listen to the local dramatic society trying to do *Tosca* and failing badly.

- Your cat/dog/goldfish/hamster has eaten/been swallowed by/is missing/has damaged your neighbour's cat/dog/goldfish/hamster (delete as appropriate)

- You spent your last money on a winning lottery ticket, which you have lost.

- Your husband/wife/boyfriend/girlfriend thinks you are too fat/thin/tall/short.

If all the above apply to you already, then I'm sorry for you. Please buy a second copy of this book and keep it safe, as something bad will probably happen to this one.

The picture isn't exactly the best, is it, but then we aren't aiming for something to hang in the Tate. The above is just to get your mind into how someone might be feeling in the series of circumstances, i.e., not great.

So, when driving to your appointment, for which you are already late, you could possibly be forgiven for being a touch irate if a badly-driven minibus happens to cut you up. Sally Nail, on her way to an interview for a customer services manager at a helpline, was having a day from hell. Maybe not level seven hell, but at least two or three, and so when she was cut-up by a badly driven minibus, she was furious. As they both pulled up at a red light, she got out of her car, ready to start shouting at the driver. Did

I mention that though Don is a good driver, sometimes his lane control isn't totally brilliant?

Shouting is an act of control. I am in control, Sally chanted to herself under her breath. Her anger management therapist told her it was good to shout; it relieved pent-up energy, without the hitting people part. She was looking forward to a good shout at the driver. It was a shame therefore, halfway down the side of the minibus, that she made the mistake of looking in…

She was still standing there, mouth open, two minutes later when one of the drivers stuck behind her got out of his car and came marching up, the minibus long gone.

Chapter Sixteen:
Crate Scot!!

It was the Arctic, it was a few days later, and it was business as usual aboard the Waddling Duck, as Andy and Paul were lost, again. A new GPS was on order, but that was currently being lost somewhere over Brazil by another freight operator.

"Right, Andy, let's work backwards. At what point did you think we were lost?"

"When you said 'We're lost'."

"So you thought we were fine up to then?"

"Well, not really, but I didn't have a clue. I left my map case in the crew room back at the airport. I was hoping you would know where we were."

"I thought you were looking at a map earlier?"

"Nope. That was a letter to my mum I just found stuffed down my seat. To be fair, the stamp is one of those Christmas ones with snow on it, so it's similar."

"So you have no clue where we went wrong, then?"

"None."

"Damn, neither do I."

Now, were I a passenger on this particular flight, I would be quite worried at this point. However, I can assure you that Paul and Andy have been in this position more than once before, and will doubtless be so again. They always find some fortuitous way to get their bearings, some sign or other. Just then, the loadmaster came up and poked his head around the cockpit door.

"Hey, guys. Weren't we meant to be looking out for a big ridge sticking out on its own about now?"

"Yeah," replied Paul, "it should be coming up in a few mins."

"Well, isn't that it over there?" said the loadmaster, pointing out to the right of the aircraft. There, in plain sight, and thus easily overlooked, was the very sign they had been seeking. Paul and Andy looked out to where he was pointing and then they dragged up the map.

"The time is about right. Yeah, yeah, you're right; it is. We just decided to approach it from a slightly different direction," Paul replied, trying to sound confident as he banked the aircraft sharply.

He didn't want to admit that the chart he had bought with him was useless. Actually, that's a bit unfair to the chart in question. If Paul hadn't spilt coffee over it, then there wouldn't have been a problem. So, he was very relieved that he knew where they were again. Now all they had to do was pass the ridge, swing right and the drop was another ten miles further on. The ridge rushed up and then passed as they banked the plane round to the right. It was just unfortunate that they should have swung left instead.

A couple of minutes later the ramp was lowered and the three crates were ready to be sent over the side. With the aircraft really reducing the power and running in very low the snow was whipped up into large flurries that totally obscured the ground.

"Load away, door secure," called the loader on the intercom. Now came the relatively simple task of contacting the camera crew to confirm the location, and then heading for home.

"Camera 1 Camera 1 this is the Waddling Duck. Cargo dropped on schedule. Report."

"Waddling Duck. Did you just say you have dropped the crates?" demanded Hattenburg, praying that he had misheard the report.

"Camera 1 that is correct. The crates are there on the target. Where are you?" asked Paul. It seemed strange that they were not waiting for the crates at the drop zone.

"Err... Waddling Duck, we are in the middle of the target area. We have not heard any aircraft. Repeat your drop position."

Paul did so and then waited for the reply. When it came he almost had to take his headphones off, so loud and angry was the voice on the other end. Through the barrage of unprintable abuse, Paul vaguely wondered whether he had dropped the crates in the wrong location. After a further ear bashing lasting ten minutes, he was positive he had.

Oh well, it will give them some exercise. That can't be a bad thing, he thought.

Nevertheless, it was probably as well that Paul was safely on the plane; the camera crew would have loved to get their hands on him. Gloomily they signed off and set out on the twenty-mile, overnight trek to get the supplies from the crates.

"This could be a blessing in disguise," Hattenburg commented. "Hopefully then we will get a sighting of these bears. Why they aren't around baffles me."

The two penguins some twenty miles away could have answered him easily, had they been asked, as they stood looking down from a ledge on the ridge at the three supply crates.

"Why did they have to drop them here?" Vadek asked the air around him. "There must be people coming to get them."
For two long months they had, as leading members of the penguin Council, managed to keep a lid on the slightly minor secret of the penguins' existence in completely the wrong continent, and now that was being threatened by badly dropped beans and Spam.

"What do you think we should do?" he asked the slightly taller penguin to his side. Both were large, their pelts showing a faint silvering as age started to creep up on them.

"We have either to hide ourselves, or hide the crates. I know what they are for. I saw one of the Baron's satellite programmes on this. They are crates of supplies for humans."

"Supplies? Out here?"

"Yes. They sometimes do really weird things, like trying to cross a landscape like this with two bits of wood strapped to their feet. They need supplies, and so they get them dropped down where they can fetch them. Problem is, they normally have cameras to film them getting tired and upset."

"How can we keep the whole colony hidden from humans with cameras? If your theory is right and the bears have been swapped down to our home world, then they won't have seen any bears, and they can't find us here! Think of the problems."

"Yes, you're right. Well then, we have no choice. We must hide the colony. Samil, Nanic, Toril, come here quick!"

The three summoned penguins made their way over.

"We have a small problem. The colony must be hidden as quickly as possible. Suggestions?"

The three stood there for a second as if they could not believe their ears. They bombarded Vadek and Romic with mental questions. By now a group of young penguins had come over to see what was going on. They could not read

201

the mental thoughts of the adults and so, finding nothing exciting happening, they waddled off to watch the sledging practice on the other side of the slope.

Most of the colony was deep underneath the ridge on which the group of penguins were standing. One of the experiments that the Baron had got right was the ability to create large spaces in spaces that look a lot smaller, similar to the type of thing you might find on a science fiction program. So, the main living space for the penguins was hidden out of sight; but penguins are curious creatures, quick to get bored, and so quite active. Even now, about 60 were outside, either taking part in or watching a sledging practice.

"The only way I can see to do it is to block up the exits and wipe out traces of ourselves outside," suggested Nanic after a short while. "If we keep a couple of spy holes further up the ledge, we can see what happens when they come to get their crates."

"It could work," agreed Samil. "There wouldn't be any need to go outside for anything and we could always open a back way out of the place if it proves necessary to leave for any reason."

"Then we will do it," said Vadek, receiving nods from the others. "Right, Toril. Get everyone in as soon as possible. Anything that is outside, we get them to bring in with them. We mustn't leave a trace."

Toril, the leader of the Junior Council, sledged off immediately to get started, whilst Vadek was finishing his instructions.

"Nanic, organise the building work. The entire face must be covered and a back way out made as soon as possible. Samil, sort out the help for Nanic and find some good watchers for later."

The four sledged off to set about their various tasks, Vadek and Romic splitting up to inform everyone what was going on. Already, Toril had gathered all of his junior leaders and was issuing instructions to them. There was no panic, no worry. Everyone knew what needed to be done, and they did it.

Samil sent four of his best scouts out to try to locate the camera crew, to see how much time they had.

It was over seven hours later when one of the scouts, Nalla, came in. She found Samil and together they made their way over to where Vadek and Nanic were inspecting the back of the ridge, deciding where to place the exit to the camp. They stopped when they saw the two approaching them.

"What did you find?" asked Vadek as Romic joined them.

"We should have until the morning," Nalla replied, hardly showing the fact that she had just sledged nearly fifty miles. "I think this storm will keep them in their camp until then." Her voice showed no sign of the distance she had just sledged; it was just a little trip. It was this ability which had helped her to gold in the penguin equivalent of a marathon for the last three years running, or rather, last three years sliding.

"They are miles off at the moment, and were just starting to set up camp as I left. They must have wanted to get under shelter before that snowstorm arrived. I doubt if they will set out until tomorrow now." She smiled faintly. "It seems that they don't like snow storms."

"Just as well for us that they don't," said Romic, relieved to find that they had enough time to finish the job. The storm had only been a minor one from their point of view compared to some of the storms they had to endure on Antarctica before the Baron came.

"Many thanks, Nalla. I suppose that's just a training sledge for you. Another title this year?"
At that, Nalla just laughed and left to have a little rest.

Everyone was ready the next morning; the colony was safely hidden from view a couple of hours before the humans came over the ridge to get their supplies.

"Hold on, there's something funny going on here," commented Hattenburg.
He had many years' experience of tracking in the wild and missed very little that was under his nose. (If it was a few feet off, then he could overlook it.) He had quickly noticed

the tracks that were all around the crates. Vadek and Romic had tried to keep everyone away from them, but could not prevent some curious penguins coming up to have a look.

"I knew we'd miss something," stated Vadek matter-of-factly, as he looked down at the crew. "We didn't clear around the crates."

"It couldn't be helped," answered Romic. "Let's just hope they get their supplies and disappear. After all, it's their supplies they are looking for, not us."

"We could always try to make them disappear," commented Samil, who was standing with the other two. Quite what he had in mind, the others preferred not to know. His preference on the Baron's satellite system had always been American mafia films, and he never missed a re-run of any of the Godfather trilogy, along with two of those currently in London.

"No. If we did that, others would start searching for them. They knew where the crates were dropped," Romic countered, removing the option of 'death by Mafioso-addicted penguin'. They continued looking down.

Back down at the crates, whilst the rest of the crew started to open boxes, Hattenburg studied the tracks on the ground. A dusting of snow an hour earlier had obscured most of the detail, but in the back of his mind, he couldn't help thinking that he knew them. He was distracted by the

205

crew as they got the first crate open. It was like listening to children around the Christmas tree at present time. He left them to it and went to stand a little distance away, lost in thought.

"This doesn't make sense," he told the others after they had finally finished and re-joined him. "All the tracks go around the crates and then lead off into that ridge, but I've had a look and cannot see anything. No openings. It's like the tracks go straight through the ridge."

Martin and the others joined him as he led them back down the faint trail, right to the point where the tracks disappeared into the face of the ridge.

"You know, daft as this sounds," said Martin, "the one thing these look like is some sort of bird track." The others laughed at that, but Hattenburg considered.

"If I had to say what they were, I'd say they were penguin tracks."

Three years previously, he had spent a month in the South Atlantic and had seen many penguin tracks.

"Maybe there's a new research programme that we don't know about?"

The sound of his voice carried to the penguins watching from their hideout on the hill.

"Let's have a look around, then," suggested Martin, although not too enthusiastically.

Nestling there in his bag was a very nice bar of chocolate,

which was beginning to dominate his will. It was almost as if the chocolate was asking him to eat it. Never having been one to be strong-willed in the first place, Martin knew that if he did not do something to distract himself, the chocolate would be doomed.

"Right then," agreed Hattenburg. "Let's start by having a look around. The weather should hold enough for us."

The penguins could do nothing but stay hidden and watch, whilst secretly hoping that the author was on their side.
The author is neutral.
"Oh flip," grumbled Romic.

Nearly an hour later, the humans gathered back in front of the crates, out of sight and sound of the penguins, who were, by now, in a right flap.

"What are we going to do? What are we going to do?" chanted Selac, one of the Penguin Council, and uncle of the nervous wreck in Don's house. Selac was extremely jumpy and was now in almost as bad a state as his younger relation, and with no pharmacy on the Arctic ice, Valium wasn't an option.

"Just relax, Selac; there's nothing much we can do about it. I doubt that they will find anything."

"I've found something," stated Martin. It is probably

better that the penguins could not hear them. Selac would have been doing cartwheels had he heard this.

"What have you found?" asked Hattenburg impatiently; it was starting to get colder.

"It's the other side of the ridge. Those tracks we can see; well, I've found one set more, except that they seem to lead *into* the ridge. There's a sort of small opening there, and it doesn't look natural."

"Are they definitely the same tracks?" asked Hattenburg. He had checked in his reference book of animal tracks and had narrowed it down to only one creature, a creature that was only found in the Southern Hemisphere. It was definitely penguins; either that, or some polar bear had had major foot surgery. *Oh well, the books aren't always right*, he thought, which was a pity, because he had written the book.

"Let's not make it too obvious. There's another cold snap on the way, so we had better be quick. If we take the second camera and set it up to cover the entrance, that way we can check if anything uses it. Harry and Willy, if you start setting up the camp, we'll go out this way and swing round to the back of the ridge, hopefully unnoticed."

The two started to set up the camp, as quick as they could, to get out of the cold, and Martin and Hattenburg started out.

Just my luck. I knew I shouldn't have said anything, thought the poor cameraman as he accompanied Hattenburg. It took them over an hour to make their way around to the back of the ridge. Martin showed Hattenburg the entrance and the tracks. They went unnoticed, because Vadek, Romic and the others had seen the men start to set up camp and had thought they were safe for the night.

"I think we had better let everyone know what's going on," said Romic, and he sent out penguins to call everyone together. "We can let anyone who wants to have some time outside go out for a bit afterwards."

Just over two hours after they had set up the camera, the first penguins came out. The camera was one of their special thirty-six hour models and it was perfectly concealed, another mark of Hattenburg's long life of filming animals in the wild. With absolute professionalism, and a great deal of shivering, the camera recorded all the activities, including a rather special Games practice. It only switched off as the sun eventually set below the horizon.

Chapter Sixteen ½ :
A Baronial Update

Down in Antarctica, the Baron was preparing for an experiment he didn't want to perform, but knew he had no choice about. He intended to transfer himself out of his ice world for a few short hours, on a kind of matter transfer yoyo, which would transport him where he wanted to go, and then bring him back a precise time later.

The risk was severe. If his calculations were wrong, he could end up in the middle of an ocean, which would not be a good idea without a boat, and he didn't have one of those handy. If he lost his yoyo device then he wouldn't get transferred back to the castle and would be stuck thousands of miles away. And if he couldn't get the supplies he needed, then he would have to come back and make yet another trip, something he wanted to avoid given the slightly less than fully functioning status of the transfer system.

"I'll wait until it's dark up there, then go," he muttered to himself for the tenth time. "Let's just hope they can supply me the goods," he continued, trying to convince himself that it was just going to be a quick, simple trip with no hiccups.

As he hadn't even tried to read a draft of his parts in the book, he had no way of knowing it would be anything but.

Chapter Seventeen:
No Well, Oh Well, Well Well

Don's house had seen many things in its time. Numerous parties, rows and relationships. One thing it had never seen, however, was attempted murder. Until now.

Cyrille was not a bad goldfish. He did his job, just like any goldfish out there. In fact, he did more than some. He swam backwards as well as forwards, and he slept upside down. What more could you ask? He had never had a day off, and had only been slightly ill once, when Don had tipped food dye into the bowl, mistaking it for an algae treatment. Cyrille had turned green for a couple of days, until Don changed his water, almost tipping him down the sink in the process.

For Cyrille, this was just another ordinary day, the 1942nd of his life, to be precise. It was also very nearly his last, as the penguins killed time in various ways, waiting to leave for their second meeting with the marketeers.

To be fair, it would not be right to blame any of the penguins, as none of them had ever even heard of a goldfish before, and here was one slowly swimming blissfully around just inches from Perec's beak. It was only natural that he would be interested in what one tasted like.

Perec was sitting watching the fish when his resolve broke. He could not stand it any longer. Dara and Nela were also in the room and could see what was about to happen.

"Perec, don't do it. It isn't fair on the fish or us."

"I know, but I can't help it. We could always get Carlota to get another one. She says that quite a lot of people have them in their homes, so there has to be a large supply."

All the time, while he had been talking, the tempted penguin was edging nearer and nearer to the bowl. At last, he reached into it and picked up the totally bemused Cyrille, who found himself floating on the air, or rather, dangling between the flippers of an errant penguin.

"Alas, poor goldfish, I knew it well, Dara."

"NO!" screamed an irate voice.

Almost as a reflex, Perec let the fish go and it dropped rather unceremoniously back into its bowl, but it was not really complaining, considering the circumstances.

"No, no, *no*. He never says the word *well*, for God's sake. It's 'knew him', not 'knew him well'!!" Don cried, revealing a pet hate, and an uncharacteristic but conveniently suitable liking of Shakespeare.

What Cyrille would have thought had he been able to understand the conversation above him is unknown. So much for the life-saving Don! Never mind his faithful goldfish!

"I'm really sorry, Don," said Perec as Carlota picked up the goldfish bowl to find a safer place for Cyrille. She had heard the commotion and had rushed in, just in time to see what had happened. Now she found a much better home for the fish and planted the bowl down.

"Now, no-one is to touch that bowl. Is that understood?" she demanded.

Even if they wanted to, the penguins would now have to scale a bookcase to get to the unfortunate Cyrille.

"Let's get loaded into the minibus; it's time we were off."

So off they went.

What's that? You want more detail than that?

We're on a word budget here.

Okay then, those readers who now wish to have details can read the following:

Penguins put on their disguises and long coats. Minibus backs up to the garage door, penguins sneak in, Don gets in. Minibus drives to destination. Well, technically Carlota drives, not the minibus – that would be silly.

Right.

Happy? We continue...

It seemed that the marketeers liked abandoned warehouses, the group realised, as they pulled up outside yet another run down building, on yet another run down industrial estate. This would be the location for the crucial second meeting to get the plutonium.

Carefully, Don and Carlota entered the dilapidated building, followed by pairs of shuffling feet. It was dark and damp and there was a peculiar smell about, although they could not locate it. The smell was not actually there, having decided to take a week's vacation at another run down warehouse, after being disturbed that morning. The reason for the disturbance lay in the middle of the warehouse, long, dark unmoving and silent. Clearly, the marketeers liked conference tables as well as run down warehouses.

The group approached the table like a gaggle of schoolchildren would approach a caged lion at a zoo; cautiously, first one then another, as if they expected it to suddenly jump up at them. Gradually, they got a bit braver and moved forward as a group, until they were finally at the table, and stood looking down at it in respectful silence. The table had to be given credit; it really knew how to do its job, sitting there, solid and immovable. When they were sure that it would not bite, they sat down on the accompanying chairs, and waited.

They did not have to wait long. Mr Amber and Mr Mauve had placed lookouts all around the area and so knew when the group arrived. Five minutes later, their cars pulled up on the gravel outside.

"Now remember, this time, just relax. Don't go blurting anything out," Carlota warned, "and no jokes, either. If we can sort it out this time, we could get the goods soon." Everyone sat there and said nothing. They all knew how important this was, just like last time. Then they heard the two dealers enter. Their footsteps echoed in unison as they made their way up to the table and sat down, nodding to the others.

"Okay then, let's start. We've checked with our suppliers and can get the goods; now, what about that contraption of yours?"

In reply, Carlota reached down to several sheets of paper on the empty seat next to her.

"Hold on, just a minute," said Mr Mauve, who had just noticed the empty chair. "Who's missing? Last time, there were eleven of you. Where's the other one?"

"He's ill, and is in bed; he couldn't come."

This was just short of the truth. Senik had been slipped a couple of sleeping tablets mixed into a tin of finest tuna. The others had watched as he drifted off on his feet, keeling over onto his back. Between them, Don and Carlota had carried him up to Don's bedroom. As the rest of the group sat in the warehouse, Senik was purring his head off in Don's bed.

"Well, do we need him here?" asked Mr Amber.

Normally, he tried to conclude all deals in three meetings, as it was good security. What he did not want was meeting four.

"We can do this without him," Carlota confirmed. "Now, you wanted to know about the plan. Obviously, it isn't here, but I can explain what it involves. Basically, it's an engine design that uses totally renewable fuel, so there is no problem about oil or electricity."

"And, just out of interest, how did you get this thing?" asked Mr Mauve, still doubting that it could exist, but realising the financial potential of such a device.

"Sorry, that's confidential. All I can say is that it was a famous scientist who designed it, so it should be reliable."
Had the two dealers known the scientist in question, they would have taken her assurances with a great pinch of salt, although where they would have got the salt from when they were sitting in the middle of a deserted warehouse is a very good question.

"Right then. We want the plans of that engine. How long to get it?"

"We have them already. As soon as you have what we are after, we can deal."

"Of course, you wouldn't think of tricking us. After all, we know where you live, Mr Castor."

"There'll be no tricks," Carlota replied firmly.

"Well then, that's all we need to discuss for now. We'll be in touch when we are ready to do the swap. I'd expect it in a week or so."

With that, the two dealers got up and offered to shake hands with Carlota, Don and Sevac who had all gotten up too. The former two were no problem, but Sevac was not concentrating and stuck out the tip of his flipper from his coat. Mr Amber took it automatically, before stopping in mid-shake to look at what he was shaking. There was a brief pause, and then he shrugged and turned to join Mr Mauve in heading for the door.

"See you soon."

They walked out the door, with Mr Amber turning to Mr Mauve as they headed for their respective cars. "I know they are in disguise, but I think that is taking it a bit too far."

"Well, they are probably just being careful, Mr Amber. After all, they aren't really penguins!"

"True," Mr Amber agreed, getting in and then nodding to his driver who pulled away, leaving eight penguins, two humans and a conference table in the old warehouse.

Chapter Eighteen:
The Winter Games

"On tonight's menu," intoned Harry, imitating a favourite sports reporter of his, "we have a whole selection of sporting events. Let the Games commence."
The others laughed, or threw things at him as they waited for the show to start.

It appeared that skating was the first item on the agenda, something that the crew had not yet seen on their secret camera, and so for the next hour, they were treated to a wide variety of penguins pirouetting, pivoting and positively prancing on the ice. It was clearly a practice session for something or other and the crew all agreed how impressive it looked. The synchronised skating was the highlight of the hour, with a performance to rival any opening ceremony of the Olympics, which was in fact what it was, although the crew didn't know this.

One thing that they did notice was that no matter what outrageous manoeuvre the penguins tried, they never fell over. The secret, which most human skaters would give their right leg for, is quite simple, though how they would skate on one leg is open to question. Penguins have long beaks, relative to their body size. They have devised the method of using them as a stabilizer by skimming them across the surface of the ice.

As they watched the transmission, the crew realised that there was one slight hazard to this artificial stabiliser. Put simply, if the penguin let the beak dig into the ice, it had an effect similar to a spin dryer going into overdrive and bursting out of its casing. Dozens of times Martin and the others watched in amusement as a penguin tried to be too clever, ending up spinning around and around and then hurtling across the ice, scattering penguins all over the place.

The camera crew quickly devised a points scoring system for the session, with a graceful glide scoring three points, a superbly executed move five, and ten points gained for each penguin floored!!

The unofficial competition was won by a particularly striking penguin who scored a knockout one hundred and ninety-six points in just four and a half minutes. The crew toasted her success in appreciative silence, until Harry came up with one of his usual bright ideas.

"Why can't they have that at the Olympics?"
Immediately several empty cans, two books, a carton of something, and four socks were launched in reprisal for such idiocy. Their short parabolic arcs were soon completed and they all impacted on their huddled target with exact precision, all except one sock which appeared

to be missing, probably burned up on re-entry. No-one could be sure, but after all, the question of the odd-sock is older than time itself.

The next item on that night's roster was an event which, unbeknown to Hattenburg, he had helped begin. Ten years previously, Hattenburg had been on Antarctica filming penguins when, surprise surprise, his supplies had been dropped in the wrong location. (It tended to be a regular occurrence on his expeditions!) In this instance, a tremendous storm had swept the area just a couple of hours afterwards and such were its effects that Hattenburg and his crew never found the cases. There was nothing they could do but order more supplies and berate the pilots concerned in completely un-repeatable language!

One of the missing cases had come down on top of another, and then both were covered with a blanket of snow which hid them from view. It was only several weeks later, after another storm, that most of the snow around the crates moved, leaving a hill with these two cases forming a level outcrop a third of the way up. Given typical penguine inquisitiveness, it was inevitable that sooner or later a penguin would slide down the hill and off the crates.

This was why, ten years later, Hattenburg and his current crew were now watching an altogether new form of ski-jumping. The penguins used no skis and a totally different technique to their human counterparts.

Whilst the occasional jumpers, or those in it just for a laugh, go sliding down on their feet, invariably ending up face-down with their beak embedded in the snow, the serious jumpers adopt a totally different method. They slide down on their backs, gaining extra speed with their flippers. To get top marks, the penguins have to be able to land on their feet within a set zone. The further into the zone, the higher the marks. Hattenburg could only watch in awe at some of the distances achieved. While he watched, part of his mind thought about making a new, hoax documentary about flying penguins, wondering whether anyone would fall for it. He mentioned it to the others.

"Speaking of falling, look at that one," laughed Martin, pointing to the screen as another penguin had just taken a nose, or rather beak-dive, flippers splayed out in the snow. Ten minutes later, the event changed.

"Oh, good, snowball again."

Chapter Nineteen:

Bits And Pieces

With darkness setting over London, as it tends to do in the late evening, Mr Amber was getting rained on as he returned to the north London flat that he shared with Mr Mauve. As he reached the steps up to it, he tripped over. With a bumped head, he looked behind him and could have sworn that he saw a couple of rats and a mouse doing a little dance. This was hardly surprising, as that was exactly what he did see.

The rats had been annoyed ever since the two men had got rid of the neighbour's cat. The cat had been old, and no competition for the rodents, who had played with it unendingly. Now it was gone, they felt bored and had taken it out on the pair who, they felt, had deprived them of their fun. In fairness, the two dealers could have claimed that it was gang justice, as they suspected the cat of pawning off several bottles of their milk.

Groaning and muttering, Mr Amber dragged himself up and walked up the remaining stairs to the door, fingering what felt like the beginnings of a bruise on his nose. Because his hand was in front of his face, he failed to see the figure lying on the last but one step, and so he found himself hurled into his front door. Just for good measure, his nose graduated to broken status, feeling that it might get more attention now.

Hearing the crash, Mr Mauve dashed to the door and flung it open, only to send Mr Amber stumbling into the hall, ending up in an undignified heap sprawled by the telephone table. The telephone, which received quite a mouthful, and not to mention an earful, decided to fall off its perch, to add further injury to the insults.

"What the heck's going on?" asked Mr Mauve in annoyance, thinking that they were being raided. "Oh, it's you."

"Of course it's me, who'd you expect, Father Christmas?"

The hall light had momentarily given up shedding light and was instead shedding tears of laughter at the spectacle, but then, its professionalism returned and it went back to its proper job. In the light, then, the two men looked out. They could see that the other figure was just coming round. How it came to be there in the first place, they had no idea.

The rats could have told them. Usually, they never had visitors, and so the rats had set several trip wires on the stairs, believing that this would partially atone for the pair's crime. Unfortunately, the mystery stranger had come along that night.

"Rats!" exclaimed the mouse, as he and his two companions had spied on the stairs earlier that evening. They had been five minutes too late to catch Mr Mauve, and now with their snares set, awaited Mr Amber's arrival. Unfortunately, it was a clearly delusional figure who had stumbled into their trap.

"Well, of course we are. What did you want to check that for?" asked one of the others.

"No, look," the mouse had said, pointing.

"Double rats," said one of his companions, drawing a stare from the other. "Why tonight of all nights do they have to have a visitor!"

They had then watched in silence as the stranger proceeded to trip on the stairs.

"At least the trip wires worked," was all they had commented at the time. They hastily re-set the snares, and then had returned to their vigil.

An hour later, they had watched as Mr Amber likewise took a tumble, and this had cheered them up immensely. Seeing him then go sprawling over the mystery figure had been the icing on the cake.

A minute after they had observed all this, the figure on the top step started to come around.

"Where am I?" he asked, having recovered consciousness after being tripped over.

"Here!" came Mr Mauve's irritated reply. Mr Amber was too busy feeling his broken nose to do anything.

"Oh, good," answered the figure. He stood up and offered his hand.

"No thanks, I've got two of my own," said Mr Mauve as he stood back to look at the stranger.

After a few moments, during which all they did was stand looking at each other, the figure on the stairs spoke.

"I'm looking for Mauve & Amber Property Locators."

"Well, you've found us."

"Oh good. I should introduce myself. The name's Ess, Baron Ess."

***

"So let me get this straight. You are saying that you live on Antarctica with a group of penguins," stated Mr Mauve.

It was an hour and a half after the unorthodox arrival of the Baron, and the three men were now down in Amber & Mauve's *special* basement, the one they used for 'discussions requiring a modicum of persuasion'. The sound-proofing, ceiling hooks and vaguely disturbing stains on the walls may give this room a more edgier feel, if you are that way inclined.

Mike Mauve rolled his eyes at Alex Amber. He just could
not believe what he was hearing, and was strongly of the

opinion that the Baron was probably no more than another escapee from the nearest Harley Street clinic.

Alex gestured to Mike and the two men left the basement. The Baron was not going anywhere, securely strapped to a chair that was not too happy with the arrangement. The chair had been quite happy on its own in the dark of the basement for the past few months, and until tonight had been close to formulating its plan as to how to turn itself into a table, the ultimate goal of any chair. (Try asking one and you will see.)

"Well, what do you think?" asked Mr Amber.

"It's hopeless. His story is just stupid. He must be a total nutcase. We might just as well let him go again."

"Hmmm."

"What, you don't think anything of this, do you?" asked Mr Amber in astonishment, catching the other's look.

"I've just thought."

"Painful, at this time of night."

"Very funny. It seems a strange coincidence, though."

"What does?"

"Well, he said the penguins were clever and could talk like normal humans."

"I know, it would make a good storyline for a book. You'd have to be pretty strange to write a book about penguins, though. Especially one about penguins that could talk. After all, who on earth would buy it?"

"Well, you could make it into a sort of odd-ball type comedy. However, that's not the point. The point is that the timing is quite convenient for it."

"For what? What are you on about?"

"He said the penguins were getting annoyed at all the experiments and had checked about how to set up their own systems."

"I know, I was in there."

"Oh, come on. Surely you've worked it out by now."

"Of course I have, I was just curious how long we could drag this bit out before the author gave up."

For quite a long while, neither of the two men said anything. Instead they just stood and stared at each other, partly in shock, partly evil anticipation, and partly because the author hadn't yet decided which of them would have the next line of dialogue, or whether to just turn them into canaries.

"Think about it, Alex, we could make a fortune."

"Flipping heck! All we have to do is work out another meeting and trap them there. We'd have the Baron *and* the penguins."

"Exactly. We have to figure out what to do with that detective and the reporter."

"We could send them fishing," Mr Amber suggested.

"Fishing?"

"As the bait."

Laughing as only evil villains can, the two men turned away from the window.

"By the way Mr Mauve, number sixteen is parking in one of our spaces again," mentioned Mr Amber as their voices faded away into the interior of the house. "I've sent them a reminder not to by cutting their brake cable."

Unbeknownst to them, the person standing conveniently under the window was thinking furiously. The brake cable wasn't his concern, but the other conversation he had overhead was. The penguins needed the plutonium, and they would only get that by meeting the two marketeers, so it looked like it would be necessary to wait until they were trapped before helping out. The timing would have to be perfect, but this particular person was used to working out timing and courses of action. Still working out a plan, the shadowy and mysterious figure turned away and went to make preparations.

Chapter Twenty:
Calls And Camouflage

"We've got the meeting date!" Don cried excitedly, as he burst into the lounge. He went two paces before falling over.

"Who moved that table leg?"

As the table leg was part of the table, Don considered it a strong possibility that the table was to blame. This was probably because he had burnt a ring into it the day before, when he placed a hot cup on its polished surface. There was nothing he could do to the table in revenge and so, instead, he got up off the floor, handing Carlota the unsigned letter that had just been posted through his letterbox.

"How long?" asked Senik.

"What, the table leg?" asked Don, just to string him along.

"No, the letter."

"Oh, about A4 size, I think."

Senik gave up in frustration.

"Four days, Senik," said Carlota, putting the poor penguin out of his misery. Immediately, Senik left the room, heading for the kitchen, to make sure he had enough Valium to get him through such a long period. No doubt to him, it would seem like four decades.

Senik wasn't the only penguin who wasn't happy with the timing. Elyd and Henec were both disappointed with the announcement, but for different reasons. Elyd had been coping as well as he could, but he was getting more and more homesick with every day that passed. Eternity in London seemed to stretch out before him. Even once they had got the plutonium, *if* they got it, they would still have to find a way to get back to Antarctica, which would take more time. His only recourse was to hide, which is why, whenever Don opened his freezer, he did so very carefully, not knowing if the sight of a sleeping penguin would appear before him.

Henec felt totally the opposite to the others. Being a *cordon bleu* chef in the middle of Antarctica wasn't very fun, because the amount of ingredients that one had to work with were very limited, even with the Baron's help. Now, in London, he was surrounded by so many implements, ingredients and recipes that he never wanted to leave. At the least, he knew that he would be taking a few books with him when they left, and the Baron would no doubt be presented with quite a large shopping list when they got home, although one item would not be on the menu. Despite trying several times, Henec had failed to master the fundamentals of the upside-down cake.

"Do we all need to go?" asked Sevac.

He too was thinking of Senik. This meeting would be the

crucial one, and he didn't want to have to start all over again. This time, there could be no mistakes.

"I think we all have to," commented Don. "If we don't, then they might wonder whether this is a trap. We can hardly say that he's ill again. We had better make sure he's got enough Valium."

"Weren't you listening to the author just now?" asked Senik as he came back into the room. "I've just checked and yes I have, just about."

"Good. In that case, then we have nothing left to prepare. The plans are ready, so now we just wait. What are the others up to?"

"I think Dara and Nela are practising again; Henec's in the kitchen with Ishy. Don't know where Perec and Torac are ..."

As it happened, Perec and Torac were in Don's upstairs bedroom, and somewhat worryingly, it appears they had mastered the art of using a cordless telephone. As Don asked his question, Perec was in fact waiting for his call to be answered.

Sally would never forget that it was half past two when she answered the call. She had only been in her new role for a week or so, and had thought that things were turning out fine...

"Good afternoon, Consumer Information. Sally speaking, how may I help you?" she asked, immediately putting on her best Customer Service voice.

"Erm, hello. I'd like to book one of your penguins, please, only I don't want it with the chocolate. What are the charges?"

Sally sat there for a moment, lost for words. Luckily, she rediscovered some of them.

"I'm sorry sir, I didn't quite catch what you just said, could you repeat that please?" The caller promptly did so.

"I know your penguins come with chocolate, but we only want the penguin. What are the fees?"

"Fees, sir? What fees? What for?"

Sally was, by now, very confused. Why had she agreed to do this little spot on the line? She had staff, this wasn't her job. All she had wanted to do was set a good example, as the brand new occupant of the Customer Services Manager role. She had a very nice desk waiting for her in her office, and there was a chair with it, too. She hoped the caller had the wrong number.

In fairness, the caller was just as confused. Why had she said 'what charges'? Surely they didn't operate a free service? There was no harm in asking.

"Is the service free, then?"

At last, thought Sally, *a normal question, almost.* It was an 0800 number and the caller surely knew that.

"Yes sir, the service is free."

"Oh good. Well, in that case, can we have two penguins please, both without chocolate."

OH NO!!

"I'm sorry, sir. I think you must have the wrong number."

"But that is the Penguin Consumer Line?"

"Yes, sir."

"Well, isn't it the one for booking the penguins then?"

"What penguins?"

"The penguins in your TV adverts! I want to book two penguins, one night only."

Sally couldn't believe what she was hearing and had to pinch herself to make sure this wasn't a dream. When she found out that pinching herself hurt, she knew she was awake, unfortunately, although she couldn't work out what she had done to deserve this.

"Sir," she said, trying to put on a brave face, until the brave snatched it back. "Those are not our penguins. They are clips from a wildlife documentary."

If she thought that this would appease the caller, she was mistaken.

"Well, why do you advertise a penguin ordering service if you haven't got the penguins? What sort of escort agency is this?"

"Escort agency?!" exclaimed Sally. "I'm sorry, sir, you must have made a mistake, thank you for calling."

Very quickly she put the phone down, wondering whether the RSPCA should be informed.

"Well, that's daft," commented Perec, as he too put the phone down.

He turned to Torac.

"Fancy running an escort agency, without any escorts. I'm going to go and ask Carlota about this. It doesn't make sense."

A minute later, Carlota was on her way out of the lounge when she found a very puzzled penguin coming to find her, clearly with a problem. Two minutes later, it was a very wise penguin who went blushing out of the study.

It was another very wise penguin who stood watching the camera crew once more return to their base, up in the cold Arctic. In fact, it was three wise penguins who stood there, each hoping their plan would work.

They had found the camera the afternoon before, purely by chance. There had been a heavy snowstorm which had swept the entire area, leaving a fresh covering of snow which had partially covered the camera. When the penguins had ventured forth once more, some had started tobogganing. It was only when one unfortunate penguin suddenly hit the camera that they found it.

The poor penguin was going quite fast at the time and the effect was like a ski-jump. The unfortunate creature soared through the air, setting a new ski-jump distance record. As it was, the landing was the only problem. The penguin fell flat on her beak, and when she got back up there was a deep impression of a penguin, flippers splayed out, in the snow.

The discovery of the camera was immediately reported to Vadek and Romic, although the penguins didn't know what it was. This is why, when the camera crew watched the film, they saw a multitude of penguin faces coming up and staring into the lens. It was only when the two leaders arrived and saw what was going on that they took control. Having seen many programmes with the Baron, they instantly realised the danger and quickly called everyone away. The camera crew noticed that everyone suddenly disappeared, but thought that it was probably because the weather was getting worse. Never for an instant did they dream that the penguins knew they had been discovered. This type of thing would only happen in fanciful books, about intelligent penguins trapped in the Arctic.

What the camera did not show was the debate which followed. The penguins were faced with four options. They could ignore the camera, take it, leave the area or try to trick their way out of the situation.

The first two options they immediately dismissed. Even if they took the camera, there was no guarantee that the camera crew wouldn't plant another, perhaps even guard it somehow. There was always the possibility too that the camera was sending its signal direct as well as recording it.

"It looks like we have to leave, then," declared Nanic.

"But they could always try to follow us!" argued Samil.

"And if the mission succeeds we must be in the same area as we started in, or else we might not get transferred back home," added Vadek.

"Right, well, in that case," stated Romic, "we don't know how long we have left here, so the only option we have left is to try and trick them into thinking we have left, and hope that it buys enough time for us. Right?"

Confused with all the left and right? So am I, and I'm the author!

"But how do we trick them? That's going to be the problem," Nanic pointed out.

"Maybe not," suggested Marel, another leading member of the Council, who had decided that he wanted a bigger part.

"What do you have in mind, Marel?" asked Romic.

"Well, it won't be easy, but if it works we should be able to fool them. It must be done today though, or else they might come and get the camera. The first thing to do is block the back entrance up. We've still got that small one on the west side. Then, what we do is this..."

***

It came as a shock to the camera crew that the first thing they saw on the tape, after going to recover it, was a penguin face peering into the lens. Now Hattenburg had the proof required that this was real. Penguins are one of the most inquisitive species on earth, and their curiosity was self-evident, watching the tape. After the penguins disappeared, at the time when Vadek and Romic had arrived, the tape was blank for several hours. Unfortunately for the crew, the camera had slid round to the right, when it had been bumped, and so they missed the departure of twenty penguins, all of them accustomed to long distance travel. They had a special mission.

"The camera must have frightened them off," said Martin, which was a bit unfair on the poor camera. It wasn't like it suddenly got up and shouted 'BOO!' or anything like that. The crew had watched in silence as a small group of penguins appeared and sledged off, followed soon after by another group, and then another, each group heading west, and soon out of sight. Had the crew actually been there, they would have appreciated the deception. For each group sledged away until they were out of sight of the camera and then doubled-back. The group that had set out earlier, headed by Nalla, had spent all day sledging backwards and forwards over a distance of forty miles, creating the impression that all the penguins had sledged off together. The plan was that the camera crew would follow this trail, but one of the storms that regularly visited the area would wipe out nearly all of the last part of the trail, so the crew would think they had just lost them due to the weather.

"Let's just pray it works," commented Vadek as the last penguins, who had wiped out the tracks of everyone returning, entered by the small western entrance. Now they had to wait.

For Hattenburg, seeing the penguins sledging off was a disappointment, but he knew that the location meant they couldn't sledge too far. He planned to track them as best as he could and see if an opportunity arose. As it was, all he had were penguins, on tape, but no proof of whether they were in the Antarctic or Arctic to back his story up.

Chapter Twenty-One:
This Title Is Under Construction

For the eleven in London, the waiting was over. The big day arrived. This was it. The final hurdle. The crux. The heart of the matter. The last chance. The ultimate barrier. Oh, you get the idea by now. And if you don't, where have you been?

Once again Don had hired a minibus. This time, wisely, it had tinted windows. He thought that had seemed safer. He wanted to prevent any possibility of being a driving hazard to other motorists. After all, the last thing you expect to see when you are driving along is a group of penguins in a minibus in front of you.

What's that?

You do see them? Quite often?

Oh, it's you again. Didn't you read the opening lines of Chapter One like I suggested at the time? You did? Well in that case, sit quietly in the corner until the end of the book. Sorry, readers. We continue...

The exit of nine penguins, Carlota, and Don from the house went relatively unnoticed. This was because the nosey neighbours who boxed Don in – metaphorically, of course – were at their day jobs as shop assistants. The penguins made it into the minibus without so much as a twitched curtain, and they set off for the final meeting.

There were no prizes for guessing the location of the critical final meeting. It was another abandoned warehouse, none other than the one Don had rescued Nancy Boi from just a few weeks previously. Getting in this time was not a problem, except that they had to clamber over a whole stack of rusting sardine tins, which had recently been thoughtlessly knocked over by someone!

"Whoever knocked these over could have made sure they were put back," moaned Torac as they clambered over the mound of tins.

Don said, and thought, nothing. That way he was safe from criticism.

Eventually, they reached the door and entered the building. The first foreboding of what was to come came from Don. He walked forward, showing off the fact that he knew the layout of the place, only to go head over heels. It appeared that he hadn't bothered to pick up his lamp last time either. Well, no-one's perfect, he reflected.

"You can think that again," said Nela.

"Definitely," agreed Dara, adding for Carlota's benefit, "Don thinks that no-one's perfect."

Carlota wasn't really listening to her. Something was

wrong; there was something missing. Don noticed it too.

"Where's the table?"

"Mmm, I was thinking the same thing. I wonder why it isn't here."

The reason for the non-presence, and some might even say the absence, of the table was that the two dealers only allocated two tables per deal. They were short of tables. This was why they had a three-meeting rule. They liked to get things concluded swiftly. As the group looked around they saw, up ahead, a large sign with an arrow on it. Funny enough, it looked like a diversion sign.

"Well, I suppose that they must want us to follow the signs," Don concluded, after staring at the sign for a couple of minutes.

The others simply gasped in feigned amazement. Clearly Don was thinking as fast as ever today!

"That doesn't make sense," Torac said.

"What doesn't?" asked Don.

"Well, how can we follow the sign? It's just standing there. What are we meant to do? Stay here? Or will it get up and walk?"

Don was feeling too nervous to understand the joke.

"That's a good point. I hadn't thought of that."

Finally, he caught everyone else up and realised what he had said. In an effort to patch things up he added "What do you think I am, stupid?"

The others declined to comment out of respect for his self-esteem.

"Never mind, don't answer that."

"We weren't going to," replied Nela.

"Can we get on with this?!" moaned Senik, his nerves working overtime as ever. He couldn't understand how the others were able to joke.

"He's right. Let's get it over with," said Carlota. She too wanted to get away from the warehouse. They didn't have too much time, as they had parked on a meter. Or at least they had, until Carlota had reversed off it and parked on the road beside it.

"Okay then, we should go this way," pointed Don, stating the obvious.

Torac led the way across the warehouse, in the direction of the sign. They were approaching an office complex, but it was all shut up and quiet. Clearly it had nothing to say. The two men watching the group from one of the darkened rooms however, had.

"This should be easy," Mr Mauve stated as they both peered out at the group.

"Agreed. I don't think there'll be any trouble. They don't seem to suspect anything."

The two men watched until the group passed down the passageway and out of sight. They then left the offices, and headed over to where they planned to meet the group. As they did so, they were completely unaware that another, completely independent figure, was watching events unfold.

"I wonder what they wanted us to follow this diversion for," pondered Dara as they rounded the far corner of the offices.

"Probably wanted to make sure we were alone," replied Carlota. "I thought I saw some movement in one of the offices as we went passed. I suppose they wer... Hello, what's this?"

The object of her surprise was leaning up against some stairs.

"It's another of those diversion signs," Don called back.

He had gone ahead to have a quick look and for once he was actually able to tell everyone something useful. He felt quite proud of himself. He stood there beaming for a minute.

"Well, which way does it say to go?" asked one of the group.

"What? Which way? Well... Er... I forgot to look. Hold on for a second."

Don wandered back to the sign, realising that he now looked a complete idiot. No change there then.

"This way."

The others hurried to catch Don up as he started to walk down the back of the offices. Had they taken the time to look around, they would have realised that they were being watched, from a distance.

"Now this is taking things too far," commented Torac. They were half way down the passage past the offices and to their left was a road-works sign. In front of them stretched a long line of traffic cones and a red traffic light.

"I agree," agreed Don agreeably.

"At least the diversion signs made sense. Maybe they are thinking of starting a construction business," put in Dara, helpful as ever.

"Never mind that. Come on!" urged Senik. He was already running over budget with all the overtime his nerves were working. Soon, they would start asking for bonus pay. Without waiting for them to follow, Senik waddled past the red light and started down past the cones. He had gone only a few paces when he tripped over a floor tile left unsecured.

I know – even in a novel you can't get the staff these days.

"Senik, Senik, can you hear me?" asked Sevac, as he tapped a flipper against Senik's face.

"Is he hurt?" asked Torac.

"Can he walk?" asked Dara and Nela in unison.

"Of course I can't walk if I'm lying down," Senik replied as he came around. Whilst the others relaxed after seeing that he was alright,

Senik slowly got back onto his feet, feeling both delighted that he was the centre of attention and a total idiot for getting knocked down in the first place.

By now, Ishy had waddled up. She had a disturbed, or thoughtful look on her beak, until it hopped off to have a good snigger at Senik, who quickly chased it off with an angry look of his own.

"That light is green now. We can carry on."
Very cautiously, Senik took up the lead once more. The fall seemed to have calmed his nerves; he felt bold and adventurous for once. Three paces later his nerves woke up and returned to command stations and he stopped dead, almost causing the others to crash into him. He gladly let Nela and Dara take his place in front, whilst he took station beside Torac in the centre of the formation.

The party passed along the lane of cones, noting the exposed pipe work on the other side.

"It looks like the council works here too," commented Don.
Up ahead there was a 'Delays Possible' sign. The date was blank. It obviously belonged to the local council. It had an all too familiar ring to it.

"A sign doesn't ring though," thought Don aloud.
Most of the others nodded in agreement, until they saw Perec reach into his ever-present bag and silence his ringing alarm clock.

"Why on earth have you brought that clock with you?" asked Don.

"Well, it couldn't have got here by itself, could it?" Perec replied.

Don thought and thought, but he couldn't find any answer to that. Who could?

"Look, another one of those diversion signs," he called out instead.

"Yes, it's the last diversion, too," said Nela, who was closer to it.

"How do you know that?" asked Carlota. "This is a pretty big warehouse."

"It says 'last diversion sign' on it."

"Oh, well yes, I suppose that explains it."

"So this is it, then!" breathed Senik. "We should find out soon."

He was a very happy penguin. Not only was he relieved to see that they were nearly there, but also his nerves had given up their clamour for bonus pay at the sight of the sign.

They had reached the end of the long passageway and now turned a corner. Finally. Up ahead they spotted the two dealers leaning casually against the wall of another set of disused offices. At sight of the group, the two men stood, and started to walk across towards them. Don took a careful look around. As far as he could tell, there was no-one else about.

The two groups met in a clear space, between the two sets of offices. Behind the dealers were four small silver cases, with bio-hazard labels on the side. The cases were open, and quite clearly empty. Everyone stopped.

"Well, we're here," offered Don.

"So I can see," replied Mr Amber. "Now let's not waste time," he continued, "have you got those plans?"

"We have, but those cases behind you are empty. Have you got the plutonium?"

"We have. It's in the office behind us," Mr Mauve answered. "These cases are from another deal."
He was as anxious to proceed as Carlota, but not because his minibus was on a parking meter. He didn't have a minibus.

"I want to see the plutonium," Don stated.
He trusted the two men about as far as he could throw them, which given the fact they were fairly bulky, and he wasn't, wouldn't be far.

"I want those plans first," countered Mr Mauve.

"Plutonium," replied Don, standing his ground, privately glad that the author had finally given him a backbone.

"Plans."

"No, plutonium," Don insisted, stretching his newfound backbone further.

Carlota, Mr Amber and the penguins watched this argument go backwards and forwards for a short while. It reminded Dara of a match at Wimbledon that she had seen on TV.

"I insist."

"No. Plans."

"I asked first."

"Did not."

"Did too."

Finally, Sevac stepped between the two men and raised his flippers, commanding silence. The two men looked down at him and shut up. It's not often that you get ordered around by a penguin.

"I hate to interrupt such an intellectual debate, but if we leave things to you two we will still be here next year."

Behind him, everyone else nodded.

"Don, why don't you two go and check the plutonium whilst Carlota shows Mr Amber the plans?"

Mauve and Amber exchanged a look, and then nodded.

"If you'll follow me, Mr Castor," said Mr Mauve, deliberately not thinking about what he had planned. He knew exactly what he would show Don, but wasn't going to give it away in front of the penguins! He waited whilst Don murmured something to Carlota and then turned and headed for a door, leading into one of the offices.

"This way."

Chapter Twenty-One ¾ : An Arctic Assignment

Whilst Don was following Mr Mauve into the warehouse offices, up in the Arctic, Hattenburg was coming back into the main camp.

Even before he said anything, the others could tell that he didn't have good news for them.

"Well, now we've got a problem," he confirmed.

"What's that?" asked Harry.

"It's something that's difficult to do," Martin replied with a straight face.

"Oh, ha ha!"

"The slight problem we have, gentleman, is simple," said Hattenburg. "Our beloved bosses want us to do a little task for them."

"What's that?" asked Martin.

"It's a small job," answered Harry.

"Touché. What's the task, Charles?"

"Oh, it's quite simple really. They want us to capture a penguin and film ourselves doing it. With proof of where we are, and when."

"Oh," came the collective reply.

No-one tried to joke about that.

Chapter Twenty-Two:
Flipping Heck!

Up in the shadows of the rafters that were holding up the roof (which is always a good idea), the mystery figure knew that it was time.

As quietly and slowly as he could, so as not to call attention to himself, he had slid along a rafter, following Mr Mauve and Don away towards the offices. Once he was out of sight of the main group, he lowered himself slowly down a convenient ladder and onto the roof of an office. He heard a door open, then shut.

"As you can see, Mr Castor, the plutonium is here as arranged," Mr Mauve was saying.
The two men were looking at yet another set of large silver canisters marked 'Plutonium' and 'To prevent danger of nuclear explosions, do not use in a bomb'.
"Four canisters, two hundred and fifty grams in each. That satisfies your order. Providing you have those plans, then we can conclude the deal."
"Carlota has got the plans, so we can do that now," said Don, turning towards the door.
"I'm afraid not, Mr. Castor," Mr Mauve said coldly, even though the office had central heating.
Don turned.

"It's so nice of you to confirm you have brought the plans with you. Saves us the bother of having to torture it out of you. Shame though; I enjoy that."

Don stood exactly still, not so much at Mr Mauve's words, but rather at the sight of the gun in his hand.

"I should have known this was a trap. I suppose these canisters are empty, too."

"Oh no, they aren't empty. They contain the plutonium. It's just that we are selling it to someone else. Speaking of which, they'll be here soon, so if you wouldn't mind walking this way, we must sort this out quickly."

Given the fact that Mr Mauve had a gun, and the fact that he would probably use it, Don had no choice but to comply with the 'request'. They passed through another office into a long corridor.

Don stopped. Mauve prodded him with the gun.

"Keep going. That door on the left."

Don stopped by the door Mr Mauve indicated, until he felt the gun pointing into his back once more.

"In you go. You can keep each other company," ordered Mr Mauve as he opened the door and shoved Don inside.

He switched on the light as he did so. Don fell to the floor, onto the legs of what he realised was another captive. Don recognised the face. Baron Ess!

Back on the main warehouse floor, Carlota and the penguins stood and waited. Don and Mr Mauve had been a little while.

"As you can see, everything's here. Once Don has confirmed the plutonium is here, we can do the deal."

"And that's the only copy of those plans?" Mr Amber asked pleasantly.

Carlota had to remind herself of the type of person she was dealing with.

"Yes. As soon as Don has checked your part of the deal, we can sort this out. The sooner we disappear, the better. We're on a meter."

"Oh, don't worry, Miss Pey," said Mr Amber, as Mr Mauve came back into view without Don. "We are just as anxious to see you disappear as you are."

Don's absence had already told Carlota that something was seriously wrong, but the tone of Alex's voice, more than his words, confirmed her worst fears. Then she caught sight of the gun in Mauve's hand. She knew there was no point trying to run; they wouldn't have a chance.

"Now, Miss Pey. I suggest you and your friends come with us. Don't go doing anything stupid, now. I'd hate to have to stop being pleasant. Not straight away, anyway. There's no fun in that."

"So much for your deal."

"Oh no, no; please don't misunderstand, Miss Pey. We were more than happy to do the deal after our last meeting."

"So what's changed? We've kept our side of the bargain."

Carlota waved the cardboard tube she was holding, wishing for a moment that Amber was a little bit closer. On reflection, hitting him probably wouldn't solve anything.

"Well," Mauve explained, "we had a visitor after our last meeting."

"A visitor?"

"Yes. It's someone who turns up to see you. That visitor told us some very interesting things about your friends here. Very interesting indeed. Once we heard what they had to say, we simply had no choice but to change our plans. After all, you deceived us first."

"How did we deceive you?"

Carlota couldn't help but feel slightly sick. She was sure she knew what was coming next.

"Your clients aren't who they say they are."

"I don't understand." She did.

"You can drop the act. We know they are real penguins. Why do you think we're wearing these?" Amber asked, pointing to a small black box clipped to the belt of his trousers. "Latest in electronic scramblers. Prevents your penguin friends from reading our thoughts."

"What? That's absurd. I told you, these are costumes and prosthetics."

"So how about we cut open one of the costumes, then?" Mr Amber suggested, a small knife appearing in his hand.

Carlota heard a crash behind her but didn't have to look to know what it was. Clearly Senik had fainted again. She knew there was nothing more that they could do. Mentally, she apologised to the penguins.

"We can do this any way you want, Miss Pey," Amber continued. "Either you give us the plans nicely, or you give us the plans the hard way."

"What choice is that?" retorted Carlota.

"Oh, sorry, I forgot to tell you. There is a third choice. You hold out on us, we'll kill one of your little friends slowly, and in great pain."

"What do you want with us?" Sevac asked suddenly.

"It's very simple, my penguin friend. You are penguins. You think. You talk. You equal money. Lots of it, to the highest bidders."

"You're going to sell us?"

"Some of you will go to private collectors. Some of you will probably go to a research lab. I dare say someone would like to get their hands on you for the odd experiment or two."

It was probably just as well Senik had already fainted. A couple of the others almost joined him!

"Two problems with your plan," commented Torac. "What makes you think we'll talk? And what about Don and Carlota?"

"Two questions. One answer," Mr Amber replied. "You'll co-operate, or we kill Don and Carlota, who we won't be letting go any time soon. Now enough talking. We don't have time for chit-chat. Are you going to give us the plans, or do I pick someone? That one on the floor would do for starters."

"Hmmm, that's a tough one," Carlota replied. She couldn't help being sarcastic, as she was so frustrated at having no way out. "Let's see. I think we'll give you the plans."

"I'm so glad you have seen sense. Now, if you would come with me, we'll do business."

"Some business."

Carlota felt a gun pressed into her back, and had no choice but to walk with Mr Mauve as he led the group into a large office. Behind him, Amber gestured to the group to get hold of Senik, and they followed.

"What have you done with Don?"

"Don't worry, he's comfortable, for now. Whether he, and you for that matter, stay that way depends on your penguin friends. Let's see if they co-operate over the next couple of weeks. Now, show me those plans."

***

Back in the corner office, the Baron had woken when Don had fallen on his legs.

"Who are you?" he whispered, as soon as Mr Mauve had closed and locked the door.

"The name's Don Castor. You're Baron Ess, right?"

"Yes, how did you know?"

"I've been helping some friends of your from Antarctica."

"Antarctica. You mean…?"

"Indeed. It was quite a surprise for me too at the time. Given that the bad guys have double-crossed us, I'm guessing they might know the secret, especially if you're here."

"Oh, they know alright. They had plenty of time to get the information out of me, I'm afraid. It's all my fault. Again."

Don was less than pleased to hear this, but still couldn't help feeling sorry for the Baron. He was clearly dejected.

"Do you know what they are planning?" asked Don.

"I think they want to use them to make money. I overheard some form of bidding war or something."

"What about us?"

"They keep us alive until every penguin's paid for. Then we're history."

"Oh, deary me," was not quite what Don said at this point. "I hope Carlota works it out."

"Carlota?"

"Long flashback. She's introduced in Chapter One. If you get out of here, you might want to read it. I just hope she manages to get them away somehow."

"I wouldn't hold out much hope of that. They're going to threaten to kill us both if they don't get their way. To be honest, it's all looking pretty hopeless."

"Yes, it's like one of those times in a book where it looks like it's all over, and only the author knows what's going to happen next," Don commented.

"I've always thought those types of books were exciting, but I guess it isn't in reality."

"I don't much like those types of book anymore."

"Me neither. Especially when you have a load of pages to go so it's clear that the author has something up their sleeve. I don't know why they bother."

"I guess there's nothing we can do then."

"Well, we could make idle chit-chat, and fill in a bit more back-story while someone works out how to get us out of here." Clearly the Baron didn't enjoy doom-laden silences either. "You say that you were helping the penguins?"

"Yes," said Don as he sat back against a wall. "They turned up one morning with Carlota and asked for my help."

"Well, you must be good if they chose you."

Don decided not to pursue this line of argument, simply shrugging modestly. He didn't want to admit that his recent cases amounted to a stroke of luck, a cat he still hadn't discovered the identity of, a paranoid window-cleaner, and his current predicament.

"It doesn't look too good from where we are sitting now does it?"

"No," said the Baron, deflated. "Not quite."

Don looked around the empty office. Only one door, no windows. No other obvious means of escape. Not even a lamp to defend himself with. Nothing. He sighed.

"So that's it then," he whispered as reality hit home. "Carlota and I are finished. Maybe not today, but soon."

"Join the club."

Just as the Baron finished speaking, there was a loud thud, then the sound of a key turning in the lock. It swung open, and a figure that neither Don nor the Baron recognised gestured them out. They were too shocked to move. Was this a trick?

"Come on, we haven't got all day," the figure

whispered, glancing anxiously over his shoulder. "We need to get the others and get out of here."

Don's brain gave him a mental slap and pointed out to him that this could be a way to avoid death. Thinking that this was a good idea, he helped the Baron up, and they hurriedly followed the stranger out of the room.

***

"Well, then, now that we have the plans, I think we have everything sorted out," Mr Amber was saying as he rolled up the blueprints and stood smiling grimly over the penguins and Carlota.

He appeared slightly disappointed that it had all been so easy. Fortunately for the captives, the fact that he had to handle another meeting that afternoon meant there was no time to torment them. Not yet, anyway.

"Now, Miss Pey. You'll be spending some quality time with Don. Meanwhile, we'll be taking the penguins with us for a little ride. For that, we'll need the keys to your minibus."

"You forgot to say 'please'!" called a voice.

Mr Amber spun around, just in time to see a lamp hurtling at his head. A moment later, he felt a blow on his head and fell unconscious.

On hearing the voice, Mr Mauve too had started to turn,

but he didn't make it. The instant he was distracted, the eight conscious penguins launched themselves at him. Now, having one oversized five-hundred-kilo penguin launch itself at you is painful. Eight of them piling on top of you leads to only one result. Within a second, Mike was lying dazed on the floor, and Carlota was holding his gun.

The fact that the two dealers were unconscious, meaning that she was safe, took a long time to sink in. Finally, she looked up to see Don smiling at her, and a dishevelled man in a grey lab coat, who looked very familiar.

"Don? I don't understand. Are you alright? Is this...? How did you get out?"

"We'll explain everything later. Right now we need to get out of here. The plutonium's here too."

"What if there are others we haven't accounted for? And what do we do with these two?"

"We'll tie them up for now. As for any others, I doubt these two would trust anyone else with a secret like this. If there are, we've got a diversion planned."

"How? We're all here."

"Trust me. Come on!"

Carlota didn't have any other choice. Quickly she helped tie Mauve and Amber up with some spare rope that was just lying around.

Isn't it amazing how that happens?

When was the last time that you watched a film and

someone had to visit a DIY store for rope?

Anyway, we digress.

With Mauve and Amber tied up, Carlota then followed Don as he led the way out of the office. Up ahead, they heard voices in the last office in the block. They stopped.

"Why don't we rush them? We've still got the gun," suggested Carlota in a whisper. "The exit is only beyond that office. We could make it."

"We can't risk it," answered the Baron. "Just sit tight. Marcus will deal with it."

"Marcus?" asked Carlota.

She had a feeling that she'd heard that name before somewhere. If she hadn't had such a fright, she would have known where from.

Before she could think, there was a loud crash from somewhere on the far side of the warehouse. It sounded like another stack of sardine tins had been tipped over.

"What the hell is that?" they heard one of the voices shout.

"We'd better check it," came the other voice.

As they heard footsteps fading quickly away, Don peeked into the last office.

"Okay. The exit's clear, come on!"

Carlota and the Baron, carrying Senik, and eight penguins waddled for the exit. Then Don, Carlota and the Baron realised they didn't need to waddle, so ran instead.

They darted out into the afternoon sun, to find their minibus parked, its back doors open, with the plutonium canisters inside. Don jumped in and Carlota followed. One after the other the penguins hopped in and lastly came the Baron, who positioned Senik safely across two seats and then shut the doors behind him.

"Okay Don, we're all here. Let's go," Carlota said. She didn't understand why Don shook his head and leaned over to open the passenger door. Finally, a familiar figure came around the side of the building and dived into the minibus. He hadn't even shut the door before Don accelerated away. It was only when the door was shut and the figure turned around that Carlota realised who it was.

"Hello again, Carlota. Sorry it took so long, but I had to wait until they had the plutonium loaded before I could do anything."
Carlota was shocked and puzzled. Facing her was Marcus Visal, the captain of the Arctic Adventurer.

Fifteen minutes later, with the minibus purring along like a relaxing moggy, Carlota felt that her head was finally catching up with reality. She now realised what Don must have felt on the first morning, when he came down to find Carlota and the penguins in his lounge.

She listened as Marcus explained that he had overheard

Carlota and two of the penguins talking one night, hidden at the back of the ship. After getting over the initial surprise, and thinking over what he had heard, he decided to follow Carlota once they had docked in England.

"Why didn't you tell me that you knew?" asked Carlota.

"I wasn't sure that you would believe I wanted to help. I thought you'd give me the slip. We've been in dock getting some minor repairs done. I knew from your conversation that you might need backup at some point, so I've been following you since you got here. Once I saw you meet those dealers, I decided to follow them instead. Luckily for you, I overheard them planning to capture you, so I was able to help."

"Just as well for us that you did. Still, at least now we've got the plutonium."

"Speaking of that," Elyd spoke up, "now that we've got it, how do we get it back to Antarctica?"

"Easy," replied Marcus, "I knew you would need a ship, so I've prepared mine. All the repairs have been done, stores are on-board. We can go whenever you want."

"First stop is home," said Don from the front, secretly relieved at how things had worked out, as were all of them. "Home and perhaps some food," he continued.

The others started laughing.

Chapter Twenty-Three:
Beam Me Up, Scotty

"Don, I think you'd better take a look at this."

"But I'm only using my overdraft now. I don't owe them anything," Don replied, quite confused.

"What?" Carlota was confused by Don.

"The bank."

"The bank what?"

"What you want me to look at. Another letter from the bank."

"Oh, no. I wish it was."

"I don't. One meeting with that bank manager was enough, thanks. Still, what is it?"

They were in Don's kitchen, taking a little breather after racing back from the warehouse. In the lounge, the penguins were bringing the Baron and Marcus fully up to date with everything that had happened.

"That," Carlota said, pointing to a piece in the tabloid Don ordered daily.

He had found from long practice that a daily order was the best way to have a paper because, as the newsagent said, it prevented a bill from mounting up. In the darker moments when Don considered this, he wondered whether the newsagent did not trust him to pay a weekly bill. Clearly, he was a very wise newsagent.

"I think we had better tell the others," Don said as he read the piece.

They hurried into the lounge, where Sevac was just finishing off the story.

"So that's how we got back there."

"One thing I don't understand, though," commented Marcus, "is why were you going to give that new engine design to a couple of marketeers? They would have had a lot of power."

"Oh no, we wouldn't leave it like that. If they had seemed like good guys then the plans would have given them enough to then talk to major manufacturers. As it was, I could tell there was something dodgy about them, so the plans were slightly modified. They would still work, but nowhere near as efficiently. Eventually someone else would have made the changes required to make it more effective," Sevac explained, before noticing Don and Carlota.

Everyone paused. They instantly knew something was wrong.

"What is it?"

"Unconfirmed reports, leaked from a source within the BBC, suggest that a film crew, headed by the famous Charles Hattenburg, have discovered penguins in the Arctic," Don read out to the horrified group. "The source says that they believe the reports to be a practical joke, but strangely, the BBC has refused to comment officially on the matter. In other news, yet another celebrity has alleged they have eaten a small pet rodent. Join our online forums to discuss..."

Everyone just sat there in absolute shock, all except Senik, who took the easy way out and fainted. By now, this was so common that no-one took any notice as his inert form toppled to the floor. They were too busy trying to work out what to do next. *Pet-eating celebrities??*

"If they find the colony then there'll be major trouble," Torac said finally, which was something of an understatement. "What can we do about it?"

There was more silence as everyone wracked their brains; all except Senik, who started snoring. Finally, the Baron broke the silence.

"The way I see it, there are only two options. Either the colony must disappear, or the camera crew must. Now, we're not ready to do the swap, and we're too far from home, but there is a way we can stop the camera crew."

"How?" asked Sevac, although he was certain that he knew the answer already.

"Use my matter transfer system. If we can assemble the equipment together, we should be able to rig a system that works. I know how to do it properly now. I've sorted out the problems."

The penguins had heard that one before, but quickly

realised that it offered them the only possible way to save the Arctic colony from discovery.

***

It had not been an easy job, creating a matter transfer system in Don's basement, and an hour later the contraption that sat there would not have won any awards for its aesthetics. Ludvig had cannibalised virtually every electrical appliance in Don's kitchen. Now, they just had to hope that it worked.

The hardest part of the whole job, however, had been clearing up, as Don's basement was the only part of the house large enough to do the job, and he didn't know the last time that he had been down there. First things first, the important task was to fit a light bulb. This was thought necessary after Don fell down the stairs.

"I'll be okay," he had groaned, sprawled on the bottom step. "Just give me a minute. What's that whistli....oooff!"

"Oh, I'm sorry, I thought that you were out of the way," said Dara.
Clearly, the whistling noise had been her sliding down the stairs.

"That was fun. I'm going to do it again," said the

impossible creature, and promptly started to hop back up the stairs to repeat the exercise.

Don got up quickly, to get out of the way, and banged his head on one of the cupboards.

Things did not improve much, until finally, using simple logic, Torac had asked Don, who by now had a large lump on his head, "Haven't you got a torch anywhere?"

"Yes, it's in the shed," Don had promptly replied and then, in answer to the stony silence of the others, "Well, no-one asked!"

Carlota returned quickly with the torch and passed it to Don, who soon located the basement light. Fortunately, the light was still where he had left it about a year before, suspended from the high ceiling as normal, which was sensible, as it would be useless anywhere else.

"Well, can you reach it?" asked Dara, on the ninth of her slides down the stairs.

"Not without help," replied Don, who did not have the advantage of being twelve feet tall to replace the light bulb twelve feet up. He tried a chair, but was persuaded that it was not suitable after going through it for the third time. They had to find another answer.

The scene a quarter of an hour later was comical to say the least. Perec, on Don's shoulders, was supporting Torac, who was trying to remove the old light, which was not quite within reach. All the while, they could hear Senik flapping around, nervous as ever.

"Senik, go and get some water, we'll need to clean the mess up in here before I can get to work," said the

Baron, who had sensed the penguin's nerves. "Here's the old bulb," said Torac, passing it down to Perec, who passed it down to Don.

"You're sure the light is off?" checked Torac as he got the new bulb, Sevac now using the torch to illuminate the holder.

"Yes, of course," reassured Don.

The instant that Don knew something was wrong came just after Torac had fitted the bulb. Carlota threw the switch and the room was flooded with light. A split second later, Don seemed to magically hurtle straight into one of the basement walls. Perec found that there was nothing under his feet, and that the only way was down. The actual fall was not that bad, but Torac tended to weigh a bit, and he was balancing on top of Perec.

The first thing that Don noticed when he awoke was Carlota, sitting by his bed with a strange look on her face, clearly concerned, yet almost laughing. Groaning, Don turned to her and asked precisely what went wrong. He did not need to ask who caused it.

"Senik spilt some water onto some of the loose wiring that Ludvig had to strip. The water caused a surge, and you were standing on some of the wires."

"I should have known," the weary detective sighed. Sevac, who had come into the room, stood up for his errant companion.

"It wasn't his fault; you know how strung up he is. His nerves couldn't handle a full bowl of water whilst trying to hop over all the wires. It's not something we do on a daily basis. Blame the author."

Grudgingly accepting this, Don sat up in bed. It was then that he caught sight of himself in his bedroom mirror. At his look of shock, Carlota laughed.

"Don't worry, it's fading all the time. You should have seen it when we brought you up here. You could always say it's a new fashion."

She was talking about Don's new shockingly white hairstyle that had replaced his usual brown mop. Don just sat there in apoplexy, clearly not believing what he was seeing. His mouth opened and closed like some hungry fish, although no words came out. Even as he sat there, his mind on low power, he could see that Carlota was right. It was fading very, very slowly. A couple of days in bed and he would be all right.

"Anyway, the experiment worked," said Sevac, taking three paces back and breaking the news as gently as he could. "Oh, by the way, we have to leave tonight; otherwise we'll miss the tides."

It was probably just as well that Elyd had taken Don's alarm clock; otherwise, it would have taken on a new role as a penguin-seeking missile. Don continued to stare into the mirror at the huge white frizzy cloud on top of his head. Wisely, Sevac mumbled some excuse and left the room, avoiding danger. Even as he made his way down the stairs, he heard Don's distraught cry to Carlota.

"I can't go out like this!"

Chapter Twenty-Four:
Blissfully Unaware

You can perhaps forgive the penguins for feeling slightly relieved, given that a captive camera crew were occupying Don's basement. However, if the penguins thought that their problems were eased, then they were sadly mistaken. Unfortunately, whilst there was a captive camera crew in a basement in London, it was the wrong crew.

On finding themselves somewhat unceremoniously dumped in the basement, they had immediately been gagged and tied up securely enough. This meant they were not able to tell the group that they had, in fact, been down in Antarctica, hoping to film penguins. Just like Hattenburg's crew in the Arctic, they had been baffled as to why there was no sign of the creatures they sought around. They were on the verge, not to mention the hard shoulder, of giving up when they found themselves transported into Don's basement. At last, they had found their penguins, but not quite as they had anticipated.

So, whilst everyone in the house thought that the Arctic colony was safe for now, back up in the Arctic the opposite was the case.

After watching the video of the penguins leaving the area,

Hattenburg had led the crew and they had followed the penguin tracks. They took an overnight trip and managed to follow the tracks for nearly twenty miles, before a vicious snowstorm wiped them away. After travelling further ahead trying to rediscover the tracks, and meeting with no success, they decided to head back to their base camp. Now, they had the extra problem of what to tell their bosses.

"I'll call them tomorrow; that should give us enough time to work out an answer," said Hattenburg when they reached the camp.

As it turned out, no excuse would be necessary.

Having spent nearly two months looking for polar bears, and not finding any, the crew were strongly of the opinion that there was little point staying on the ice.

"In that case," said Martin, "I might as well go and get that camera back that we left out. It's not like it'll be needed."

Hattenburg nodded in agreement and so, an hour later, Martin set out.

Vadek and Romic still had penguins watching the humans' camp, and the instant Martin left, they were informed. They soon guessed where he was heading, but did not feel particularly worried. The camp was secure enough. They knew where Martin would go and there would be no sign of their presence on his route. That, they had made sure of.

It didn't take all that long to trudge through the snow, but by the time that he reached the camera, Martin realised that he had misjudged the weather. Until he had rounded the end of the ridge, he had been unable to see the rapidly approaching storm. He could see clearly now that there was no way he would make it back to the camp by the normal route. There was no choice but to take a short cut across the ridge. Admittedly, it was potentially hazardous, but probably rated a better option than freezing solid in the middle of nowhere.

Martin could see it would be a close-run thing, even though he was walking. Already, the strengthening wind was whipping the snow up in front of him, obscuring him from the penguins' view.

"We should be alright," stated Vadek. "The storm should ensure that there are no traces around, if we missed anything."

Normally, this would be true, but Martin was a weak cameraman. He had a very strong predilection against the cold, and so hurried along. Suddenly, even though the snow was starting to fall and the wind was extremely bitter, Martin stopped dead.

Just to his right, there was a very small gully, and in it were not one, but two penguin tracks. There was no time to follow them, but Martin quickly shot a few seconds of film before hurrying on. He reached the camp out of breath, having had to run the last part of the way as the storm closed in. He burst into camp as Hattenburg was about to contact London.

"You haven't called London yet, have you?"

"No. Just about to. I might as well get it over with."

"Don't."

"Why not?"

"They're still there, or at least some of them are!" Martin exclaimed, walking over to their tape deck. "Watch this."

Everyone gathered around and Martin ran the handful of seconds of footage.

"Where did you shoot this?"

"Around the edge of the ridge. About half way up the slope. I had to take a shortcut across otherwise the storm would have beaten me."

Hattenburg had spent more than long enough in the wild to be able to tell how old a track was at a glance. The fact that a snowstorm had destroyed all possibility of there being any tracks around their camp kind of helped too. The author is good like that.

"So that means that those tracks can only have been made after we saw them all leave on the camera," Hattenburg concluded.

He was shocked, too, that clearly the whole concept of penguin intelligence would have to be re-analysed. On the evidence of the tape it would appear that they could not only identify threats, but could put complex plans into action.

"This will represent a completely new field of study," he told the group. "For now, though, the priority is to get the evidence."

"Couldn't it just be that a couple of penguins didn't leave with the rest?" asked Harry.

"I had thought of that, but it would make a mockery of the whole plot up to this point."

"True. Okay, they tricked us."

Everyone nodded, and the author breathed a sigh of relief.

"Right," Hattenburg continued. "What we'll do is use the end of the storm as a cover to plant another camera, by this new path. We'll use one of the live-broadcast ones. That way, we can broadcast a signal back to camp."

"Meaning that we don't have to go anywhere near it," nodded Martin, quite glad to stay warm whenever possible.

Then he realised, as cameraman, he would have to go and plant the camera. He groaned.

In London, whilst Don had been recovering from his shock, there was no time to waste, and the rest of the group had been extremely busy. After tying up the camera crew, the Baron had started to pack up the equipment, ready for the journey to the Antarctic.

Whilst Don helped pack the equipment, Carlota went out to hire a van that would transport them all down to the port. They had all agreed this was the best policy. While she was out, Carlota rang the local police, giving details of where they could find the two dealers. They were still there, left in the warehouse.

"Well, that's all the loose ends tied up," she said as she returned, parking the van outside the front door, because it was too big to fit inside.

She just about navigated the hall, as it was crammed with lots of boxes of packed equipment. Marcus was on the phone in the kitchen. With him were Sevac and the Baron.

"It's just as well we're going tonight," said Sevac. "Senik's run out of Valium."

He glanced into the lounge, where Senik was trying to watch television. Quite a challenge given that the satellite dish had been requisitioned for the basement. The poor animal was a painting of marginally controlled nervousness.

Actually, that's a lie. The poor animal was a penguin, not a painting.

Nevertheless, if penguins had opposable thumbs, there is no doubt Senik would have been twiddling them. Out of all the penguins, the Baron had declined only Senik's help with the final packing, murmuring something about 'expensive', 'one piece' and 'good condition'.

Meanwhile, Dara had taken it upon herself to keep the camera crew entertained. She still insisted on not using the easy way down the stairs into Don's basement, preferring instead to slide down. The camera crew's heads swivelled in unison as Dara flew down the stairs, then they nodded together as she hopped back up each stair to repeat the run.

"Sorry about this," she told the crew as she slid to a halt for the umpteenth time. "It's just that we can't risk you exposing us."

"Mmmmhmm hmmf fhhmmm," pointed out one of the captive crew.

Now, unless you are used to deciphering words from those wearing gags (in which case, avoid the authorities), you may not know that what was said was actually:

"What do you mean, expose you? All we were doing was minding our own business, when we got grabbed and dumped in here. And where is 'here', anyway? Who are you? What are you doing here? Why are we here? How can you talk? Are you real?"

As you can see, the language of Gag is very expressive.

283

Dara simply turned to begin her hop up the stairs once more.

When Don finally emerged, an hour later, his hair was still noticeably white. Everyone tried really hard to not look, or laugh. This was mostly accomplished, although Don did spend an hour with everyone looking at a point just below his chin. Finally, the author was kind enough to leave a woolly hat lying around, which Don promptly crammed onto his head.

"About time too," he grumbled.

Just then, Marcus put down the phone.

"Well, we'll definitely have to go tonight," he informed them. "The forecasted meteorological information for this trans-hemispheric voyage shows an extremely oversized cumulo-nimbus formation of evaporated water molecules building on the opposite shore of the colossal expanse of combined hydrogen and oxygen molecules that borders this singular landmass."

He had only put it this way to make it hard on the poor author of the book. This was due to a dispute over the size of his part. The shorthand version he explained to the confused penguins.

"It means that there's a set of storm cells in our path, as we head south. The last thing we want is rough weather, that'll lengthen the trip."

The penguins nodded at the explanation, while the author made a mental note to get his own back.

"This way, I take it, we get the best currents?" asked Nela, who could not resist.

"What a shocking thing to say," Dara replied.

"Well, she always was a bright spark," Elyd concluded.

"Oh'm not that bad," Nela responded in defence.

"What? What? Not that bad? No, I agree, the charge is even worse," Perec added, trying not to burst out laughing.

"Oh, very funny," Don groaned, who had been expecting it.

He knew he should have been more grateful for the hat.

"Now can we get on with things?"

"We'll have to be careful," Dara said to her sister as they went out of the room.

"I think you are right," Nela answered, raising her voice. "You never know, he might have a short fuse."

That did it. Everyone started laughing, and there was nothing Don could do. In fact, Perec was so busy rolling around the floor in hysterics that he rolled completely under the sofa, which only added to the occasion.

There was only one penguin who didn't laugh at Don's misfortune, and that was Henec. Not because he didn't think it was funny – he did, and was only just controlling himself – but rather because he was a penguin on a mission. As Don walked out of the room, Henec followed. There was no harm in asking, he thought.

As it turned out, Henec left Don's house with more than he expected. He had wanted several of Don's cookery books, so that he could cook a greater variety of dishes back home. He had already asked the Baron to secure most of the necessary extras. Even so, he did not expect Don to be so generous. He left with not only nine cookery books, but the re-assembled food mixer (complete with lid), various cooking implements and an even greater supply of ingredients, which included, as pride of place, a box of herbs and spices. Once Henec had placed these items in the van he stayed in there, to make sure they did not run off, although how they could do that without legs is an interesting question.

Each of the penguins ended up taking some small memento of their stay with them. Elyd already had his, tucked away safely in his, or rather Carlota's, bag. He made a last check to see it was still in there, reassured by the noise of it ticking away.

Torac chose a football training video, and a copy of the previous year's FA Cup Final. Don thought he wanted it to teach new skills, but Torac sadly had to disappoint him.

"No, all I want it for is to give them a good laugh

before the match. Should relax them nicely."

Ishy was given a gold chain from Carlota for a jewel she kept somewhere on her person, or penguin. Don thought better than to ask where.

Dara and Nela, although sisters, had two totally different mementos. For Nela it was the whole *Godfather* series on DVD. For Dara, however, it was a single book, which Don had specifically purchased for her. A copy of *Hamlet*.

Senik also had books. The first was a book on building self-confidence, a must for any architect, and the other was a book on relaxation. As a just-in-case measure, they added a ten-year supply of Valium.

Sevac and Perec only wanted photographs. For Sevac it was a photograph of the whole group. One of the shocked camera crew in the basement was asked to press the button on the camera, with the group assembled down there for the photograph. She was too astonished to refuse.

Perec's photograph was of Cyrille. As the poor fish was not being eaten this time, he was more than happy to pose for the camera, and Perec guarded the picture even more than Elyd did his alarm clock. Even so, if you ever get the opportunity to study the photo, you might notice that one of his flippers is definitely moving towards the opening of the bowl!

With all the mementos, equipment and penguins loaded into the back of the van with the Baron and Marcus, Don and Carlota locked up the house. They had made sure that the captive camera crew were still locked in the basement, complete with their supplies that they had conveniently had with them when they were transferred. Well, we wouldn't want them to starve, now, would we?

Giving the locks a final check, and looking around to make sure that everything was loaded, Don closed the front door and locked it. Once in the van, they all started to think of their next steps. An hour's drive to Southampton, and then the voyage to Antarctica.

Chapter Twenty-Five:
Sea Stories

The Arctic Adventurer was a good ship, unless she was sailing; the kind of vessel that was perfectly happy to sit in a dock for weeks on end. It was only when she was taken out to sea, which after all was her designed role, that the problems started to mount up.

Marcus had become very adept at seeing the problems in advance and so, recently, all the maintenance work that had needed to be done had been carried out on land. It saved the hassle of finding out that one of the screws had just dropped off for the third time when in mid-Atlantic. This all meant that the crew of the vessel were kept very busy in preparation for the voyage, which they all felt was at very short notice for such a journey. One or two of them would have said so, but a little thing called money prevented them. Also it wouldn't add anything to the story.

And so it was, that the crew did not see the penguins come aboard. They did wonder at the crates of fish going into one of the holds, especially as they didn't normally transport foodstuffs, but they were so busy coaxing the ship to life, that they had no time to pay much attention.

The same lack of attention could not be said for the arrival of the human cargo however. Don was not the only one to find that Carlota could be quite an attraction, and had it not been for Marcus' stern discipline in controlling the crew, it is doubtful that anything would have been done whenever she was around.

Having finally made ready, the journey began, and the Adventurer headed for the Atlantic, where, once in full steam, Don found he had an uncanny knack of being perfectly seasick. Carlota helped him through it until he found he could manage fine, as long as he never looked at the ocean, a bit of a difficulty considering their surroundings. Most of the time, he stayed in his cabin, and when he did go out, he tried to obey the maxim of not looking. This caused some difficulties, namely that Don was introduced the hard way to several of the doors and ladders on the ship. He either looked sideways, towards the superstructure, or straight up. This might possibly be what caused one of the crew to complain to his shipmates about Don, describing the detective as very uppity. In his defence, Don claimed that he did not see the poor man, as he was looking straight up at the time. Surely, it was not his fault he had almost knocked him overboard?

Whilst the crew got to see a great deal of the passengers, the same was not true for the cargo. From a very early stage, Marcus had demanded that, out of the crew, only he had access to one specific hold. The cargo was apparently a very important secret.

Even so, the galley hand on the boat did not expect that the cargo would lead to him finding a penguin in the galley.

Especially not a talking one in the middle of the night! He was rightly pretty shaken up, and the penguin, none other than the *cordon bleu* Henec, looked fairly surprised himself.

"Ah, hello... goodbye," said the penguin, making a quick exit from the scene.

"Goodbye," said the hand, too shocked to follow the penguin.

He sat down for a few minutes and then, having recovered his senses, he walked up to the bridge. Marcus was on watch.

"Captain... well... er..."

"What is it, lad? Spit it out."

"Well, I saw... or at least I think... I don't think I was imagining it. Maybe I was?"

"Imagining what?"

"It was in the galley, sir."

"What was in the galley?" asked Marcus, still feigning puzzlement. He knew very well what it was. Indeed, he had made an accurate guess as to whom.

"It was a ... It was a penguin sir," rushed the crewman, thinking that he'd be put off ship at the next landing as insane.

Given that the next stop was Antarctica, he hoped this wasn't the case!

"A penguin. Ah. Did it speak?" Marcus asked.

At this, the other crew on the deck looked at him as if he

too was short of more than just a few of his senses.

"Well, yes sir. It did."

"Oh, I should have realised. Don't worry, you did see it, but I should explain. This is the secret cargo."

"Talking penguins?" asked his first officer. "But that's impossible."

"No. They're a camera crew in disguise. Meant to be completely confidential. They're going to do some filming on Antarctica, in amongst the penguins, so they have these special suits to wear. They have to get used to them before they get there."

"So that's what's in the number one hold?"

"Yes. They did the same thing a few years back, so they've got all the materials they need, except frozen fish to provide baited food for in front of the cameras, and some other equipment."

Apart from the first bit, Marcus realised that the rest of what he had said was mostly true.

"Now, they mustn't be disturbed by anyone, as before, and no-one is to talk to them if ever they come above decks. Make sure the rest of the crew are informed."

His deck crew nodded at the instruction, and the message was soon passed around the boat, although no-one thought to wonder where Don and Carlota came in to the arrangement.

Meanwhile, down in the hold, the group went over some of the highlights of the past weeks, to fill their time, and to get us nicely down to the Antarctic without making the journey seem very short.

"I couldn't believe it when you turned up at the party," commented Carlota as she sat with the penguins in the hold. Don had just left for some tablets, having found that his seasickness had come back, after a half-day holiday.

"You haven't heard the worst," answered Henec, and he explained.

It appears that gaining entry to the party had not been a problem. No-one knew anyone else in costume, so he was let in. In fact, the author can exclusively reveal that it was lucky that they had left the party rapidly when they did meet.

The organiser of the party, who busy trying to do the rounds dressed up like a paperboy, made a terrible mistake. A police officer came calling to ask that they turn the music down, as several neighbours had complained. The organiser took it as a joke and turned the music up, whilst several others jeered. The police officer was wise and retreated, calling for assistants, and assistance. Each reveller who remained was asked to remove their headdress, if they were wearing one, so the police could identify everyone. What would have happened if Henec had still been at the party would be anyone's guess!

Still, there Henec was, standing in the packed room, after receiving several compliments on his costume from a six foot blue and red parrot, and a pair of slippers. Now came the slightly difficult bit. How was he to find Don and Carlota when he did not know what they were wearing? By the time he had arrived, the party had been going for more than a few minutes and there was seemingly no end to the available drinks. It looked an impossible task, and Henec was beginning to feel worried when he felt two strong arms crash down onto him and he was whirled around.

"What a sshmaaa..shmasshhi... nice costume!" slurred the figure Henec found starring down at him.

"Scott's the name," continued the stranger, thrusting out his hand. Gingerly Henec shook it with his flipper.

"Err... hi, I'm... a penguin," said Henec, who could not think of anything better to say.

"HAAA, HAA, HA!" roared the figure at a volume that would have woken a hibernating tortoise. "Where, where did you get your coss...cosssshhh...your outfit?"

"Ah, well. I made it myself," Henec replied. "Or rather, my mother did."
They both laughed, although not quite sharing the same joke.

"I say, look what that Roman is doing to that hen!" exclaimed Scott, and look he did.

Whilst his attention was otherwise engaged, Henec made his exit.

The paperboy had looked around the party and was satisfied that the guests were so drunk they would eat, so he brought out the food. For him this was a big mistake. To say that Henec was first to help himself would be like saying buttered bread has the slight tendency to land face down on a carpet. It was all a question of self-restraint, but where the most prime salmon in the world, or at least in the local corner shop, was concerned, Henec just could not help himself. Faster than an Olympic swimmer he dived into the pile of food, soon rooting out the salmon paté and sandwiches. Very carefully, he separated the fish from the bread and ate it. He could hardly put the bread back, so that is why, the next day, the paperboy found several slices of buttered bread and several crackers behind his sofa. He never could work out what had happened. Maybe I should send him a copy to explain.

Back at the party, however, Henec was no closer to finding Don and Carlota, and was wandering around worried when he had a stroke of luck. He had made his way out into the large dining room, again packed with people in fancy dress, when he saw another penguin wandering about too. For a split second, he almost made the mistake of trying to talk to it mentally, but then realised that it was only a costume. Nevertheless, Henec took a moment or to two to watch the figure and thought the costume was not bad. Suddenly, though, the other penguin appeared to have problems. Someone had pulled its headdress off, revealing a balding man in his late forties. Henec recognised the culprit as Carlota and hurriedly made his way over, only to have his beak nearly taken off.

"And the rest you know," Henec concluded. "It was something that I don't want to do again in a hurry, either."

The others laughed, imagining the scene, and then Sevac spoke up.

"There was one thing that I've been meaning to ask you, but it slipped my mind. How come you have invisible pelicans in Britain?"

"Invisible pelicans?" asked Don, who had just come back into the hold.

"Yes, you see what happened was this... "

Cue swirling visuals and flashback music.

Apparently, the penguins had had their little swim in the Thames and had come out of the water near a sign for London Zoo. On an impulse, they decided to visit and quickly waddled their way to it, luckily avoiding all but a paperboy who thought they were in fancy dress. The paperboy was in fact none other than the host of the party

Don and Carlota were headed to. For a moment, he had kittens, thinking that they were going to the party too. Fortunately, they turned the other way and he could relax. He didn't like cats.

"We got up to the zoo and were on the wrong side of the street so had to cross. Then, up ahead, we saw this sign with some black and white lines and a yellow light or two."

"A pelican crossing?" asked Carlota.

"Yes. The little sign said 'pelican crossing ahead'," Sevac explained. "We waited half an hour though, and didn't see any."

Finally, the penguins had gotten tired of waiting and decided to cross. It was typical penguin logic that as pelicans were clearly black, white and yellow, and as they were of the same colours, they could use this special crossing too. Don and Carlota were already several steps ahead of them in the story and could guess what came next.

"It was so quiet, we thought it would be fine. And we thought that any traffic would stop, you see..."

On the night in question, there was little traffic about, but one couple that were out on that night were the Headbangers, a retired couple from Los Angeles who were in Britain on a sightseeing holiday. The penguins left them with holiday memories they would never forget.

The couple had wanted to see London by night and so were driving along past the zoo, towards the Thames. Suddenly, out of the shadows, waddling straight into the path of their car, came a penguin.

Tex Headbanger slammed on the brake pedal. The brakes responded by squealing loudly and smoking. They had tried to quit for a month but did not have the strength.

It is questionable who was the more shocked: Dara, who had stepped out, already starting to party in her mind, or the Headbangers. It was a pretty close-run thing and luckily, Dara dived forward out of the car's path. Tex had driven on, thinking what a strange country Britain was. First, the thing with the airport baggage trolleys that would go any way but in a straight line, and then this. His wife, Martha, was also thinking about it, but along slightly different lines.

"Well, say Tex, isn't it cute an' all, having penguins all over," although this was the first penguin they had seen. "We should have them back home."
Tex had to destroy her illusion.

"Don't be foolish Martha. It was one of those darn politicians on his way to some weird adult party."

"Maybe we should have given him a lift then. I didn't know they had penguins in the Houses."
Tex said nothing; it was better not to!

"That was a lucky escape," said Sevac. "If anything had happened there, we would have had real problems. As it was, we hopped over and got into the zoo, found the others and started to party. It was only when Senik tried to get back over that he found we couldn't. The only thing to do was contact Henec and then wait for you. It seemed pointless to not party in the meantime, though, and so we did."

Sevac did not have to explain. The most important words in the penguin language are food, warmth, shelter and parties, and sometimes they do not have to be in that order.

"What I want to know Ludvig," Don commented, squatting on one of the heavy wooden cases that were meant to contain their 'research equipment', "How did you end up a captive of those guys up in London? I mean, it's not as if you simply walked up to their front door and knocked..."

Behind the Baron's back, Don was suddenly aware of Perec waving his flippers rapidly, shaking his head as he looked at Don. Ludvig turned, probably due to the draft of air generated by the flippers. Perec immediately turned the waving into a set of stretching exercises.

"What!? I want to keep fit," he replied to the Baron's stare.

"Of course you do," Ludvig smiled dryly. "As you can probably tell, Don, knocking on their front door was precisely what I did do. Or at least, that's what I intended to do. They tracked down a couple of highly accurate clocks for me years ago when I first started out. Nothing dodgy. I knew that if anyone could track down what I needed, it would be them, and then they could get it shipped down to me."

"Couldn't you just have phoned?"

"They aren't that modern, Don. No online booking system for the black market. Anyway, I transferred myself. Unfortunately it appears that humans need to be inside a building if they don't want to be delirious for a few hours at the other end of a transfer. I was rambling apparently when I met them. That's how they found out about you. Sorry."

"Oh."

There really wasn't much else Don could say.

As the sun gradually set, and the stories continued, the Arctic Adventurer sailed on towards Antarctica, whilst several thousand miles away, sitting on a packing case, Hattenburg could only watch the monitor in amazement as the penguins continued to re-write everything he had ever written about animal intelligence. He had realised what an excellent opportunity this was to study penguins really close up and so had got permission to film them for a couple of weeks, before attempting to trap one. That way, they could get some decent evidence to support their story.

"Another two weeks of filming, and I think we'll have enough material to work with," he commented to the others, as they watched that night's entertainment.

"Two weeks until we are famous," Martin whispered to Harry.

"I'll drink to that."

Chapter Twenty-Six:
The Start Of The Race

The days seemed to go slowly for every one of the group on board the Adventurer, although for the homesick Elyd and Senik, they seemed to tick away slower than for everyone else. Still, tick away they did, during which time the penguins and the Baron explained a great many things about their lives to the other three humans. They explained all about the Penguin Games, and talked of their lives and history. It was clear to Don that, despite the Baron's obvious failings, the penguins didn't mind him living there; some of the things he did provided them with a great deal of entertainment.

When Marcus entered the hold one afternoon, Perec was re-telling a favourite penguin legend, of a time when a great cold came to the world, when ice seemed to stretch on and on and on without end, and there was fish by the thousand for everyone. On seeing Marcus, Perec stopped.

"Sorry to interrupt, but I thought you'd like to know we've spotted land."

He had hardly finished the sentence when Elyd shot past him, quickly followed by a blur of other penguins. They all crowded to the side of the vessel, the penguins lined up like black-and-white bowling balls in a rack.

"Home," Elyd whispered, and that was all he, or any of the penguins said for the next hour, as the ship got closer and closer to its location.

Eventually, with many a glance back, the penguins made their way back down below decks. All except for Elyd, who remained, a flipper resting on the side of the ship, as he neared home. Finally, with a sigh, he turned and went down to join the others. They had already made their plans, but wanted to go over them, to be certain.

At the other end of the world, Hattenburg and his crew were also cooking up plans, whilst Martin cooked their latest pre-packaged, and decidedly bland, meal. There was a temporary hitch when Harry, who was slightly hard of hearing, thought Hattenburg had said 'make pants' not 'make plans', but that was soon sorted.

"Okay. The editor wants us to capture at least one penguin. If possible, they want two. We will all have to be involved, but they still want it on tape. We're to use one of the newspapers dropped to us the other day as proof of when it is. Suggestions?"

"I think the best way would be to have a good look around and find an area which is easy to surround."

"Why not just rush them one morning and grab one?" interrupted Martin.

"Too risky. If we miss, then they may scatter. We'll never catch them then."

"And," continued Hattenburg, "if they didn't run then we could get injured. Those penguins weigh a lot. You wouldn't want one jumping on you. No, the best way is to spring a trap if we can. We need to work out how to get one or two on their own."

"If I remember right," said Martin, "there's a place just round that southern spur which forms a sort of cul-de-sac. We could go and see if it gets used by any of them."

"How long have they given us?" asked Harry.

"That's up to us. My orders are to make sure it works, so we go when we are ready. I'd figure five or six days to get everything ready and rehearse the plan. I'm sure none of us want this to fail. We'll have to leave the area to practise, which is a risk, but it doesn't look like the penguins are intending to go anywhere, otherwise they really would have left when they had the chance."

Secretly, the rest of the crew agreed. Each of them was imagining how famous they would be when they returned with the penguins, and each was certain that their part in the plan would be 'the' most important. Unfortunately there was nothing they could do that evening, as a storm was storming through the area, as storms normally do. Instead, they settled down to watch the transmission from that day. First event – skating.

Twelve hours later, on the other side of the world, Marcus woke the penguins as he came into the hold. Their discussions had gone on into the early hours and even though they were so close to their goal, eventually they had become so tired that they had to sleep.

Torac heard the door open and slowly raised his head. He realised Don and Carlota had awoken earlier because they were nowhere to be seen. From his sleeping companions came a low thrumming noise. He turned to Marcus.

"How far away are we?"

"We'll reach port about six hours from now. Early afternoon at the latest."

"Listen, Marcus, I never got a chance to thank you for what you did for us."

"All I did was give you a little helping hand. You are the ones who did the hard work, although from what Don and Carlota said, not without the odd bit of partying."

"Well, you know, it had to be done."

"Of course," grinned Marcus. "Anyway, swimming all that way; helping Carlota; meeting those dealers. You had the hard job. I knew if you got what you needed, you'd need a vessel back to the Antarctic. You could hardly fly it down there, so I thought I'd follow and see if I could help."

"Good thing you did. Otherwise we'd probably

have been sold by now, and who knows what else."

"It had to be done."

Six hours later, the hold was a hive of activity, although no bees could be seen. All the penguins were checking and re-checking and then, just to be sure, checking again. Once they were finally satisfied, which involved dragging Senik away by his feet as he wanted to un-pack and check everything for the fourth time, they started to load some of the equipment onto sleds, ready for the trip across the ice.

"Half an hour until we dock. Once the crates and supplies are unloaded it should be dark enough for you all to head away without too much notice."

"We'll radio you when we arrive to confirm all's gone okay," confirmed Carlota.

"No problem. We'll be here. Time I went above and made sure the crew are ready," said Marcus as he looked at his watch.

"Don't look at me," replied the watch. "You're the captain."

Marcus headed back to the bridge to oversee the docking and unloading operation, which went smoothly. Just as the area was getting as dark as it would at this time of year, he watched three humans and the penguins leave the ship and head off across the ice.

"Good luck, folks," he whispered.

"Skipper, I've been meaning to ask something,"

said the galley hand as he bought up coffee.

"What's that?"

"How come there's so many of them? Surely they would stand less chance of being spotted if there was only a few of them?"

"Well, I was talking to one of the team," said Marcus, thinking fast, "and apparently they are going to split up and cover two groups. That's why there were so many crates; they needed double of everything."

Marcus knew he could get away with this explanation. After all, if his crew were daft enough to believe that there really was a human camera crew dressed up as penguins, then they would believe anything.

"Oh, that explains it."

Marcus, and the author, rest their case.

On the ice, there was no time for any rest. As soon as darkness fell, everyone helped to unpack the remaining cases and load everything onto the sleds. All that was left were two large crates of fish, which they would tow behind them.

"Three days, four at most, and we should be there and all set up," said the Baron confidently. He saw the penguins look at him.

"Trust me; I know what I'm doing this time."

He started his sled and the group slowly started their long journey.

It was probably just as well that he couldn't read the collective thought of the penguins at that moment.

Chapter Twenty-Seven:
See Him Here, See Him There

Just over three days later, we find the group in the Baron's castle, and, just for a change, Senik is nervous.

"It must be nearly ready by now, surely?" moaned Senik as he paced backwards and forwards, flippers behind his back, like some anxious relative outside a maternity ward. For once, he wasn't alone in being worried. Beside him, Dara and Nela also paced, keeping in sync with their normally more nervous cousin.

"After everything we've been through, we can't fail now, surely? Not this close."

Quite who this Surely character Senik is talking to, the author has no idea, he hasn't put him there. However, I am sure that, having followed their adventure this far, you wouldn't wish them to fail, either.

What? You've flicked to the back of the book to read just the ending?

No cheating!

Right, sorry about that. Where were we?

That's right, three penguins are pacing back and forth on the plush red carpet lining the Baron's hallway floor. But why, you ask, are they so worried? Read on...

It was about three hours after they had returned to the castle that the group realised just how serious their stranded relatives' plight was, up in the Arctic. Purely out of curiosity the Baron had, quite illegally, hacked the email of a producer at the BBC to see if the camera crew had escaped from the London basement. What he found instead chilled him to the core.

A quick, and irregular, use of a military mapping satellite confirmed his fears, once he had warmed up.

"What do you mean, *the wrong ones*?" demanded Don, when the Baron had explained. Don was privately glad that he wasn't the one to have messed up for once. And why not? After all, it certainly made a nice change to have people not looking at him in annoyance.

"We've captured the wrong crew."

"I heard you the first time. And what's with this 'we' business? I didn't do anything."

"Oh I don't know, Don," chimed in Perec, "I thought you were the shining light last time, almost the creative spark even."

At this point, Perec stopped, aware that he was within grabbing distance, and Don, who had been interrupted in mid-rant, was clearly in grabbing mood. The fact that the author has momentarily lost the ability to make any more electricity jokes, we will kindly overlook.

"Don, it doesn't matter who did what, none of that matters now," Carlota interrupted before turning to the Baron. "Can you fix it?"

"Yes."

"Sure?"

"Trus... no, I can't really say that, can I?" the Baron answered ruefully.

"Not really," said Don, trying to regain the high ground, whilst also feeling slightly hypocritical.

"I can give you ninety-five percent odds. I know everything that went wrong, and now I finally know why. There is no reason why this should not work."

"Should?"

"That's the best I can do."

Well, given the choice between ninety-five percent odds, and doing nothing at all, ninety-five percent odds seemed the best option, and so once again Don found himself helping to set up a matter transfer job in a basement.

Quite why eccentric scientists prefer to build their weird devices in basements was something Don didn't understand. He was about to question this, but yours truly stepped in and re-wrote his character to understand that the author was simply following historical precedent. I mean, you wouldn't demand an answer of Bram Stoker now would you?

At least this time, lighting wasn't a problem. The Baron's basement was the size of an indoor tennis court, and lit almost like one. Nevertheless, the scale of the operation was substantially larger than the transfer performed in London. Don, very surprisingly, was the first to spot the flaw in the plan.

"Don's right," said Torac.

"What about?" asked Carlota which, given that Don hadn't yet said anything, was understandable.

"There isn't enough room in here," objected Torac. Don felt quite proud at this, and decided to store this feeling deep in his memory, as it didn't happen very often.

"How's this going to work, Ludvig?" asked Torac of the Baron. "You can't fit our whole colony in this basement!"

"We won't have to. Back in London, I had to use what I had available, which meant the crew had to come directly to us."

"So how is it any different now? And for that matter, what about the bears outside?"

"For a start, we've got proper equipment, and now I know why it didn't work. The bears will naturally go back as part of the process, their locations won't matter. As long as we can pinpoint the colony, then whatever came this way will go back the same way."

"You're sure?"

"Yes. You see, the truth is that I was a lot closer to

313

getting the experiment to work last time than I realised."
There were various glances and mental thoughts amongst
the penguins at this.

"No, really, I was," stressed the Baron. "It was a
two stage process. First, making a transfer happen. That's
easy enough, as it turns out; you just need to understand
the fundamentals of the Time Hypersensitivity Unilation
Dimension. Quite why it took me so long, I don't know. All
of a sudden one day, it just hit me."

"So if it's so easy, what went wrong?"

"Well, breaking something down into its
component molecules and putting them back together
again is easy. It's like a jigsaw puzzle in reverse. You see
what the picture is, then break it apart. As long as you put
the pieces back together again in the right places, the
picture is back again."

"How does moving the colony to the Arctic come
into it, then?" asked Sevac.

"Well," the Baron warmed to his theme, "the trick is
moving the molecules somewhere different to where they
started. After all, what's the point in moving something to
where it already is? It might as well stay there in the first
place. To get something to move, you have to factor in the
Movement Outside Velocity Expectations quotient. Once
you've got that, you can calculate how to move the item to
a new place."

"And it was this second bit that was the problem?"

"Yes. Transferring the colony should be fine. I realised I had missed a zero off the end of one of the calculations."

… !!!

Silence.

No, even more silent than that.

The kind of silence that occurs only when you ask 'Who died?' only to find out that someone has.

Dead Silence.

Lots of very angry penguins.

"All of this because of one missing zero?" Torac finally asked.

"Yes. That's the trouble with buying a calculator from a pound shop, I guess. That's why things went slightly wrong last time."

Now, assuming you were sane before you started reading this book, and haven't lost your sanity since (except you who are sitting in the corner since being told to do so), then you might think that displacing an entire colony of a species to the opposite end of the earth is just a teensy, weensy, ever so marginally, little bit more than 'slightly wrong'!!!

From the collective looks of astonishment of those around him, the Baron was probably aware of this, but chose to ignore it. He didn't really have a leg to stand on in defence. That's a lie actually, he had two perfectly good legs, but he needed them.

"Let's get started, we've not got much time. From what those emails said, the trap looks imminent – probably when it gets light in the morning, their time. We've got a lot to do."

"So how do we help?" gasped Senik.

The poor penguin had been holding his breath, trying not to yell at everyone to get started. As he spoke, he picked up a curiously curved piece of metal, which he promptly lost his grip on and watched fall to the floor.

"Why don't you go keep an eye on that satellite feed? Let us know when it gets light up there. They will need daylight for the trap."

Senik nodded and set off at once, glad for something to do. Dara and Nela quickly followed; the last thing they needed was a broken monitor on the satellite feed.

That was why, hours later, Senik, Dara and Nela paced backwards and forwards in the hallway, only interrupting their vigil to go and take a look at the satellite images every few minutes. Finally, after a quick check, Dara waddled hurriedly up to the other two.

"It's getting lighter up there; definitely changed since last time."

"We better go tell the Baron. Senik, watch the

316

monitor and let us know if you see any movement."

"Nicely done, sis," said Dara after watching Senik waddle off. "Last thing we need is him nervous around all the equipment down there. Let's go."

The two sisters waddled down the steps into the basement, and were just in time to hear the Baron announce, "It's ready."

"So what are we waiting for?" asked Don, who had taken on the mantel of nervous person in Senik's absence; not that Senik is a person, of course, but by now you should have read enough to know what the author means.

"We need to test it. I'm not making the same mistake again. We'd be in real trouble if we ended up transferring up there, instead of getting them all safely back down here."

Everyone agreed this would be less than ideal.

"So how do we test it?" asked Don.

A fraction of a second later, his brain suggested to him that this may not have been a wise question, as it implied assistance from Don in the testing process.

"Good of you to offer, Don. It's better if it's you to prove it can handle large masses," said the Baron at once. He too had picked up on the possibility and wanted to use Don before he had a chance to back out. A hint, perhaps, of revenge for the hard time Don had just given him.

"Well," Don started, but then realised he didn't really have a choice, "oh... I .. umm... what do you want

317

me to do?" he finished lamely.

"Nothing. Just sit on this chair," said the Baron, pointing to what looked like a stainless steel stool.

As you may have realised, Don is not one for too much exertion, so on hearing that all he had to do was sit on a chair, he became quite happy, even if it wasn't the plush armchair that we mentioned way back in Chapter One.

"Oh, this is quite comfortable," he said in surprise.

"Yes, that's because it isn't totally there, so in fact you are half floating on air just above it. You just rest there a minute, while I find something to go on the other chair."

"I'll do it. We know it's safe on us from your tests ages ago," volunteered Torac. Without waiting he waddled to the other chair, took off the empty bucket that was sitting on it, and was helped up by Carlota.

It was only then that Don noticed the identical chair sitting a few feet away, elevated slightly on a very polished metal plate. He glanced down. Another shiny metal plate underneath his chair also. Finally, the Baron's words seemed to penetrate his head, and he understood that when the Baron had said his only task was to sit, he might have left a little piece or two of information out. He wasn't alone.

"What's going to happen to Don?" Carlota asked, in a tone that was aimed at being 'just casually asking, don't mind the answer', but came across as more like 'how many pieces is the poor guy going to be left in, and should we say goodbye now?'.

"Nothing at all," the Baron soothed, "really, he won't feel a thing. In fact, he won't notice anything happening at all, until he sees the result."

"The result? What's going to happen to me? I like me the way I am."

"You'll still be you. Right, let me explain. Torac is going to sit on this chair here. When the transfer happens, you and he will simply swap places. We need to prove that not only can we get the penguins home, but that we can put the polar bears back where they should be."

"And I won't feel a thing?"

"No. Once you start to be de-materialised, you'll literally know nothing about it. It should feel like time has stood still, and you've just re-appeared in a new place."

"And you are doubly sure I won't feel a thing?" Don repeated.

Getting a paper cut was in the top ten of Don's most painful experiences. The thought of being 'de-materialised' sounded infinitely worse!

"If it's any easier, Don, I'll ask Senik to come down with something electrical and a jug of water," suggested Torac. "Then you won't feel a thing."

"No no, it's okay. Let's do it."

Quite surprising, really. The thought of being knocked

unconscious by Senik was, in Don's brain, a more dangerous event than being dematerialised. Perhaps the slightly lop-sided logic that bought him to that conclusion explains why he has never been that good a private detective.

"Hey, don't blame me, you created my character! If you want me to be more successful, re-write the first couple of chapters."
Excuse me dear reader, a slight author-character negotiation is required for us to continue.
"Shut up and get back to work, else I'll make it a bucket of water and a lawnmower with a dodgy cable!"
Negotiation over. Story continues.

"Right, now we've got that out of the way," said the well-behaved Baron, who will find his castle repaired and upgraded at the end of the book, "let's do the test. We're running out of time. I want everyone except Don right back over by the stairs. No sense in taking unnecessary risks."
"No mention of risks in my contract," the detective tried to grumble under his breath, but given that the author is the one writing his dialogue, this was unsuccessful.
Still, given that Don was perched on a chair about to undergo a very dangerous experiment, he can be forgiven, this once.

With a few backward glances at Don, and in a couple of

cases a flipper that started to raise in farewell, but then thought better of it, the group moved back towards the stairs. The Baron remained at his controls at the back of the room. Don perched nervously on the chair, fighting the urge to bolt. Torac meanwhile was waiting patiently, unfazed.

"Right, Don, close your eyes."

"Why?"

"I don't know really, I just thought it might make it easier for you."

Eyes were closed. Then the Baron remembered he needed to keep his open.

"Okay, on three. One, two, ..."

"Wait!" cried Don, eyes still firmly shut.

"What?"

"Don't know."

"We aren't going to go through that type of game," said the Baron somewhat decisively, and without warning he stabbed his thumb down on a big purple button, situated just next to the obligatory big red one that is always present in any control panel, normally to torment those of us who cannot resist pressing them.

Now to be honest, if you could ask Don what happened next he would tell you that, except for one thing, he doesn't remember. It all happened so fast. However, given that this transfer malarkey is the whole reason we are in

Antarctica at the moment, a brief description is perhaps called for. So let's slow things down a bit. Like how time seems to dilate when you drop a drink onto a carpet.

Clunk. The button is pushed.

Don's eyes start to open, but never quite make it, quite possibly because by the time his eyelids have started to open, half his forehead has already dematerialised, and the rest is following rapidly.

Blankness. Not an uncommon state for Don, but not due to his normal nature this time.
Consciousness with eyes still starting to open.
A weird tingling sensation.
A weird floating sensation.
A painful thudding sensation due to the floating sensation being Don falling off the other chair.
Darkness.
And a smell of fish.

"I think we can say that works," Don heard the Baron say, slightly muffled in the darkness. "Now we tweak the settings to do the real transfer. Should only take a few minutes. Let's hope they are all together up there."

"Can someone get this bucket off my head?"

322

Chapter Twenty-Eight:
A Non-Revealing Chapter Title

At the other end of the globe, the plan was ready. Everything was set. Nothing was left to chance. It all led up to this point. Every 'i' had been dotted, every 't' crossed. Yes, this is going the same way as the opening of Chapter Twenty-One, but there's a shortage of chapter openings at this point.

Each member of the camera crew was well aware of what was at stake. If their capture plan worked, the crew would be famous throughout the whole world. There would be book deals, interviews, and supermarket openings in obscure towns in the middle of nowhere. If the plan failed, then they would have a lot of explaining to do.

Out of the corner of his eye, Martin saw Hattenburg lift his hand. This was it. Even more slowly than an errant schoolchild on their way to see the headmaster, the five men crept forward. A mistake now would ruin everything.

As he popped his head over the edge of the ridge, Martin saw the penguin below, totally oblivious to the trap about to be sprung. Between them, Martin and Harry carried a large net that had been airlifted to them especially for this purpose. The plan was simple: capture a penguin, whilst

Hattenburg filmed the event.

The two men paused, looking across at Hattenburg.
Ready.

Suddenly, Hattenburg dropped his hand and Martin and Harry rushed forward with the net.

For a split second, Martin heard warning bells in his head, but he dismissed them. It was probably due to him putting his alarm clock too close to his head the night before. Then, he realised he was right. Something was wrong, terribly wrong, and it was not the fact that Harry had fallen over, or the fact that Hattenburg appeared to be sliding down the ridge, due to the huge vibrations running through the ice all around them.

Martin stopped. Something was happening and he was sure that it was not good. The very air felt heavy around him and then, out of nowhere, came a tremendous humming noise.

What the heck? he thought in confusion.

He saw the others turning and running in panic, and was just about to do the same when there came a vivid green light which blinded him, followed by a thunderclap of an explosion. He fell over, stunned. When he looked again, he was barely able to believe his eyes.

The very first thing he noticed was that somehow he was underneath the very net that should now contain a penguin or two. The second thing he noticed was that whilst there were a couple of things in view, he could no longer see the large black bulk of a penguin anywhere in the vicinity.

It was probably due to these points that Martin was slow to examine the things he could see. He realised there was a seal under the net with him. He didn't see that outside the net, two eyes were watching him. Finally, getting tired of waiting for Martin to catch up with the plot, the seal hit him with its tail and quite clearly gestured to The Eyes.

Martin looked, and saw them at last. Then he saw that those eyes, which were looking at him with a look of barely concealed amusement, seemed to belong to something that bore an uncanny resemblance to a very large polar bear. Cream coat? Check. Four paws? Check. Black snout? Check. Liking for fresh meat? Che...

Martin threw the net, seal and all, hurtling ten feet away and got to his feet. From the look on the bear's face, Martin knew he had better move fast, or else he would be roasted.

In fact, he was wrong. The bear had no cooking equipment, but as far as Martin was concerned, the difference was immaterial. He turned and ran for it. The seal, who had been stalking penguins for its own culinary reasons, decided to also scarper. It had no plans on being on a polar bear menu.

Chapter Twenty-Nine:
Fun And Games

In Antarctica, life had settled back to normal surprisingly quickly. The eight original penguin adventurers, and Ishy, had received a hero's welcome when they had hopped out of the castle to find a multitude of penguins. There were the traditional back slaps and high fives as the group made their way slowly forward to where Romic stood awaiting them.

Don, Carlota and the Baron hung back, outsiders to a private ceremony that, to Don, seemed to involve lots of head bobs, flipper waves and occasional trumpeting.

Finally, with the group greeted and clearly approved of by their leader, they led Romic and Vadek back up to the castle to meet Don and Carlota. As they did, the vast majority of the other penguins began sledging for their heated caverns. Well, it is cold down there!

The homecoming celebrations lasted a whole day before the serious business of an over-late Penguin Games became the only topic of discussion. So it was that five days later, Don, Carlota and the Baron sat by the side of the bobsleigh run, ready to watch the first competitor.

"The Games should have been held a month ago,"

Sevac had explained when the announcement had been made, "but of course they couldn't risk it up there. Instead the others kept up a kind of training for the competitors, and decided that if we ever got back, we would start the Games straight away, so we could hold it before breeding season."

"So how does it work, then?" asked Don.

"Pretty much like your winter and summer Games do, except we don't do all your activities, especially those weird ones like that funny walking race. You'll see over the next few days."

And see Don most certainly had. The iceball tournament had been like watching a combination of ice hockey, football and rugby all rolled into one. Intensely competitive, highly accident-attracting, and played at breakneck speed, Don had found himself cheering, wincing and ducking all in good measure (the ducking mainly due to badly played shots).

The iceball tournament covered the opening two days of the Games, mainly as some of the competitors were also entered for later events. After iceball had come ice skating, then more traditional races and relays, even including a penguin version of hurdles, except instead of having to jump over hurdles, they had to sledge under ice bridges.

"I still think we could learn a thing or two from their ice skating," said Don to Carlota as they waited for the bobsleigh competition to start.

"It was quite impressive, wasn't it?"

"Closest I think we'll ever come to seeing a flying penguin – well, except for the ski-jump event next week."

Once again, penguins had taken a human competition to a new level, simply by introducing their beaks as a way to perform better tricks. Forget 'triple salcos', write off 'two and a half twists', and definitely set aside that weird spinning move people do where they start standing up, then crouch, then stand again. (I mean, what's that all about?). Don knew that if he could record the penguins and show their techniques to an Olympic judge, the sport would be revolutionised overnight.

"The highlight for me," remembered Carlota, "was that one who managed to go thirty feet through the air, spinning like a top. How they didn't win first place I'll never understand."

"Something about putting a foot down wrong on the landing. I agree it was a bit harsh. Anyway, look, there's Dara. She must be about to start."

Don had been looking forward to the bobsleigh ever since the events had been announced. He still remembered his trusty old sledge from his childhood. Bright blue with silver ropes – the sledge, not his childhood.

"The bobsleigh course is made of natural ice, with the fastest competitor the winner," the Baron explained, mostly for the reader's benefit. "The only difference to human bobsleigh is that the penguins are the rider and the sleigh!"

Originally, the standard way for sledging the course was designed by Malus Kalvor, one of the greatest penguins to ever bobsleigh. The competitor went down on their back, feet first, using flippers as a way to steer, with their head up to see where they were going. Recently though, a new technique had been evolved and was now standard practice, designed by no other than Dara herself, as she had explained the previous evening.

It had all started by accident one day, when Dara, Nela and their cousin Melia had been on the slopes for a practice. They had agreed on a slope and had started sleighing the normal way. After a while, they had gathered at the top of the run for a rest, and Dara was messing about. In the middle of an impression of a ballerina that she had seen on the satellite the night before, she pirouetted too far and plunged onto the run, head first on her stomach. Being typically Dara, she thought it might be fun and so did not stop herself. Very quickly, however, she noticed that she seemed to be going a bit fast, and was getting faster. She called to Nela and Melia to help and they started to sledge down, but found that they had no chance of catching her.

Dara meanwhile was having the time of her life, although

she was still hurtling along. She had tried everything she could think of to stop herself, but nothing worked. Suddenly, she saw the end of the run looming up, but there was no way she was going to stop, instead racing through the finish line, and, incidentally, knocking a whole four seconds off her personal best time. The best time looked around, found the missing seconds and went to see his doctor.

"Get out of the way!!" she screamed out as a group of old age penguins made their way slowly across the run.

Too late. She scattered them like bowling pins as she zoomed through. She kept on and on, trundling through the middle of an ice hockey game and gliding serenely, albeit very quickly, through an ice party.

No-one could really believe what they were seeing and several thought they must have been seeing things. They were not. By now, Dara was just a trifle concerned about how she was to stop. Even if she just waited until she glided to a halt that could be some distance away. She saw a rapidly approaching ice pillar and reached out to grab it with a flipper, but only succeeded in sending herself hurtling along a new heading.

Then, suddenly, salvation loomed large in front of her. An obstruction so solid that when she hit it, she actually bounced back a couple of feet.

"What was it?" asked Don as he listened to Dara's account.

"Norgid." Dara replied.

Don and Carlota laughed.

"It wasn't funny. He could stop anything, and it hurt!" Dara responded.

"Tell me," said Carlota, "if you go so fast like this, how do you stop in the competition?"

"Well, the answer's obvious. I don't know why I didn't think of it then. We use our beaks as brakes. We just have to be careful," she added, not sharing with them the time when she had been too casual and ended up digging her beak in too far and somersaulting over it. It had actually looked pretty impressive, but counted zero towards her marks. Shame she was not a gymnast!

An hour later, and after watching penguins whiz, whoosh, whirl and some other descriptive word beginning with 'w', Dara was crowned winner of the bobsleigh competition, in one of the closest finishes ever. It actually came down to a photo-finish between her and another competitor, with Dara taking the title by a beak, although this then had consequences for her ability to stop before the wall of ice at the end of the run. Still, she was pleased once she had been dug out of the mound of packed snow.

After receiving her medal, she followed Don and Carlota over to the Underwater Challenge event, where Nela was waiting to compete.

"Well done, sis; now it's my turn," Nela congratulated her as they waddled up.

Don still had not got out of the habit of waddling when he

was with the penguins, something Carlota found quite amusing, and also secretly quite endearing.

"I still think you're mad. That water is worse than freezing," Don told Nela as she prepared, although technically he was not correct; after all, if it was freezing, it would be ice, not water.

"It's a challenge," she replied as her turn came and she slipped into the water.

Quite a few minutes later, everyone found themselves holding their breath in anticipation. Some looked worried, some anxious, others awed. The clock was running, or at least it would have been if the penguin holding it would put it down. The poor thing was cold and wanted to get indoors. Well, wouldn't you?

"12 anatics," intoned the Intoner.

Don looked over at Carlota and grinned.

"Well, she's won."

"Mm. I wonder how long she'll stay down there."

"13 anatics."

"14 anatics... Stop the clock!"

Everyone stared at the water in confusion. Nela hadn't yet come back to the surface.

"I said stop the clock! It's getting away!" the intoner shrieked.

And it was true; the clock had slipped from its penguin's grasp and was already a fair distance away. Immediately, two penguins began to sledge after it, to give it a right ticking-off.

Fortunately, the backup clock was made of sterner stuff and a minute later recorded a new penguin record as Nela finally broke the surface.

"15 anatics, 12 anatocs," the intoner proclaimed once Nela had slid out of the water and began to get her breath back.

With a noise like several hundred penguins congratulating a champion diver, the several hundred penguins gathered congratulated the champion diver, now holder of the record for three years running.

"That's the third year running," Dara said, just in case any reader had skipped the previous line.

"She must be mad," Don replied, as he applauded.

"Takes one to know one," said the penguin as she gently tapped Don on the back with a flipper.

With the Games finally over and the penguins slowly starting to return to their now plutonium-powered lives, Don and Carlota knew it was drawing towards the time for them to leave. Before they did so, the Baron had given them a guided tour of his rambling castle.

The Baron's castle looked in serious need of urgent repairs on the outside, but as soon as Don and Carlota had first stepped through the door, they entered a different world. Far from the cold, silent stone shambles they were expecting, they had been transported into a palace. This impression didn't change with their last visit to his home.

The entrance hall was massive. Not ordinary massive either, but the type of massive that is even more massive than that. The red carpet was so thick that their feet seemed to sink into it as they walked.

"This must be worth a fortune," Carlota remarked to Don as they meandered down the hall. "I mean, just look at all these ornaments," she added, looking all around.

It was as she was looking that she noticed that Don was no longer with her. In fact, he had taken only three steps inside the hall before coming to an abrupt halt. He never usually said much anyway, so Carlota hadn't noticed.

"What's the matter, Don?"
Don could do nothing but point in reply, having been struck dumb by one of the paintings on the wall.

"Oh, so that's where the Mona Lisa ended up," said Carlota, as she came up and saw what Don was looking at.

"I always liked seeing it when I came in," said the Baron as he walked out of his study.
For a moment the three of them stood in silent admiration of the masterpiece, until the Baron turned away and said

"I'll miss that there. Still, never mind. Shall I show you around some of the other little surprises of the place?"

The other little surprises of the place, as the Baron had put it, included the genuine World Cup, several of the most valuable paintings in the world and a space, the plaque of which simply said 'Bucket'.

"I know this must sound like a really daft question," said Carlota, standing in front of the non-bucket, "but why should there be a bucket here?"

"Hold on, I'll go and get it," said the Baron who disappeared, quickly re-appearing holding the same bucket Don had discovered the inside of, down in the basement.

It looked like an ordinary bucket, only it was highly polished and shining like a lamp, which had the added advantage of lighting up this section of the room without the need for a bulb (the Baron being very money-conscious). The bucket practically glowed and the two puzzled humans listened with astonishment to the story the Baron now told.

It was all down to the matter transfer experiment that the Baron was working on. This, the two had already realised as the bucket was grouped with several, extremely valuable pieces. At first they assumed that the bucket was an accident, but no...

"At the time, I thought I had finally cracked it and so tried another swapping experiment, and got the penguins to help me. What I did was position two chairs on either side of the room, and the plan was for the penguin to sit in one and be transferred to the other."

Unfortunately, the experiment didn't go according to plan, due to another chair, which couldn't really be blamed; after all, the Baron had put it there.

"The penguin sat in the chair and I powered up the system. All the dials showed that everything was working and so I activated the beam. That's when something went wrong. The penguin disappeared according to plan, but the bucket of fish on this other chair also disappeared. Then, something started to appear on the chair across the room, but it wasn't a penguin; it was the bucket, but without the fish."

"When was this?"

"Five months ago."

"I remember that! Some fish randomly turned up on a quiz show. Everyone thought it must have been a practical joke by one of the crew!"

"I didn't know how it could have happened, but as I later found out on the satellite, the bucket of fish must have somehow become locked in time and caused a mix-up."

"Well, that explains what happened to the bucket of fish," said Don, remembering the incident, "but what happened to the penguin in the other chair that was meant to be transferred? I didn't hear anything about a penguin turning up anywhere."

"No, you wouldn't have done. We didn't know where the penguin had gone either until someone tried to sit in the chair. The penguin hadn't gone anywhere, in fact, but was merely invisible and asleep. It took about eight weeks for the invisibility to wear off. It was quite weird. There were penguins walking into something that they couldn't see for the first few hours, so in the end, I tied an orange scarf around the penguin to prevent any further accidents. It was quite weird to watch this orange scarf wandering around the place, but in the end we got used to it. I never did get my scarf back, though," he concluded wistfully.

The tour continued throughout the day, as around every corner there was always something new to see. Finally, they came back to where they started and met Darik, Perec, Nela and Melia on their way out.

"I shall be sorry to see these go," said the Baron wistfully, looking at the treasures. "I think I'll have to go and visit them sometime. Have you thought of how to get them back yet?"

"Not yet," said Don. They knew it would be difficult. They couldn't just hang them back on the walls!

"There is one way you could do it," said Nela.

"Couldn't you put the items in one of the warehouses that you met the dealers in, and then tip off the police?"

As ever, the answer was obvious.

"Why didn't I think of that?" Don wondered aloud. The others just looked at him. There was no need to say anything.

"Fancy coming to see how our machine is coming along?" Melia asked.

"I had wondered where the plutonium had got to," Don nodded. Melia led the way out of the castle with Don and Carlota; the Baron told them he would catch them up. Apparently Henec wanted to see him.

"He says it something about a shopping list for food," commented the Baron. "I wonder what he means."

"I hope you've got a large freezer," was all Don would say by way of explanation as they went out of the door, leaving the Baron even more puzzled and now very uneasy.

Chapter Thirty:
Time To Disappear

Had anyone told Don a year previously that he would find himself crying when saying goodbye to a group of penguins, he would have undoubtedly laughed at them, yet this was what he was doing when the time came to say goodbye.

Don and Carlota had stayed with the penguins for nearly three weeks, but now it was time for them to leave, otherwise you'll never reach the end of the book. To simplify the script, and allow for possible sequels, it was decided that the Baron would be staying on, until such time that Don and Carlota had managed to return the 'borrowed' treasures back to their rightful owners, and his name had been cleared.

Marcus had fooled the crew by telling them that the 'penguins' had problems, which the specialists, thus explaining the human passengers' role, had to help them with. This was causing the delay. It was not that much of a problem. The ship had sailed prepared for a long time at sea.

"Well, here we are," said Carlota, for once lost for words as they approached the water.

"Looks like it," agreed Perec, looking around the

group, desperately trying to lighten the mood, unsuccessfully.

"Try to stay out of trouble won't you," Don suggested.

"I will," Ludvig replied, hurriedly hiding a scrap of paper out of sight.

The ship was anchored just out of sight, in a bay just the other side of the ridge that the group were standing on. It was probably just as well, as there were nearly a hundred penguins gathered on the slope. In the centre were eight of the original nine adventurers plus Ishy, Vadek, Romic, and the three humans. They were some twenty kilometres from the main colony, but quite a few penguins had made the trek as a 'thank you' to Don and Carlota.

"We really should go; the ship is waiting," said Don when the silence had dragged on.

"Well, don't go forgetting where we are, will you?" said Ishy, now flipper in flipper with Sevac.
Well, it is the start of breeding season!

"Of course not," Carlota replied, although they knew the likelihood of them meeting again was practically nil.
With heavy hearts and tearful eyes, the two made ready to leave.

"Just before you go, I want you to have these," said Elyd, stepping forward.

To Don he handed a small square packet. To Carlota, a slightly larger one.

"Go on, open them," urged Sevac, who knew what was inside.

The humans slowly unwrapped the items, taking their time, desperate to stay for those few moments longer. A small sad smile came to Don's face as he unwrapped a new electric alarm clock.

"It switches itself off after a minute, so you won't need to hit it," explained Elyd, whilst Don looked across at Carlota's new Gucci bag.

"Thank you, thank you all so much," Don whispered.

Once again, your ever generous author had supplied a modicum of backbone to our trusty detective, removing the need for tears. Even so, Don knew that had he the choice, he would quite gladly stay on the ice forever. The plot, not to mention sequel possibilities, prevent this.

The whole group gathered together, sharing one last moment.

"This really won't do, you know," said Dara. "We can still keep in touch. You have heard of the internet, haven't you? You can always email."

Don realised that he would have to pay his phone bill more regularly from now on.

"Yes, you will," agreed Nela. "And as you would

say, any time you're in the area, pop in for tea."

Despite their sorrow, they all smiled. Now, if ever, was the time to leave. The two humans picked up their packs and turned to the ridge.

"Don't look back. It won't help," whispered Don to Carlota as they reached the top of the ridge.

They were now standing on the ridgeline, looking down on the ship. Yet despite his own advice, on an impulse they both turned round, hand in hand, looking back to the group standing, watching them. In an instant, a hundred or so penguin flippers raised and waved. Don and Carlota waved back and then, with their feet feeling like lead, they slowly dragged themselves round to face the ship once more. Every step felt like the most difficult they had ever taken as they slowly started down the other side of the ridge. In a moment, the penguins were hidden from view.

Back on the other side of the hill, the penguins were still standing there long after the boat had sailed away. The eight London adventurers and Ishy slowly stepped up to the ridge and watched in silence as the boat headed towards the horizon, becoming smaller and smaller. Finally, in the distance, Ishy could just make out the shape of the boat... and then it was gone. At the same time, she thought she momentarily saw a camera crew blink in and out of existence.

Chapter Thirty-One:
Yes, Another One

Now you may think that, with the penguins safely back on the ice and Don and Carlota on their way home, that this is the end of the tale. A quick glance, however, will show you that this is not so. There are a few pages left yet before the Epilogue.

And so it must be, because as Don and Carlota sailed northwards they knew that there was still unfinished business in London, for a variety of reasons. Although they agreed on how there were going to achieve most things, there was one item they were still debating.

"Why not?" asked Don, as we join their conversation half-way through.

"Because we can't."

"Not even one?"

"No," Carlota insisted firmly, "they all go."

"But…"

"No 'but's, Don. You know we can't."

"Oh, I suppose you are right," Don admitted, reluctantly, in defeat. "Still, it would be nice to have kept at least one."

"I agree, but we can hardly get the reward for tracking down the List of Ten if you keep a Da Vinci hanging on your wall."

It is perhaps understandable that Don had grown attached to art in the two weeks that they had been back at sea; well, at ocean. As well as the List of Ten, so called because they were the most high profile of the items that had unexpectedly relocated to the Baron's castle, there were more minor but still expensive paintings, pictures, and sculptures that had also been 'accidentally acquired'. As Don wandered the hold, off-limits to everyone except for Marcus, Carlota and himself, he couldn't help lifting the occasional create lid to stare at some of the contents. It was only now, as they were only a couple of days' sailing from home, that he could finally understand why the Baron had not made more of an effort to return the artefacts to their rightful owners. Although, given the Baron's somewhat less than successful progress up to the time that he vanished, it is likely that putting items back would probably have meant more disappearing. After all, you will remember standing in the Tower of London earlier in the book, witnessing the failure of one of his attempts.

What's that? You don't remember doing that? You're another one who's cheated, haven't you, and skipped to the back of the book? Go back to the beginning and start again properly!

Sorry about that – some people!

Anyway, as we know, the Baron didn't transfer any of the items back and so it fell to Don and Carlota to do so. That wasn't their only job. In fact, their first would involve the 'guests' that they had invited into Don's basement.

Three days later, with their bags dumped in the hall and a vanload of treasures currently in a secure place, Don and Carlota made their way slowly down the stairs to the basement. In his hand Don held the gun that Carlota had grabbed at the warehouse when they had fled.

Now, don't worry, this is a comedy, the author isn't going to put in a twist that Don is a homicidal maniac at weekends. The author has simply given him this prop as a way to control the camera crew who should be desperate to get out of the basement. I say 'should be', not 'are', for one simple reason.

"They aren't in here!" exclaimed Don in surprise, after the two of them had checked every corner of the basement. All that was left were some discarded food wrappers and plastic bottles filled with a yellowish liquid. "I don't get it. The door was locked. How could they have escaped? There are no windows, and the floor is concrete."

"I really don't know, Don. You're sure the door was locked?"

"You saw it was."

"I know, but I don't understand either. Let's check the rest of the house and see what we can find."

They didn't find any sign of the camera crew anywhere else in the rest of the house, not that they expected to, given that the door had been locked.

I'm sure by now you too are also wondering where they could have gone (or whether the author has made a mistake that he couldn't go back and type over). Well, there is no mistake, and with the judicious use of one of the last flash-backs in the book, we will for a final time rewind and drop into the corner of the same basement, two weeks after the camera crew had been captured, and a week after they had gotten over the shock. No talking, now; they aren't allowed to know we are here.

"Hey Paul, what are you doing messing around with that stuff?"

"There's lights on it," Paul, formerly Sound Recordist (Antarctica) replied. "This is the first time that there's been a light on it."

"What did you touch?" asked an unimportant, one-dimensional, dialogue character.

"Nothing, but I've been studying how this is all rigged up and think I have an idea of what it is."

"Well, what is it then?"

"I think it's some kind of transporting device," Paul explained.

He had come to this conclusion mainly due to the number of *Star Trek* programs he had watched as a child.

"I'm guessing that these batteries power it, and it must have taken them this past fortnight to re-charge."

"You sure? Stuff like that doesn't exist in real life, only in fiction."

"Well, it's the only thing that makes sense. Question is, if it got us into these rooms, surely it can get us back out again... if we can just figure out how."

"Maybe it's worth a go."

They decided to find out.

And that's precisely why Don and Carlota found an empty basement as Paul's theory was, of course, correct. Quite where the missing camera crew had gone, not even the author is totally sure of, as, with the exception of that one quick glimpse we had a couple of pages ago, he is still waiting for them to reappear.

"Well, at least that's one problem solved," Don was glad to say, quite relieved that what he had thought was going to be a difficult problem to solve, had appeared to have resolved itself.

"Yeah, weird, but like you say, it's one thing less to worry about. At least now we can focus on getting the treasures back to their homes."

"And getting a reward into the bargain."

"I thought you'd like that part."

"Well, business has been a bit slow."

"Hmmm. Well, once we've got it all back, then you'll have had two successful cases in only a few weeks, assuming you find out the cat's identity. That's an improvement."

"Three cases."

"What's that?"

"Three cases. You said two."

"Who's the third?"

"Lady Boi."

"That wasn't really a case, though, was it?"

"Yes it was."

"You weren't hired to find her."

"No, but I still found her, and got paid, so it's really three cases."

Carlota thought about this for a moment. Realising that the author wanted to get onto how they were going to get the goods back, she decided to stop arguing, and change the subject.

"Right. So let's go over the plan for how we are going to get the goods back. Are you happy with what we came up with on the ship?"

"I think so. I just hope those marketeers aren't waiting for us. That would scupper everything, including us living."

"They won't be. Ludvig showed you the satellite of them being in that prison. His matter transfer does really work now. They won't be leaving any time in our lifetimes."

"I know, just they make me nervous. What happens if they decide to settle their scores on us?"

"Oh, I don't think you need to worry about that."

"Why not?"

"Didn't Ludvig tell you? When we called the police that day we left London, it was in the press what prison they were taken to. When Ludvig got everything working, he transferred them out of it for a couple of minutes. A bit of a diversion."

"A diversion?"

"Yes. He transferred them to the top of Everest for a moment, then down to his basement. He made it quite clear that if anything happened to either of us, he could get to them no matter where they are. And he told them that he's set up some kind of protection so that if anything happens to him, someone else will make sure the same thing will happen to them. I think he told them he would put them back on top of Everest."

"How do you know all this?"

"It was in an earlier draft of the last chapter, but must have been removed for some reason."

"Ah, I see. Well, in that case, I'm happy with the plan then."

"Good."

"There's just one thing."

"What's that?"

"Well, it's just, when you … You know…"

Don stopped. Then he heard Torac's no-nonsense voice in his head, from a private conversation they had together the morning before Don and Carlota had left.

"I don't understand why you don't just tell her how you feel," the penguin had told him.

"It's not that simple."

"Why not?"

As Don had stood there, he found that he had not been able to answer that question. He still couldn't.

How do I say it? he now thought in frustration, until the author, in an unusual moment of Don-related kindness, stepped in.

Slowly, Carlota reached out a hand and gently touched his arm.

"Don, don't worry. I'm not going anywhere."

Epilogue

The next few weeks that followed Carlota's words had moved quite quickly, which is just as well given that this is the Epilogue.

Their plan on how to return the List of Ten worked perfectly, although not without Don's attempt to 'accidentally' leave one of the Picassos behind. Carlota's prepared cover story was accepted without any doubts, to prevent any further chapters being required, and also to leave the possibility of a sequel. Even authors have to eat.

After the initial interviews, both police and journalistic, followed by the subsequent offers of magazine, TV and film deals, Don and Carlota had escaped to a very private Pacific island courtesy of the Baron, who simply transported them, their luggage and two weeks' worth of supplies in the blink of four eyes.

For Hattenburg and the Arctic crew, an explanation of 'extreme hallucinogenic effects' was blamed on a batch of extremely suspect 'mushroom risotto' ready-meals. The camera footage of the penguins practicing for the Games, and the iceball matches, was deemed too implausible to be believed and so every copy was destroyed.

Andy Craft and Paul Lane bought themselves a GPS that

always worked and even opened a side-line business, lecturing on what to do if lost. Andy and Paul that is, not the GPS.

The camel made it.

The cat appears in a future book and negotiations as to its identity are on-going.

The Baron had gotten so comfortable living in Antarctica that he decided to stay there, even though Don and Carlota had managed to clear his name.

Derek never did turn up for his second appointment with Don but, due to Don's lack of diarizing of meetings, he completely forgot to investigate, especially as their first meeting with Mr Amber and Mr Mauve was the day of their appointment. Mandy does, however, have a very nice patio.

And most important of all? What you are really wanting to know? Yes, that's right. Don's alarm clock. It's currently safely tucked up in its towels, the flipper of a slightly purring, sleeping penguin resting gently on it.

Finally, with a TV movie detailing the List of Ten broadcast a year since, we join Don and Carlota in Don's newly refurbished lounge. It's morning. They are munching on toast and watching breakfast TV. There is a knock on

Don's new front door, and he goes to open it.

"Don," says an ox-like black and white creature, standing on his doorstep. "We need your help."

"Flipping heck!"

THE END

About the Author & This Tale

Quite obviously rather odd, the author resides in a quiet town in Hampshire, England. He first started writing thanks to a teacher at Wolverhampton Grammar School who at one point in a creative story wrote WHAT??? in rather large letters, but still gave an A for effort.

During a bout of insomnia one summer in his eighteenth year, he found himself picking up a pen and piece of paper at 3am. Onto that first piece of paper he wrote two simple questions:

'What would you do if you went downstairs and found six penguins watching breakfast television and eating toast?'

'Why are they eating toast?'

The rest, as they say, is history. And in answer... cereal would stick to their beaks.

About the Illustrator

Graham Williams is an illustration graduate living by the sea in Brighton. He works using a range of traditional mediums before adding a touch of digital wizardry, and often addresses the human condition; exploring the trials and tribulations, the highs and lows, and the giddy chaotic excitement of life.

Graham has displayed work as part of several exhibitions since his graduation and has featured in Creative Review (2012). He is always looking for a new project and wants to keep his fingers in as many pies as possible. Please feel free to contact him with a project idea or a recipe for a good pie.

www.gwillustration.com

Graham can be contacted via the website above or by email.

gw.studio@hotmail.co.uk

5103199R00198

Printed in Great Britain
by Amazon.co.uk, Ltd.,
Marston Gate.